THE SUNS OF SCORPIO

W9-BGU-908

Also by Alan Burt Akers

TRANSIT TO SCORPIO

An Orbit Book

First published in Great Britain in 1974
by Futura Publications Limited
Copyright © Daw Books Inc. 1973

DEDICATION: For Donald A. Wollheim

This book is sold subject to the condition
that it shall not, by way of trade or
otherwise, be lent, re-sold, hired out or
otherwise circulated without the publisher's
prior consent in any form of binding or
cover other than that in which it is
published and without a similar condition
including this condition being imposed on the
subsequent purchaser.

ISBN 0 8600 78159
Printed in Great Britain by
C. Nicholls & Company Ltd.
The Philips Park Press
Manchester.

Futura Publications Limited,
49 Poland Street,
LONDON W1A 2LG

Alan Burt Akers

The Suns Of Scorpio

Illustrated by Tim Kirk

Futura Publications Limited
An Orbit Book

Contents

List of Illustrations

page

A NOTE ON THE TAPES FROM AFRICA

Some of the strange and remarkable story of Dray Prescot, which I have by a fortunate chance been privileged to edit, has already seen publication.* Yet still as I listen to my little cassette tape recorder the power of Prescot's sure calm voice haunts me. There is much in the incredibly long life of this man yet to learn and we must be thankful that we have been given what we do have available to us.

The cassettes my friend Geoffrey Dean handed me that day in Washington, cassettes he had received in Africa from Dan Fraser who, alone of us, has actually seen and talked with Dray Prescot, are incalculably valuable. Yet some cassettes are missing. This is quite clear from the textual evidence. That this is a tragedy goes without saying and I have urgently contacted Geoffrey to discover if he can trace any way in which the loss might have occurred. So far he has been unable to offer any explanation. It is too much to imagine that by some miraculous stroke of good fortune someone might stumble upon these missing cassettes—say in the baggage room of an airline terminal or a lost property office. If, as I fear, they are lying abandoned in some pestiferous West African village, unrecognized and forgotten, someone may use them to record the latest ephemeral pop tunes. ...

Dray Prescot, as described by Dan Fraser, is a man a little above medium height, with straight brown hair and brown eyes that are level and oddly dominating. His shoulders made Dan's eyes pop. Dan sensed an abrasive honesty, a fearless courage, about him. He moves, Dan says, like a great hunting cat, quiet and deadly.

Dray Prescot, born in 1775, insists on calling himself a plain sailor, yet already his story indicates that even during his time on this Earth when he was attempting with little

* TRANSIT TO SCORPIO: DAW Books, Inc.

success to make his way he was destined for some vast and almost unimaginable fate. I believe he always expected something great and mysterious to happen to him. When he was transplanted from Earth to Kregen beneath Antares by the Savanti, those semi-divine men of Aphrasöe, the Swinging City, he positively reveled in the experiences designed to test him. Something about his makeup, perhaps his mental independence, his quick resentment of unjust authority, and most particularly his defiant determination to cure in the pool of baptism the crippled leg sustained by his beloved Delia in a fall from a zorca, made the Savanti cast him out of his paradise.

Subsequently, after he had been transported back to Kregen beneath the Suns of Scorpio by the Star Lords, he fought his way up to be Zorcander of the Clan of Felschraung. Then, after his enslavement in the marble quarries of Zenicce, he graced himself—in that same enclave city of Zenicce—in the eyes of Great Aunt Shusha, who bestowed upon him the title of Lord of Strombor, giving him possession of all her family's holdings. All these experiences seem, to judge by what he says himself in the following narrative, to have touched him lightly. I cannot believe that to be true. During these early periods on Kregen Dray Prescot was maturing in ways that perhaps we on this Earth do not understand.

As to the editing of the tapes, I have abridged certain portions, and tried to bring some order out of the confusion of names and dates and places. For instance, Prescot is inconsistent in his usage of names. Sometimes he will spell out the word, and this makes transcription easy; at other times I have tried to spell the name phonetically, following what I hope are the guide lines he indicates. "Jikai," for instance, which he spells out, he pronounces as "Jickeye." He uses the word "na" between proper names, and I take it to mean the English "of" used rather in the French fashion of "*de*." But he also uses "nal." He says: "Mangar na Arkasson" but: "The Savanti nal Aphrasöe." I feel the usage bears no relation to the double vowel. Clearly there are grammatical rules on Kregen that diverge from those with which we are familiar on this Earth. Generally I have substituted "of" in these circumstances.

Prescot speaks with the characteristic lack of calculated forethought to be expected from a man recollecting past events. He will wander from one point to another as various enticing memories recur to him; but I feel this lends a certain lightness and vigor to his narrative and, at some risk of displeasure from the purists of the language among us, I have in most cases merely amended the punctuation and left the train of thought as Prescot spoke it.

So far as he has said nothing of note about the seasons, and he uses that word as a rule, hardly ever "year." I suspect the seasonal cycles to be far more complicated astronomical, meteorological and agricultural affairs than we here are accustomed to.

Geoffrey Dean said to me: "Here are the tapes from Africa. I promised Dan Fraser I would honor what he had promised Dray Prescot, for I truly believe, Alan, there is a purpose behind Prescot's desire to have his story read by people on Earth."

I believe that, too.

Alan Burt Akers.

CHAPTER ONE

Summons of the Scorpion

Once before I had been flung out of paradise.

Now as I tried to gather up the broken threads of my life on this Earth, I, Dray Prescot, realized how useless mere pretense was. Everything I held dear, all I wanted of hope or happiness, still existed on Kregen under the Suns of Scorpio. There, I knew, my Delia waited for me. Delia! My Delia of the Blue Mountains, my Delia of Delphond—for the Star Lords had contemptuously thrust me back to Earth before Delia could become Delia of Strombor. There on Kregen beneath Antares all I desired was denied to me here on Earth.

My return to this Earth brought me one unexpected experience.

Peace had broken out.

Since the age of eighteen I had known nothing but war, apart from that brief and abortive period of the Peace of Amiens, and even then I had not been completely free. What the new peace meant to me was simple and unpleasant.

The details of my wanderings after I managed to escape the inquiries after my arrival, naked, on that beach in Portugal are not important, for I confess I must have been living in shock. I had vanished overboard as far as the deck watch was concerned, that night seven years ago, disappearing forever from *Roscommon*'s quarterdeck the night after we had taken that French eighty-gun ship. Had I, as far as the navy was concerned, still been alive I would in the normal course of events have expected to be promoted to commander. Now, with the peace, with a seven-year lapse of life to explain, with ships being laid up and men cast adrift to rot on shore, what chance had I, plain Dray Prescot, of achieving the giddy heights of command?

Through chance I was in Brussels when the Corsican

escaped from Elba and aroused France for the final dying
glory of the Hundred Days.

I imagined I knew how Bonaparte felt.

He had had the world at his feet, and then he had nothing
but a tiny island. He had been rejected, deposed, his friends
had turned against him—he, too, in a way, had been kicked
out of his paradise.

It had been my duty to fight Bonaparte and his fleets; so it
was without any sense of incongruity that I found myself at
Waterloo on that fateful day of the eighteenth of June, 1815.

The names are all familiar now—La Belle Alliance, La
Haye Sainte, Hougoumont; the sunken road, the charges, the
squares, the cavalry defeats, the onslaught of the Old
Guard—all have been talked about and written about as no
other battle in all this Earthly world. Somehow in the
smashing avalanches of the British volleys as the Foot
Guards hurled back the elite Old Guard, and I charged down
with Colborne's 52nd, and we saw the sway and the recoil of
the Guard and then were haring after the ruined wreck of
the French army, I found a powder-tasting, bitter, unpleasant
anodyne for my hopeless longings.

In the aftermath of battle I was able to render some
assistance to an English gentleman who, being innopportunely
pressed by a swearing group of moustached grenadiers of the
Old Guard, was happy to allow me to drive them off. This
meeting proved of no little importance; indeed, had my life
been led as are ordinary people's lives—that is, decently, on
the planet of their birth until their death—it would have
marked a most momentous day. Our friendship ripened
during the days he was nursed back to full health and on our
return to London he insisted I partake of his hospitality. You
will notice I do not mention his name, and this I do for very
good and sound reasons. Suffice it to say that through his
friendship and influence I was able to place my little store of
money into good hands, and I mark the beginning of my
present Earthly fortune as originating on the field of Waterloo.

But it is not of my days on Earth that I would tell you.

Feeling the need once more of wide horizons and the heel
of a ship beneath my feet I shipped out—as a passenger—
and traveled slowly in the general direction of India, where I
hoped to find something, anything, I knew not what, to dull
the ever-present ache that made of all I did on this Earth
pointless and plodding and mere routine existence.

There seemed to me then little rhyme or reason for the malicious pranks played on me by the Star Lords. I had no clear conception of who or what they were—I didn't give a damn then, either, just so long as they returned me to Kregen beneath Antares. I had seen that gorgeous scarlet and golden-feathered hunting bird, greater than either hawk or eagle, the Gdoinye, circling above me during moments of crisis. And, too, I had seen the white dove that had up to then ignored the scarlet and golden raptor. There were forces in play I did not and didn't want to understand as the Star Lords battled for what they desired in their mysterious unhuman ways with whatever forces opposed them; and the Savanti—mere human men after all—looked on appalled and attempted to move the pieces of destiny in ways that would benefit mere mortal humanity.

The forces that moved destiny chose to transport me to Kregen under the Suns of Scorpio during my first night ashore in Bombay.

The heat, stifling and intense, the smells, the flies, the cacophony of noise, all these things meant nothing to me. I had experienced far worse. And on that night, so long ago now, the stars above my head flung down a sheening light that coalesced and fused into a burning patina mocking me and closing me in. I had reached that point of despair in which I believed that never again would I tread the fields of Kregen, never again look out from the walls of my palace of Strombor in Zenicce, never again hold in my arms Delia of Delphond.

From the balcony, I looked up at the stars, with the night breeze susurrating great jagged leaves and the insects buzzing in their millions, and picked out, not without some difficulty, that familiar red fire of Antares, the arrogant upflung tail of the constellation of Scorpio, I stared longingly, sick with that inner crumbling of spirit that recognized with loathing that I did, indeed, despair.

In my agony and my desperation I had thought that India might provide a scorpion—as it had bred the one that killed my father.

Clearly, that long-ago night, I was light-headed. When I looked up at the stars, at the red fire of Antares, and the familiar blue lambency grew, swelling and bloating into the blue-limned outlines of a giant scorpion, I was drained of all the exultation that had uplifted me the last time this had happened.

I simply lifted up my arms and let myself be carried wherever the Star Lords willed, happy only that I should once again tread the earth of Kregen, under the Suns of Scorpio.

Without opening my eyes I knew I was on Kregen.

The stinking heat of a sweltering Bombay night was gone. I felt a cooling breeze on my forehead. Also, I felt a peculiar scrabbling tickling sensation on my chest. Slowly, almost languorously, I opened my eyes.

As I had half expected to be, I was naked.

But, sitting on my chest and waving its tail at me, a large, reddish, armor-glinting scorpion poised on its squat legs.

Without being able to help myself, moving with a violence entirely beyond my control, I leaped to my feet with a single bound. I yelled. The scorpion, dislodged, was flung out and away. It fell among a rocky outcrop and, regaining its legs with an ungraceful waddle, vanished into a crack among the rocks.

I took a deep breath. I remembered the scorpion that had killed my father. I remembered the phantom scorpion who had crewed for me aboard the leaf boat on that original journey down the sacred River Aph. I remembered too the scorpion that had appeared as my friends laughed and I had sat with Delia, my Delia of the Blue Mountains, with the red sunshine of Zim flooding the chamber and the greenish light of Genodras just creeping into the corner of the window, as we made the bokkertu for our betrothal, just before I had been flung out of Kregen. I remembered these times of terror and despair when I had previously seen a scorpion—and I laughed.

Yes, I, Dray Prescot, who seldom smiled, laughed!

For I knew I was back on Kregen. I could tell by the feeling of lightness about my body, the scent on the wind, the mingled shards of light falling about me in an opaline glory from the twin suns of Antares.

So I laughed.

I felt free, rejuvenated, alive, gloriously alive, the blood singing through my body and ready for anything this savage, beautiful, vicious, and beloved world of Kregen might offer. With a strange exalted kind of curiosity, I looked about me.

That blessed familiar pink sunshine bathed the landscape in glory. A grove of trees before me, bending in the wind, showed the white and pink blossoms of the missal. Grass as green and luscious as any that ever grew on Earth spread beneath my feet. Far away on the horizon, so far that I knew I stood upon a lofty eminence, the line of the sea cut cleanly into the brilliant sky. I breathed in deeply, expanding my chest. I felt more alive than at any time since I had been snatched away from my palace of Strombor in Zenicce. Once again I was on Kregen. I was home!

I walked slowly toward the demarcated edge of the grass near to me on my left hand, at right angles to that distant prospect of the sea. I was naked. If it had been the Star Lords who had brought me here this time, or the Savanti, those dispassionate, near-perfect men of the Swinging City of Aphrasöe, then I would not expect otherwise. Truth to tell, I think they understood how less in my estimation they would stand had they thought to provide me with clothing, with weapons, a sword, a helmet, a shield, or spear. I was brought to this planet of Kregen beneath Antares, as I believed, for a purpose, even though as yet I might not divine what that purpose might be. I understood something of the way of those forces that had snatched me across four hundred light-years of interstellar space.

The grass felt soft and springy beneath my feet and the wind blew through my hair. At the lip of the precipice I stood looking out and down on a sight at once incredible and beautiful in its insolent power. However beautiful that sight might be and however incredible, I did not care. I was back on Kregen. Just whereabouts on the surface of the planet I had been placed I had no way of knowing, and I didn't care. I knew only that whatever faced me in the days ahead I would find my way back to Strombor in Zenicce, that proud city of the continent of Segesthes, find my way back to clasp Delia in my arms once more. If she had left Strombor, where she would still regard herself as in a foreign land, and had returned to her home by the Blue Mountains in Vallia and to her father, the emperor of the unified island empire, then I would follow her there too. I would go to the ends of this world as I would my own to find Delia of the Blue Mountains.

Below me extended a rocky shelf cut from the side of the cliff. Below that another extended. Each shelf was about a hundred yards wide. They descended like a dizzyingly disorienting giant's staircase, down and down, until the last shelf vanished beneath the calm surface of a narrow ribbon of water. Opposite me the shelves rose again from the water, up and up, stepped up and back and back, rising until I could look across five miles of clear air to the opposite lip. Here and there smaller stairways threaded the rock faces. I turned and looked inland. The perspectives dwindled away and were lost in the distance.

The supposition appeared extraordinary—ridiculous, even—but from the order of the level steps, the block facings, and the uniformity of appearance, I judged this Grand Canal to be man-made. Or, if not entirely man-made, then certainly the hand of man had been laid on what was originally a canal linking the outer wave-tossed ocean with the calmer and smoother waters of an inland sea.

I could see no sign of any living thing. However, I felt that a projecting mass perched on the topmost level directly opposite me, a rocky edifice squared and minutely distinct in the clean air, must be some form of habitation. A tremor of smoke arose from its summit, black and thin at the distance, trailing away in the wind.

The last time I had arrived on Kregen I had heard Delia's scream ringing in my ears. This time, also, I heard a scream; but I knew instantly that it was not Delia's.

Running toward the bluff from which the breeze blew and the gentle sound of the sea could now be heard susurrating murmurously in the warm air, I saw a figure break through a screen of trees and, staggering a few steps forward, fall full-length on the sward.

As I reached him I saw he was not a man.

He was a Chulik, one of those beast-humans born like men with two arms and legs, with a face that might also have been human but for the twin three-inch long upward-reaching tusks, and who in nothing else resembled humanity. His skin was a smooth oily yellow. His eyes small, black, and round like currants. He was strong and powerful, a mercenary warrior, with his mail coif from which the ventail hung open, and a hauberk that reached down to mid-thigh. He carried no weapons that I could see. His strength and power was attested to by the fact that he had screamed at all, with the red pudding that was his face all pulpy, lacerated, and bloody.

A silence descended.

I had no idea as yet which one of the many hostile and savagely ferocious predators of Kregen might have so ravaged his face. But I felt a familiar thrill of blood thump along my veins—and then I truly knew I had returned to Kregen beneath the Suns of Scorpio.

The only previous occasion on Kregen I had seen mail had been when the Princess Natema Cydones had tempted me. In an alcove a giant mail-clad man had stood, silent and motionless, bearing a rapier of such marvelous workmanship and balance, that same rapier I had captured and used in that final victorious fight in Strombor. Armor of any kind was a useful sort of clothing to wear on Kregen. Around the Chulik's waist was a white garment striped with green.

At sight of the green-striped material I frowned.

However, as you will have gathered by now, I am not overly squeamish about the small things of life, and so I stripped off the garment of green-striped white cloth and wrapped it about myself into a kind of breechclout.

Infinitely more important than clothes on Kregen are weapons, more important even than armor. This Chulik carried no weapon. This was exceedingly strange. Carefully, walking with that light springy tread that carried me soundlessly over the grass, I approached the edge of the cliff overlooking the sea.

The wind sported in my hair. I looked over and down.

The sea heaved gently a long way down the jagged cliffs. I could barely make out a curving beach of yellow sand where waves broke which I could barely hear. A few gulls and other seabirds wheeled; but they were strangely silent. That sea shone a refulgent blue. The seas that washed the shores of the continent of Segesthes were green, or gray, sometimes blue with a hardness and coldness about that blueness; this sea moved languidly, smoothly, and its blueness struck back at the eye. I had seen that blueness of water in the Mediterranean. With a sailor's eye I studied the scene, and I took particular notice of a vessel half-drawn up on that narrow curve of yellow sand.

She was a galley. Her ram beak, her pencil-thin lines, the oars now drawn inboard, all proclaimed that clearly. But she was not like that galley that had welcomed me to Aphrasöe, the Swinging City, after my inaugural journey down the sacred River Aph.

I looked about the edge of the cliff, rooting among the bushes that lined the crest. I did not find any weapon the Chulik might have dropped.

I looked further along the cliff edge, seeking the probable path the mercenary would have ascended. I became very still.

A group of creatures squatted there half-hidden by the bushes. The bushes were thorn-ivy, thickets to be avoided by those with tender skin. These creatures snuggled within the thick thorn-encrusted loops, squatting on all sixes, their coarse gray pelts matted with dirt, leaves, and excrement, their heads all turned to look down the ascending pathway up the face of the cliff.

Now I knew what manner of creature it was who had torn out the Chulik's face.

They were not unlike the Segesthan rock-ape, the grundal, some five feet in height when standing erect, with thin spiderish limbs that in their agility could take them swinging with nonchalant ease across rocks that would defeat a mountain goat. I had seen them on occasion among the distant mountains bordering the Great Plains of Segesthes, when I had hunted with my Clansmen; these fellows were of a kind: vicious, cowardly, deadly when hunting in packs. Their heads were all turned away from me, yet I knew what they would be like from a frontal view. Their mouths were incredibly large, closing in folds of flesh, and when open round and armed with concentric rows of needle-like teeth. They looked not unlike some of those single-minded predatory fish dredged up from the deep seas, all mouth and fangs.

Something like ten or a dozen waited in the bushes.

Sounds broke on the still air. The scuffle of feet, the rattle of stones, the quick chatter of people in animated careless conversation. Listening with ears trained as a warrior with the Clansmen of Felschraung, I did not hear the sound I wanted to hear. I could hear no chink of weapons.

Now the voices were close enough for me to understand what was being said. The language was a form of Kregish so close to what I knew that I was convinced Segesthes could not be far removed from wherever I was now.

"When I catch you, Valima," puffed a light eager boy's voice, "you know what to expect, I trust?"

"Catch me?" The girl's voice was filled with laughter, clear, trilling, carefree, hugely enjoying herself and the moment. "Why, I declare, Gahan Gannius, you could not catch a fat greasy merchant at his prayers!"

"You will be at your prayers in a moment!"

Now I could see them as they laughed, puffing and toiling up the slope. The explanation for their words and the young man's clear exasperation was simple. He pursued the girl up the trail zigzagging in the cliff face, and she, a laughing sprite, danced on ahead. She carried a twisted bundle of clothing over her head. From the bundle loops of pearls hung down over her ears, a leather belt, a corner of a green and white cloth, a golden buckle. Both she and the boy were naked; and despite her burden she was able to keep him at any distance she desired. She bounded ahead with a gay laugh that sounded by far too reckless for a young naked girl on a cliff face with a dozen grundals lying in wait.

Their guard, the Chulik, lay with his face ripped out.

I picked up the first stone. It lay near the edge, a large, jagged stone, satisfactorily heavy in my hand.

A man, weaponless among a world of predators, must find what he can to defend himself. It is in his nature not to let himself die easily. I had proved that, many times.

I stood up.

"Hai!" I shouted. And, again, "Hai!"

I threw the stone. I did not stop to check its flight but bent immediately, seized another from the crumpled outcrop, and hurled it. The first stone, as I threw the second, cracked into the head of the nearest grundal. When the third was on its way I saw the second smite the next grundal a glancing blow, upon that round teeth-filled muzzle so like that of a deep sea fish.

"Beware!" I took breath to yell. "Grundal!"

Six stones I threw, six hard jagged bolts of pulverizing rock, before the grundals were on me.

They were not like the Segesthan rock-apes I had known before. Each one ran on his lower pair of limbs, claws scrabbling, and his upper pair reached out to grasp me and draw my face into that grinning orbit of teeth so that it might be bitten off. But, surprising me, each one carried in his middle limbs' hands a stout stick, a cudgel perhaps three feet long.

Had they known it, that was their mistake.

Claws and cudgels and needle-sharp teeth raked for me. I sprang sideways, took the first upraised cudgel, turned and twisted and bent, and the cudgel was mine.

A grundal screeched and leaped in from the side and I in my turn leaped and kicked him alongside his head, feeling the needle-fangs' pressure through those folds of skin. The cudgel broke the skull of the one in front.

"Your back!" a voice screamed from somewhere.

I bent and rolled and the lunging grundal went over me and the cudgel helped him on his way. I could not dispatch him for the next two who attacked; these I treated separately thus: the first was caught by his cudgel and pulled forward, the second was beaten over the shoulders and, also, stumbled forward and I, with a gliding motion at once graceful and very unpleasant to them in its consequences, removed my body from the point of impact. They smashed into each other and went down screeching.

I took two quick strokes to beat in their skulls and was facing the next when a Chulik, his yellow skin extraordinarily sweaty and shiny from the run up, smote downward with a sword and split a grundal down to his shoulders.

The rest turned, screeching, beginning to drop their cudgels and to dance on their four lower limbs, a dance of rage and frustration, a reversion to their near-savage ancestry.

Not many of them were left.

Another Chulik appeared and the two semi-humans charged the grundals. The rock-apes spat defiance, but retreated and then dived over the cliff edge, swinging in fantastic overhand leaps across the rock face, disappearing into cracks and crannies and shadow-shrouded holes.

As a welcome to Kregen, I decided, staring at the girl and boy who were now hurriedly clothing themselves, at the sweaty Chuliks, and the dead grundals, this had been a fair old party. The boy, as soon as he was dressed, was cursing the Chulik guard commander. I took little notice, letting the old, familiar, hated tones of harsh authority flow over my head. Truth to tell, the Chuliks should have done their job better. They were regarded as among the best of mercenary semi-human guards, and they charged a higher premium for their services as a result. The dead one beyond the trees was no advertisement for them.

Looking at the girl was a much more rewarding occupation. She had very dark hair, not quite black, and a pleasant, open face with dark eyes. She was somewhat full about the jaw and her figure, for I had seen that whether I wished it or not, had been full, too, plump, almost; but this I suspected was merely youth and would trim off in a few years. The boy was slender, strong in his movements and gestures, with dark hair and eyes; but there was in his face a certain expression, a cast of character, a shadow I coldly felt upon me. At that time I did not brood upon him, this Gahan Gannius, for I had just come to Kregen and needed information.

He was giving orders now, harshly, meanly, the horror of what might have occurred to him still fresh in his mind. The girl, Valima, looked at me. I remained standing, the cudgel still grasped in my hand. No one had spoken to me since that swift warning shout that a grundal was about to attack my back.

"We cannot picnic here, that is certain," Gahan Gannius was saying, very disgruntled, almost sulky. "I suppose we had best go back to the shore."

"If you command, Gahan."

"I do so command! Is there any doubt?"

The Chuliks, a few more had now appeared, puffing, stood stolidly by. Their place as hired mercenaries obviated any form of inhibition from these young people, the master and the mistress. And still they had taken no notice of me.

The young master shouted at the servants who had been struggling up laden with food and wines, with tables and tablecloths, with chairs, with awnings, with rugs. Now they turned back to shore again, these men and women clad in brief gray garments with broad green borders. With the contents of a ship's stateroom upon their shoulders, they trudged up the cliff and now down, so as to fulfill the whim of these insensitive young people for a foolhardy picnic.

When they had all gone down again I was left alone.

I stood at the summit of the cliff, abandoned, and I marveled. I marveled that I had done nothing about their bad manners.

CHAPTER TWO

The Todalpheme of Akhram

From the summit of the opposite side of the canal I could look up and see the structure rising a half mile away. I had arrived here by the simple expedient of climbing down the myriads of stairs cut into the giant rock shelves, swimming the half mile stretch of water, and then climbing up again. The twin suns were low in the sky now and their light, still mingled, would gradually fade and turn into a purer greenish glow as the green sun, the one called Genodras, lingered a while after the larger red sun, Zim, had vanished.

Then the stars would come out and I might have a better idea of just where I was on the surface of Kregen beneath Antares.

The structure appeared a solidly constructed castle or hotel with stoppered windows; its many turrets covered a roof I felt sure was more than a simple closure of halls behind curtain walls. There was domes, minaret-like spires, and the gable-ends of lofty buildings. The opaline shadows fell across its gray walls. I wondered if it had been built at the same time the canal had been straightened and faced with stone, or if its builders had, like those of Medieval Rome, plundered the ancient edifice for their own materials.

I walked slowly up toward the structure in the gathering green light.

From the dead body of the Chulik I had taken his mail coif, hauberk, and leather gear. The boy and girl, Gahan Gannius and Valima, evidently had not bothered to inquire into the fate of their guard, and his companions were under constraint. I had met the Chuliks before. I knew it was their custom to adopt the uniforms, accouterments, and weapons of those by whom they were hired. In Zenicce, where for a time I had been a bravo-fighter, the Chuliks carried the long rapier and the dagger; here, they carried the weapons suitable to mail-clad men.

The long sword had turned up at last, in my search, skewered into the ground beyond a clump of the ivy-thorn. It must have flung up, somersaulting, from the dead Chulik hand. I picked it up and studied it. Much may be learned of a people by a diligent study of their weapons.

The first object of scrutiny was the point. This was a true point, yet its wedge-shaped flanks, although reasonably sharp, were not those of a thrusting weapon. The point was known here, but, confirming the mail-clad armored Chulik's, was not favored. There exists the well-known fallacy that the point and thrusting were unknown during the European Middle Ages; the truth is simply that thrusting is not the most effective way of disposing of a mail-clad opponent. So the long sword—I turned it over in my hands. It was straight, cheaply-made, well-sharpened, as I would expect of a Chulik mercenary, with a simple iron cross-guard and wooden grip, ridged and notched. On the flat of the blade, below the guard, was etched a monogram that I took to be the Kregish letters for G.G.M. There was no maker's name.

So. A cheap, mass-produced weapon, a trifle clumsy as to balance and swing; it would serve me until a better came along.

Now I stood before the strange structure with its many domes and cupolas, its square-cut walls, in the dying light of Genodras, the green sun of Kregen.

They came out to me. I was ready. If they came to greet me, all well and good. If they came to slay me or take me captive I would swing this new sword until I had made good my escape in the shadows.

"Lahal!" they called in the universal greeting of Kregen. "Lahal."

"Lahal," I replied.

I stood waiting for them to approach. They carried torches and in the evening breeze that would strengthen with the dying suns the torches streamed like scarlet and golden hair. I saw yellow robes, and sandals, and shaven heads in flung-back hoods. I looked at these men's waists and I saw ropes wound about them, with tassels that swung as they walked.

The ropes and the tassels were blue.

I let out my breath.

I had hoped they would be scarlet ropes and tassels.

"Lahal, stranger. If you seek rest for this night, then come quickly, for night draws on rapidly."

The speaker lifted his torch as he spoke. His voice was

peculiar, high and shrill, almost feminine. I saw his face. Smooth, that face, beardless yet old, with wrinkled skin about the eyes and puckering beside the mouth. He was smiling. *Here,* I thought then, and was proved right, *is a man who thinks he has nothing to fear.*

We walked back to the structure and entered through a great masonry archway which was immediately closed by a bronze-bound lenken door. I recognized the wood by its color, an ashy color with a close-textured grain; I suppose the lenk tree and lenken wood is the Kregan equivalent of our Terrestrial oak. If there were grundals out there, with jaws waiting to bite our faces off, the closing of that bronze-bound lenken door gave a comforting feel to our backs.

Conducted to a small chamber where I was offered warmed water for washing and a change of clothing—a robe similar to the yellow robes worn by the men here—and then invited to join the men for dinner in the refectory, I found everything well-ordered and calm. Everything proceeded as though governed by a routine so well-established nothing would overturn it. A feeling of pleasure, quite unmistakably pleasure, began to steal over me. This might not be Aphrasöe, the City of the Savanti, but the people here knew something of that art of making everything seem important and part of a ritual of life that would go on everlastingly.

The food was good. Simple food, and I had expected that; fish, some meat I suspected was vosk cooked in a new way, fruits including the essential and beneficial palines, all accompanied by a fine bland wine of a transparent yellow color and a low alcohol content, as I judged.

All the men gathered in the refectory were dressed in the same way and they all spoke in the same high-pitched voices. There were about a hundred of them. The men who brought in the food were dressed exactly in the same way, and when they had finished serving they joined us at the long sturm-wood tables. Many lanterns shed a golden light on the scene. Halfway through the meal a youngish man mounted a kind of stand, scarcely a pulpit, and began to recite a poem. It was a long rigmarole about a ship that had sailed into a whirlpool and been caught up to one of Kregen's seven moons. I do not smile easily and I seldom laugh. I neither laughed nor smiled at the story; but it interested me.

I did not think I was in a Kregan equivalent of a monastery. Such things did exist, I knew, and there had been the order of the purple monks in Zenicce. However, something about these people, their lack of fuss or ceremony, convinced me their lives were dedicated to something other than the disciplines of the convent.

I imagine that you who are listening to my story, as you play the recordings I make in this African famine area, will guess at my thoughts. Was this the reason I had been brought back to Kregen? Had the Star Lords brought me, or the Savanti? Tantalizingly, I had not seen either a scarlet-feathered raptor or a white dove to give me any clues.

One of the men spoke directly to me as I drained the last of my wine. He appeared older than the others, although there were many elderly men as well as middle-aged ones. The lines and wrinkles in his face belied the otherwise smoothness of his skin.

"You should retire now, stranger, for it is clear you have traveled much and are tired."

Could he have known just how far I had traveled!

I nodded and rose. "I would like to thank you for your hospitality—" I began.

He raised a hand. "We will talk in the morning, stranger."

I was quite prepared to accept this dismissal. I was tired. The bed was not too soft for comfortable sleep, and I slept; if I dreamed I no longer recollect what phantoms filled my mind. In the morning, after a fine breakfast, I went for a stroll along the battlements with the old man, whose name was Akhram. The name of the building too, he told me, was Akhram.

"When I die, which may occur in perhaps fifty years or so, then there will be a new Akhram in Akhram."

I nodded, understanding.

Over the high parapet I could see, stretching out on all sides except for those where the Grand Canal and the sea cliffs hemmed us in, broad fields, orchards, tilled land, carefully tended agricultural holdings. This place would be rich. In the fields people labored, mere ants at this distance. Were they slaves, I wondered, or free?

I asked my usual questions.

No, he had never heard of Aphrasöe, the City of the Savanti. I forced down the pang of disappointment.

"I once saw," I said, "three men dressed as you are, except that they wore scarlet ropes around their waists, with scarlet tassels."

Akhram shook his head.

"That may be so. I know of the pink-roped Todalpheme of

Loh, and we are the blue-roped Todalpheme of Turismond; but of scarlet-roped, alas, my friend, I know nothing."

Turismond. I was on the continent of Turismond. I had heard of Turismond. Surely, then, Segesthes could not be far?

"And Segesthes?" I asked. "The city of Zenicce?"

He regarded me. "Did you not ask these scarlet-roped Todalpheme, yourself, what of Aphrasöe?"

"They were dead, the three, dead."

"I see."

We walked for a space in that wonderful streaming opaline radiance.

Then: "I have heard of the continent of Segesthes, of course. Zenicce, as I am given to understand, is a not-too popular city with the seafarers of the outer ocean."

I made myself walk sedately at his side as we patrolled the battlements in the early morning suns-shine.

"And of Vallia?"

He nodded quickly. "Of Vallia we know well, for their world-encompassing ships bring us strange and wonderful things from far lands."

I was as good as back with my Delia of the Blue Mountains. For a moment I felt faint. What of the Star Lords' intentions, now—if in truth it had been the Star Lords, the Everoinye?

Akhram was talking on and out of politeness, that which had been so earnestly drummed into my head by my parents, I forced myself to listen. He was talking about the tide they expected that afternoon. As he spoke, I understood what went on here and what was the service in which these Todalpheme were engaged. The Todalpheme, in brief, calculated the tides of Kregen, kept accounts, and reckoned up with all the old familiar sailor lore I had learned back on Earth. I felt a wonder at the kind of calculations they must do. For Kregen has, besides the twin suns, the red and the green, her seven moons, the largest almost twice the size of Earth's moon. I knew that with so many heavenly bodies circling the tidal motions would to a very large extent be canceled out, the very multiplicity of forces creating not more and higher tides but fewer and less. Except when bodies were in line, when they spread evenly; then the spring or neap tides would be marvelous in their extent. Back in Zenicce I had seen the tidal defenses, and the way in which the houses along the canals had been built well above the mean water level. When tides ravaged through Zenicce tragedy could result, so the barrages, defenses, and gates were kept always in good repair, a charge on the Assembly.

Akhram told me that a great dam stood at the seaward end of the Grand Canal that connected this inner sea with the outer ocean. There were closable channels through the dam. The dam faced both ways. It had been constructed, so Akhram said, by those men of the sunrise—he said sunrise, not suns-rise—in the distant past as they had faced and leveled the canal itself, so as to control the tidal influx and efflux from the inner sea.

"We are an inward-facing people, here on the inner sea," he said. "We know that outside, in the stormy outer ocean, there are other continents and islands. Sometimes ships sail through the regulated openings in the Dam of Days. Vallia, Wloclef from whence come thick fleeces of the curly ponsho, Loh from whence come fabulous, superbly cut gems and glassware of incredible fineness: these places we know as they trade with us. Donengil, also, in South Turismond. There are a few others; otherwise, we remain willingly confined to our inner sea."

Later I was allowed to visit the observatories and watch the Todalpheme at work. Much of what they did with ephemeris and celestial observation was familiar to me; but much was strange, beyond my comprehension, for they used what seemed almost a different kind of logic. They were as devoted to their work as monks to theirs. But they laughed and were free and easy.

They showed a certain respect for my own understanding of the movements of heavenly bodies and the predictable movements of bodies of water, with tides and currents and winds and all the hazards thereto attached.

This inner sea was practically tideless. There was little wonder in this, of course (the Mediterranean tides never exceed two feet), and these dedicated men spent their lives calculating tide tables so that they might warn the custodians at the gates of the dam to be ready when the outer ocean boiled and seethed and roared in with all its power. I gathered there was no other navigable exit from the inner sea.

"Why do you live here, on the inward end of the Grand Canal?" I asked.

Akhram smiled in a vague way and swung his arm in a gesture that encompassed the fertile soil, the orchards, the smooth sea. "We are an inward-facing people. We love the Eye of the World."

When Akhram referred to the dam he called it the "Dam of Days." I realized how much it meant. If the outer ocean got up into a real big tide and swept in through the narrow gut of the Grand Canal, it would sweep like a great broom across the inner sea.

That great Dam of Days had been built in the long-ago by a people now scattered and forgotten, known only by the monuments in stone they had built and which time had overthrown, all except the Grand Canal and the Dam of Days.

I saw a stir in the fields. People were running. Faintly, cries reached up. Akhram looked over and his face drew down into a stern-lined visage of agony and frustrated anger.

"Again they raid us," he whispered.

Now I could see mail-clad men riding beasts, swooping after the running farm people. I saw a man stagger and go down with a great net enveloping him. Girls were snatched up to saddle bows. Little children, toddlers, even were plucked up and flung screaming into ready sacks.

The long sword I had found by the thorn-ivy was below, in the room I had been assigned. I started off along the parapet. When I emerged by the massive lenken door it was just closing. A frightened rabble crowded in, the last just squeezing through the little postern cut in the main doors. I lifted the sword.

"Let me out," I said to the men bolting and barring the doors.

I wore the green-striped material taken from the dead Chulik. I had been unable to don the hauberk or coif; my shoulders are broader than most. I held the sword so the men at the doors could see it.

"Do not go out," they said. "You will be killed or captured—"

"Open the door."

Akhram was there. He put a hand on my arm.

"We do not ask visitors for their names or their allegiances, friend," he said. He stared up at me, for I am above middle height. "If they are your hereditary foes, you may go freely forth and be killed for your convictions. But I take you for a stranger. You do not know our ways—"

"I know slaving when I see it."

He sighed. "They are gone by now. They sweep in, when

we do not expect them, not at dawn or sunset, and take our people. We, the Todalpheme, are inviolate by nature, law, and mutual agreement; for, if we were killed, then who would give warning when the great tides were coming? But our people, our loyal people who care for us, are not inviolate."

"Who are they?" I asked. "The slavers?"

Akhram looked about him on the frightened mob of peasant folk in their simple clothing, some with the pitchforks still in their hands, some with infants clinging to their skirts, some with blood upon their faces. "Who?" asked Akhram.

The man who answered, a full-bodied man with a brown beard to his waist and a seamed and agricultural face, spoke in a tongue I had difficulty in following. It was not Kregish, the universal Latin of Kregen, and it was not the language of Segesthes, spoken by my Clansmen of Felschraung and Longuelm, and by the Houses and free men and slaves of Zenicce.

"Followers of Grodno," Akhram said. He looked weary, like a civilized man who sees things with which civilization should be done. Then, quickly, as he saw me open my mouth to ask, he spoke. "Grodno, the green-sun deity, the counterpart to Zair, the red-sun deity. They are, as all men can tell, locked in mortal combat."

I nodded. I remembered how men said the sky colors were always in opposition.

"And the city of these people, these slavers, these followers of Grodno?"

"Grodno lies all to the northern side of the inner sea; Zair to the south. Their cities are many and scattered, each free and independent. I do not know from which city these raiders came.

I said, lifting the sword again: "I shall go to the cities of Grodno, for I believe—"

I did not say any more.

Suddenly I saw, planing high in the air and descending in wide hunting circles, the gorgeous scarlet plumage of a great bird of prey, a raptor with golden feathers encircling its neck and its black feet and talons outstretched in wide menace. I knew that bird, the Gdoinye, the messenger or spy of the Star Lords. As I saw it so I felt that familiar lassitude, that sickening sense of falling, overpower me, and I felt my knees give way, my sword arm fall, my every sense reel and shiver with the shock of dissociation.

"No!" I managed to cry out. "No! I will not return to Earth! I will not. . . . I will stay on Kregen. . . . I will not return!"

But the blue mist encompassed me and I was falling. . . .

CHAPTER THREE

Into the Eye of the World

North or south ... Grodno or Zair ... green or red ...
Genodras or Zim. ... Somewhere a conflict was being fought
out. I did not know then and even now I must in the nature
of things be unaware of all that passed as I sank down in a
stupor in the courtyard of the tidal buildings of Akhram with
the frightened rabble of peasantry about me and the massive
lenken door fast shut with its bronze bolts and bars. I was
aware of a vast hollow roaring in my head. This perturbed
me, for on my previous transplantations from Kregen to
Earth, or from Earth to Kregen, the thing had been done
and over with in mere heartbeats.

I seemed detached from myself. I was there, in that courtyard with the kindly concerned face of Akhram bending
over me. And, also, I was looking down on the scene from a
goodly height and the scene eddied around like a whirlpool,
like that whirlpool into which I had plunged in my leaf boat
going down the River Aph. I shuddered at the thought that I
might be seeing that scene from the viewpoint of the Gdoinye, the scarlet and golden bird of prey.

As I looked, both upward and downward, simultaneously, I
saw a white dove moving smoothly through the level air.

I thought I understood, then.

I thought the Star Lords, who I imagined had brought me
here to Kregen on this occasion, did not want me to go to
the north shore cities of the followers of Grodno, the cities of
the green sun; but maybe the Savanti, whose messenger and
observer the white dove was, would prefer it if I did go.

I hung as it were in a kind of limbo.

With a hoarse scream the scarlet bird swung toward the
white dove.

This was the first occasion on which I had seen either bird
take any notice of the other.

The white dove moved with that deceptively smooth wing-beat and climbed away, slipping past the stooping bird of prey.

Both birds turned and rose in the air.

I followed them into the opaline radiance of the sky where the twin suns shed their mingled light fusing into a golden pinkish glory whose edges shone lambently with a tinged green. Then I could see them no longer and I sank back and fell, and so opened my eyes again on the dust of the courtyard.

Sandaled feet shuffled by my nose. Hoarse breathing sounded in my ears and hands reached down to lift me. I guessed I had not lain on the ground for half a minute. The friendly and concerned peasants were trying to carry me. I hauled out an arm and waved it and then, still groggy, stood up. I do not smile often, but I looked not without pleasure on the courtyard of Akhram, on the peasants, on the great lenken door, and on Akhram himself, who was staring at me as though, truly, I had risen from the dead.

There remains little to tell of the rest of my stay in Akhram, the astronomical observatory of the Todalpheme.

I learned what I needed of the local language with a fierce obsessive drive that disconcerted my teacher, a Todalpheme with a gentle face and mournful eyes. His voice, as high-pitched as the others, and his face, as smooth as those of the younger brethren, unsettled me. I learned quickly.

Also, I learned that if I wished to cross the wide outer ocean to reach Vallia, it would be necessary to take a ship from one of the ports of the inner sea. Few ships ventured past the Dam of Days, and it would serve my purpose to go to a city rather than wait meekly here for a ship from the outside world to pass on her way home.

Finally, Akhram spoke gently to me, pointing out my knowledge of the sea, tides, and calculations over which we had amicably pored together. Navigation has always come easily to me, and by this time I had fixed in my head the geographical outlines of the inner sea as well as Akhram could teach me with the aid of maps and globes kept in his own private study. I was also able to give him some sage advice on the higher mathematics, and his grasp of calculus also was thereby strengthened.

What he proposed was obvious, given the context of our relationship.

He now knew my name, Dray Prescot, and used it with some affection. Because of my somewhat stupid and vainglorious attempt to rush outside and deal with the raiders, alone, with my sword, I understood he felt that he owed me gratitude. I owned no particular loyalty to any set of codes; codes, in a general sense, are for the weaklings who rely on ritual and formula; but I granted their use at the right times and places; that had not been one of them. Had I got outside I would have been killed or captured and, very probably, only further annoyed the mail-clad men of Grodno.

"You are at heart one of us, Dray," said Akhram, then. "Your knowledge is already far advanced over that normal for one of your years in our disciplines. Join us! Join us, Dray Prescot; become a Todalpheme. You would enjoy the life here."

In other days, in other climes I might have been tempted.

But——there was Delia of Delphond.

There were the Star Lords; there were the Savanti; but most of all there was Delia of the Blue Mountains, my Delia.

"I thank you for your gracious offer, Akhram. But it cannot be. I have other destinies——"

"If it is because we are all castrati, and you would of necessity have to be castrated likewise, I can assure you that is of little importance beside the knowledge gained——"

I shook my head. "It is not that, Akhram."

He turned away.

"It is difficult, to find the right young men. But, if the Todalpheme were no more, who, then, would warn the fisher folk, the sailors in their gallant ships, the people of the shore cities? For the inner sea is a calm sea. It is flat, placid, smooth. When storms come a man may see the clouds gather and sense the change in the wind, and sniff the breeze, and say to himself a storm is due and so seek harbor. But——who can warn him when the tides will come sweeping in to smash and crush and destroy if the gates are not closed on the Dam of Days?"

"The Todalpheme will not die, Akhram. There will always be young men ready to take up the challenge. Do not fear."

When it was time to go I promised the Todalpheme that I would halt on my journey to the outer ocean and give them Lahal. I also promised myself the sight of this wonderful Dam of Days and its gates and locks, for judging by the Grand Canal it must be an engineering work of colossal scale.

They gave me a decent tunic of white cloth, and a satchel in which were placed, lovingly wrapped in leaves, a supply of the long loaves of bread, some dried meat, and fruit. Over my back I slung a profusely berried branch of palines. Then, with the hauberk and coif rolled up around my middle and the long sword depending from a pair of straps at my side, sandals on my feet, I set off.

They all crowded to see me go.

"Rememberee!" they called. "Rememberee, Dray Prescot."

"Rememberee!" I called back.

I knew that had I tried, now, to take any other course I would have been flung back to Earth. Much though I wanted to rush to Delia, much though I yearned to hold her in my arms again, I dare not take a single step overtly in her direction.

I was trapped in the schemes of the Star Lords, or the Savanti—although I suspected that those calm grave men wished me well, even though they had turned me out of paradise. If I tried to board a ship for Vallia, I felt sure I would find myself engulfed by that enveloping blueness and awake on some remote part of the Earth where I had been born.

Being unprovided with either a zorca or a vove, those riding animals of the great plains of Segesthes, I walked. I walked for the better part of six burs.*

I had absolutely no concern over the future. This time was different from all the other times I had gone forward into danger and adventure. I might seek to hire myself out as a mercenary. I might seek employment on a ship. It did not matter. I knew that the forces that toyed with me and drove me on would turn my hand to what they had planned for me.

Do not blame me. If you believe that I welcomed this turn of events, then you are woefully wrong. I was being forced away from all that I held dear in two worlds. I had more or less resigned myself to the truth that I would never again return—or be permitted to return—to Aphrasöe, the City of the Savanti; and all that I wanted on Earth or Kregen was my Delia of the Blue Mountains. Yet if I took a single step in her direction I felt sure the forces that manipulated my des-

---

* A bur is the Kregan hour, some forty Earth minutes long. It is divided into fifty murs, the Kregan minute. Discrepancies in the year caused by the orbit of Kregen about a binary are ironed out at festival times. There are forty-eight burs in the Kregan day and night cycle. I have omitted much of what Dray Prescot says of mensuration on Kregen and have considerably amended his account of the technical activities of the tide-watchers, the Todalpheme.

A.B.A.

tiny would contemptuously toss me back to Earth. I felt
mean and vengeful. I was not a happy man as I walked out
in the mingled suns-shine to seek the city of Grodno; the man
or beast who crossed my path had best beware and walk with
a small tread when I passed by.

The shoreline presented a strangely dead appearance.

I passed no habitations, no small fishing villages, no towns
or hamlets bowered in the trees that grew profusely everywhere. Trees and grass and flowers grew lushly all along my
way; the air tanged with that exciting sting of the sea, salty
and zestful; the green sun and the red sun shed their opaline
rays across the landscape and over the gleaming expanse of
smooth blue sea: but I met no single living soul in all that
journey.

When the provisions given me by the Todalpheme were exhausted I used my acquired Clansman's skills and hunted
more. The water in the streams and rills tasted as sweet as
Eward wine from Zenicce. I was slowly working on the hauberk, unfixing the linked mesh along the spine and the sides
and lacing it up again to a broader fit with leather thongs. I
did not hurry the work; I did not hurry in my walk. If those
dung-bellied Star Lords wanted me to do their dirty work for
them, then I would do it in my own time.

I could not be sure it was the Star Lords who had arranged this. I did feel sure, though, that if they did not wish
me to travel where I was traveling they would stop me. I had
the idea that the Savanti, powerful and mysterious though
they were, could not, when all was said and done, overmaster
the Everoinye, the Star Lords.

No matter who was forcing me to take this course (I did
not discount the emergence of yet a third force into the
arena where actions and conflicts were being battled out
quite beyond my comprehension), I was being used on Kregen. I had been used in Zenicce to overthrow the Most Noble
House of Esztercari. I had done so, and in the doing of it
had become the Lord of Strombor. Then, in my moment of
victory when I was about to be bethrothed to my Delia, I
had been whisked back to Earth. Oh, yes, I was being used,
like a cunning and shiftless captain will use his first lieutenant
quite beyond the bounds of duty. So. I can remember the
moment well, as I walked along a low cliff line above the sea,
that smooth inner sea of Turismond, with the breeze in my
face and the twin suns shining brilliantly down. If I were to
be used in a fashion that the modern world, the world of the

twentieth century, would call a troubleshooter, then I would
be a troubleshooter for the Star Lords, or the Savanti, or
anyone else, on my own terms.

Nothing I did must interfere with my set purpose to find
Delia. But, equally, I could do nothing to seek her until I had
settled the matter in hand. Accordingly, then, I walked along
with a heart if not lighter, at least less oppressed. Still, I hungered for some tangible opponent to face with steel in my
hand.

I had not led a particularly happy life. Happiness, I tended
to think in those far-off days, was a kind of mirage a man
dying of thirst sees in the desert. I had found great wonder
and pleasure among my Clansmen, and had striven for the
achievement of Delia of Delphond only to lose her in the
moment of gaining; I wondered if I would ever be able to
say with Mr. Valiant-for-Truth, out of Bunyan's *Pilgrim's
Progress*: "With great difficulty I am got hither, yet now I do
not repent me of all the trouble I have been at to arrive
where I am."

The days passed and I had seen no human life, only
avoided a pack of grundals. I had looked out on an empty
sea and walked through an empty countryside.

What I had seen at Akhram and my knowledge mainly
gained from long hours reading during off-watch periods
made me take a long swing inland. The Todalphemes' maps
had shown the inner sea, the *Eye of the World* it was marked
down in the cursive script on the ancient parchment, as being
bean-shaped, humped to the north, and something over five
hundred dwaburs* long from west to east. Because of its in-
dented coastlines, it was studded with bays, peninsulas, islands, and the river deltas. Its width was difficult to measure
accurately although proportionally a bean-shape gives a good
impression.

The average width might be something in the order of a
hundred dwaburs; however, that would not take into account
the two smaller but still sizable seas opening off the southern

* I have left Prescot's use of the Kregish "dwabur" here. A dwabur
is one of the standard units of measurement and is approximately five
Terrestrial miles. Its origin, according to Prescot, comes from the sunset
people's army marching disciplines: they would continue for two of
their hours, that is, burs (the Kregish word for two is dwa), with a
halt. Their speed must therefore have been something over three and a
half miles an hour. More usual are the local lesser fractions of the
dwabur.

A.B.A.

shore, reached through narrow channels. I was in the northern hemisphere of Kregen still, and I had gathered that Vallia lay across the outer ocean, the sea that in Zenicce we called the Sunset Sea, east with a touch of northing in it from here. Between the eastern end of the inner sea and the eastern end of the continent of Turismond lay vast and craggy mountains; beyond were areas inhabited by inhospitable peoples around whom had gathered all the chilling and horrific legends to be expected from a land of mystery. I gathered also that these people of the inner sea, the Eye of the World, relished a tall story as much as the folk of Segesthes.

So I struck a little inland, away from that shining sea.

On the third day I was rewarded by finding myself among cultivated rows of sah-lah bushes, their blossom incredibly sweet, bright like the missal I had seen by the Grand Canal. This particular season was burgeoning with the promise of a rich, ripe harvest and every chance of a successful second crop.

I watched carefully, for I had enough experience of savage Kregen now not to rush in headlong without a surveillance; alas, a stricture I was continually forgetting in the stress of one emergency after another. Here, however, there seemed to be no emergency; in fact I would then have hazarded a guess that stress and danger were unknown. I would have been wrong; but not for the reasons I advanced to myself as I crouched in the bushes and stared out on the orderly rows of huts, the busy men and women in the fields, the sense of discipline and order everywhere.

When I had satisfied myself that this must be some kind of farm on a colossal scale, with all the usual muddle and filth inseparable from farm life removed in some magical way, I decided I had best wash myself before making an appearance. I found a stream and stripped off and thus, all naked and streaming water, I saw the mailed man ride into sight over the bank. I was to be caught more than once swimming, naked, to mutual misunderstandings, for men shed more than clothes when they strip. On this occasion I was given no chance at explanations, no chance to talk, no chance to prove myself a stranger here, not one of their people.

A man clad in steel mesh leaned from his mount and swung his sword down toward my head.

I ducked and turned, but the water stinging my eyes had betrayed my accuracy of vision, the water around my waist hampered me, and the blade caught me flatly across the back of the skull.

I have a thick skull, I think, and it has taken enough knocks to prove it tough and durable and obstinate, too, I admit. All my poor old head bone could do on this occasion was to save my life. I could not stop the sudden black swoop of darkness and unconsciousness.

CHAPTER FOUR

Magdag

"I have persuaded Holly," said Genal, looking up with a squint from where he slapped and shaped a mud brick, "to bring us an extra portion of cheese when the suns are overhead."

"You'll ask that poor girl to do too much one day, Genal," I told him with a severity that was only half a mockery. "Then the guards will find out, and—"

"She is clever, is Holly," said Genal, slapping his brick with a hard and competent hand. The sounds of bricks being slapped and patted and the splash of water, the hard breathing of hundreds of work people making bricks, floated up into the stifling air.

"Too clever—and too beautiful—for the likes of you, Genal, you hollow-bricker, you."

He laughed.

Oh, yes. The work people here in the city of Magdag could laugh. We were not slaves, not, that is, in the meaning of that foul word. We worked for wages that were paid in kind. We were supplied from the massive produce farms kept up by the overlords, the mailed men of Magdag. Of course we were whipped to keep up our production quota of bricks. We would not receive our food if we fell behind in output. But the workers were allowed to leave their miserable little hovels, crowded against the sides of the magnificent buildings they were erecting, to travel the short distance to their more permanent homes in the warrens for weekends.

I made a scratch with my wooden stylus on the soft clay tablet I held in its wooden bracket.

"You had best move at a more rapid rate, Genal," I told him.

He seized another mass of the brick mud and began to slap and bang at it with the wooden spatula, sprinkling it with

41

water as he did so. The earthenware jar was almost empty and he cried out in exasperation.

"Water! Water, you useless cramph! Water for bricks!"

A young lad came running with a water skin with which to replenish the jar. I took the opportunity to have a long swig. The suns were hot, close together, shining down in glory.

All about me stretched the city of Magdag.

I have seen the Pyramids; I have seen Angkor; I have seen Chichen Itza, or what is left of it; I have seen Versailles and, more particularly, I have seen the fabled city of Zenicce. None can rival in sheer size and bulk the massive complexes of Magdag. Mile after mile the enormous blocks of architecture stretched. They rose from the plain in a kind of insensate hunger for growth. Countless thousands of men, women, and children worked on them. Always, in Magdag, there was building.

As for the styles of that architecture, it had changed over the generations and the centuries, so that forever a new shape, a fresh skyline, would lift and reveal a new facet in this craze for megalithic building obsessing the overlords of Magdag.

At that time I was a plain sailor lightly touched by my experiences on Kregen, still unaware of what being the Lord of Strombor would truly mean. For years my home had been the pitching, rolling, noisy timbers of ships, both on the lower deck and in the wardroom. To me, building in brick and stone meant permanence. Yet these overlords continued to build. They continued to erect enormous structures which glowered across the plain and frowned down over the inner sea and the many harbors they had constructed as part and parcel of their craze. What of the permanence of these colossal erections? They were mostly empty. Dust and spiders inhabited them, along with the darkness and the gorgeous decorations, the countless images, the shrines, the naves, and chancels.

The overlords of Magdag frenziedly built their gigantic monuments and mercilessly drove on their work people and their slaves; the end results were simply more enormous empty buildings, devoted to dark ends I could not fathom then.

Genal, whose dark and animated face showed only half the concentration of a quick and agile mind needful in the never-ending task of making bricks, cast a look upward.

"It is almost noon. Where is Holly? I'm hungry."

Many other brick makers were standing up, some knuckling their backs; the sounds of slapping and shaping dwindled on the hot air.

An Och guard hawked and spat.

Now women were bringing the midday food for their men.

The food was prepared at the little cabins and shacks erected in the shadows of the great walls and mighty upflung edifices. They clung like limpets to rocks. The women walked gracefully among the piles of building materials, the bricks, the ladders, the masonry, the long lengths of lumber.

"You are fortunate, Stylor, to be stylor to our gang," said Genal as Holly approached.

I nodded.

"I agree. None cook as well as Holly."

She shot me a quick and suspicious look, this young girl whose task was to cook and clean for a brick-making gang, and then to take her turn with the wooden spatula of sturmwood. The sight of my ugly face, I suppose, gave her pause. Because I had been discovered to possess the relatively rare art of reading and writing—all a gift of that pill of genetically-coded language instruction given to me so long ago by Maspero, my tutor in the fabulous city of Aphrasöe—I had automatically been enrolled as a stylor, one who kept accounts of bricks made, of work done, of quotas filled. Stylors stood everywhere among the buildings, as they stood at seed time and harvest in the Magdag-owned field farms, keeping accounts.

For that simple skill of reading and writing I had been spared much of the horror of the real slaves, those who labored in the mines cutting stone, or bringing out great double-handfuls of gems, or rowed chained to galley oar benches.

Magdag, despite its grandiose building program that dominated the lives of everyone within fifty dwaburs, was essentially a seaport, a city of the inner sea.

And here was I, a sailor, condemned to count bricks when the sea washed the jetties within hearing and the ships waited rocking on the waves. How I hungered for the sea, then! The sea breeze in my nostrils made me itch for the feel of a deck beneath my feet, the wind in my hair, the creak of ropes and block, the very lifeblood of the sea!

We all sat down to our meal and, as she had promised, Holly portioned out a double-helping to Genal, who motioned to her to do likewise for me. We were all wearing the plain gray breechclout, or loincloth, of the worker. Some of the women also wore a gray tunic; many did not bother, wanting their arms free for the never-ending work. As Holly bent before me I looked into her young face. Naïve, she looked, dark-haired, serious-eyed, with a soft and seemingly scarcely-formed mouth.

"And since when has a stylor deserved extra rations, stolen at expense and danger?" she asked Genal.

He started up hotly, but I put a hand on his shoulder and he went down with some force.

"It is no matter."

"But I think it is a matter—"

I made no answer. A man was running toward us through the gangs of workers eating their midday meal. He thwacked a long balass stick down on shoulders as he ran, his face angry.

"Up, you lazy rasts! There is work. Up!"

With a snarled yelp of indignant anger Genal rose, his young face flushed, his eyes bright. Holly took a quick step to stand beside him. Her head came just to his shoulder. Both of them had to look up if they wished to stare into my face.

"Pugnarses," said Genal disgustedly. He would have said more, but Holly laid her slender hand upon his arm.

The man was an overseer, a worker like ourselves but selected out from our miserable ranks to be given his tithe of petty authority, a balass stick—balass is similar to Earthly ebony—and a gray tunic with the green and black badges of his authority stitched to breast and back. He was a tall man, almost as tall as me, burly, with unkempt black hair and pinched nostrils, his eyebrows shaggy and frowning above his malice-bright eyes. He was the gang-boss of ten gangs, and he would never tolerate underproduction or skimped work. Always, the threat of the whip hung over Pugnarses as it dominated our lives.

We all rose, grumbling and stretching and bolting the last mouthfuls of our food.

Pugnarses thwacked his stick down with a ferocity I clearly saw came from his own simmering anger at what he did. He was a man born into the wrong area of life. He should have been a son to some high overlord, to strut about wearing his mail armor, his long sword at his side, giving orders in the midst of battle rather than orders as to quantities and qualities of mud bricks.

We could now hear the high yells of other overseers and the long moaning chants of hundreds of workers and slaves.

"We could see the winged statue being dragged by hundreds of men and women."

As we ran down among the scattered confusion of the brick
works and out past where the masons were looking up from
their midday meal, we could see the winged statue fully three
hundred feet tall, being dragged by hundreds of men and
women. The colossal statue towered above us, magnificent in
its barbarity of inspiration and cultural attainment. Many
days had been spent carving those immobile features, that
cliff-like forehead, the feathered crown, the folded arms with
their implements of semi-divine authority, those spreading
wings of minutely carved feathers. Beneath its footed pedestal
massive rollers of lenk creaked with the weight. As the slaves
pulled and hauled and struggled in the heat, dragging that
whole awful mass by long ropes, other workers lifted their
rearmost roller in turn and carried it to the front. There the
great overseer—with the blaze of color on his white tunic and
a coiled whip in his right hand—could direct its accurate
placing for the forward rolling weight.

We were hurriedly positioned onto a rope and we tailed on
as Pugnarses, sweating, shouted and lifted his balass stick. In
time with the convulsive heavings of the other slaves we
dragged the monstrous statue up the gentle incline that been
the cause of its momentary hesitation and the consequent calling out of fresh draft-animals—us—men and women, workers of Magdag.

Between us, with much breath wasted on cursing and
swearing and the calling on Grakki-Grodno, the sky god of
the draft-beasts, and with the balass sticks and the whips of
the guards falling upon our sweating naked backs, we hauled
that divine effigy up the slope. We dragged it clear of the incline and halfway toward the shadow-darkened gateway, four
hundred feet high, into which it must pass to be set against
the wall and serve as just one more reminder of the majesty
and power of Magdag.

In the long lines toiling on the ropes alongside I saw numbers of the half-humans of Kregen. There were Ochs; and
Rapas, those vulturine-like people whose smell was so offen-
sive in the nostrils of men; there was even a handful of Fristles. I saw no Chuliks among the slaves, although there were
other beast-humans whose forms were new to me.

Other men and Ochs and Rapas with swords and whips
guarded and goaded on men and Ochs and Rapas. Truly,
creation on Kregen had leveled the species. Humanity, although apparently everywhere in the ascendant here in this
section of Kregen, was not the only Lord of Creation. I saw

a number of men greasing the ropes near their fastenings, and inspecting each roller in turn as it was dragged clear for cracks and weaknesses. Many of these men had red hair, and so might well have come from Loh, that continent of hidden walled gardens and veils, that lay southeast of Turismond in the Sunset Sea, nearer to Vallia than the eastern tip of Turismond, where only isolated cities flourished in a sea of barbarity. The thought of Vallia with its island empire I had never seen brought unbidden other memories from which I could never shake free, and I bent to the rope with a curse.

"By Zim-Zair," panted a burly slave, entirely naked, next to me on the adjoining rope. "I'd have this accursed heathen statue topple and split into a thousand fragments!"

"Silence, slave!" A Chulik flicked a cunning whip in a welting blow down the man's back. "Pull!"

The slave, his mass of curly black hair wet and glittering in the suns-shine, cursed but had no spittle to express his contempt. "Loathsome beasts," he grunted, low, as he hauled with cracking muscles. His skin was tanned and healthy, his nose an arrogant beak, his lips thin. "By Zantristar the Merciful! If I had my blade at my side now—"

On and on we hauled and heaved that mighty colossus into its appointed resting place. It would make, I knew, another fine haunt for spiders.

As we crowded out through that towering opening, jumbled together, the workers talking and laughing now the work was done, the slaves moody and silent, I made it my business to get alongside the curly-haired man.

"You mentioned Zim," I said.

He drew a brawny forearm across his bearded lips. He looked at me cautiously.

"And if I had, would that surprise a heretic?"

I shook my head. We moved into the light. "I am no heretic. I thought Zair—"

"Grodno is the sky deity these poor deluded fools worship when all men living in the light know it is to Zair we must look for our salvation." His eyes had measured me. "You have not been a slave long? Are you a stranger?"

"From Segesthes."

"We know nothing of the outer ocean here in the Eye of the World. If you are a stranger, then in peril of your immortal soul I counsel you to have no truck with Grodno. Only to Zair can men look for salvation. They took me from my galley, the overlords of Magdag; they branded me and made me a slave. But I shall escape, and return across the inner sea to Holy Sanurkazz."

We were thrust apart in the throng, but I caught his arm. Here was information for which I/ hungered. The name of Sanurkazz caught at my imagination. I have mentioned how, when I first heard the name Strombor, my blood thumped and I felt a golden splendor unfolding. Here, now, was an echo of that feeling as the name Sanurkazz fell for the first time on my ears.

"Can you tell me, friend—" I began.

He interrupted me. He looked down at my hand on his arm.

"I am a slave, stranger. I suffer the whip and the irons and the balass. But no slave or worker lays a hand on me."

I took my hand away. I did not remove it swiftly. I did not express an apology, for I have made it a rule never to apologize, but I nodded, and my face must have given him pause.

"What is your name, stranger?"

"Men call me Stylor, but—"

"Stylor. I am Zorg—Zorg of Felteraz."

We would have gone on speaking, but the overseers whipped the slaves away and shouted at the workers, and so we parted. I had been impressed by this man. He might be a slave; he was not broken.

By the time we had returned to the brick works, a temporary site among the colossal buildings all around, the time for our midday meal break had long passed and we were put immediately onto brick making again. As I checked the production and made the neat marks in the Kregish cursive, for there was always a strict accounting, I pondered on this man, Zorg of Felteraz. He, most clearly, did not share in the worship of the green-sun deity, Grodno. He was a follower of Zair. So, that was why he was a slave and not a worker. The differences between the two conditions were small; they existed and were either resented or proudly proclaimed; but for a free man the pride involved was a pitiful thing.

My days among the megalithic buildings of Magdag passed.

The sheer scope of the complexes amazed me. Men would be perched atop crazy scaffoldings of wood executing marvelous friezes along the architraves, five hundred feet in the air. The statuary varied from life size to enormous creations of many artificially interlocked masses of stone. So much art, so much skill, so much painstaking labor, and all to decorate

and beautify vast and empty halls. Some of these buildings
were truly gigantic. I heard odd comments about the time of
dying, the time of the Great Death and the Great Birth, but
little added up beyond what might be a simple agricultural
death and re-creation cycle.

I was sure of one thing. These were not giant mausoleum
sacrifices of the living to the dead: they were not tombs; they
were not Kregan Pyramids.

Most of life aboard ship is occupied in waiting, and so I
slipped easily into that life among the megaliths of Magdag,
having been well-schooled in waiting. I knew that if I tried to
break away without the permission of the Star Lords—I had
by now convinced myself they must be the instruments of my
present position—I would be punished by transferral back to
Earth.

As a stylor I could move among the buildings with some
freedom, and I spent some time searching for the man of
Zair, Zorg of Felteraz, but I did not find him. However, I
will speak only of those things immediately touching on what
followed, leaving out most of the unpleasant punishments; the
starvings that followed low production or the lack of height
in a wall by a certain date; the sporadic revolts ruthlessly
put down by the half-beast, half-human guards; the infrequent
days of feasting; the fights and quarrels and thievery of the
warrens. They made a life savage, bizarre, demanding: a life
that no man or woman should have to endure.

I said to Genal: "Why do you and your people slave and
suffer for the overlords simply so as to build them more
empty monuments? Don't you wish to live your own life?"

To which he would reply, his fists knotted: "Aye, Stylor, I
do! But revolt—that must be carefully planned—carefully
planned—" He looked about him uneasily.

Many men and women talked of revolt. Slave and worker,
all spoke of the time when they could become free men
through rebellion. At this time I do not think one of them
thought beyond a rebellion to a true revolution.

Maybe I do the Prophet a disservice in saying this.

Perhaps, even then, he had a glimmering of the true ideals
of revolution over the bloody gut-reaction of rebellion, for
afterward he proved himself nobly. He was called only the
Prophet; he must have had a name, but it was forgotten.
Slaves might be called what their master wished; in my case I
had been called Stylor for the task I performed without my
even being aware of that until the name was in habitual use.

Among the close-packed warrens on the landward edge of the city, outside the gay and noble sections where the overlords lived in luxury with the sea breeze to cool them in the heat of the day, the Prophet moved with a sure tread, preaching. He spoke simply that no man should own another in slavery, that no man should cringe to the whip, whether slave, worker, or free, that men should have some say in what happened to them in life.

I met him from time to time wandering the warrens among the slaves and the workers, speaking in words of fire, to be met with lackluster eyes and disillusioned shrugs, the sloughing away of all hope. He was constantly on the run from the guards. He was an object of pity and some affection to the workers, like a blind dog they would not see killed, and so they hid him and fed him and passed him along from hideout to hideout. In those runnels of ancient brick and mud walls, of crazy roofs and toppling walls and towers, an army could have been lost. The guards ventured into the interior at their peril, only in force.

For two days in every twleve the workers might return to their homes in the warrens, although often they contrived to spend more time there than that, until roused out by guards. Then the Prophet would speak to them, trying to inflame them, trying to arouse them.

Because he was an old man, even by Kregan standards, being, I suppose, about a hundred and eighty, his hair was white. His white mass of hair, his white beard, his white moustache, were merely the ordinary features of an old man, and their remarkable similarity to what one conceives of as a prophet's appearance was merely coincidental. His old eyes fairly snapped at me like a barracuda as he spoke, his voice a hoarse resounding trumpet easily audible a quarter of a dwabur away. Such men are known on our own Earth.

The guards, whether human or beast, seldom ventured into the slave warrens. Holly, Genal, and I were standing in a doorway listening to the Prophet, and both young people's faces were alight with their inner passions. They, at least, saw sense in what the Prophet said. Beneath scattered torchlight the mass of workers and slaves before us listened as at an entertainment; their spirits had been whip-broken. Then the shouts and shrieks broke out, the trample of iron-shod hooves, the clash of arms.

A party of mail-clad men rode in heavily from a side street, deploying instantly, yodeling and shouting, to come smashing into the mass of people. They were using their swords' edges. Blood spouted. The Prophet disappeared. Holly screamed. I grabbed her arm and Genal took her other hand and we dived back into the doorway. Even as the warped boards closed on us the mounted men hammered past.

"They're not after the Prophet," said Holly, her breast heaving, her eyes wide and wild. "This is sport for them, a great Jikai!"

I winced to hear that word in this contemptible context.

"Yes," said Genal viciously. "It is time for them to come hunting for fun." His eager voice broke. "For fun!"

"There is work for me tonight," said Holly. I stared at her. I had no idea what she meant. I was to find out.

CHAPTER FIVE

Bait for overlords

The Maiden with the Many Smiles, the largest moon of Kregen, floated free of cloud. Brilliant pink moonlight flooded down over the deserted square on the outskirts of the warrens. In many doorways human bright-eyed maidens waited. Given the size of the moon, almost twice that of Earth's satellite, the fullness and the brilliance of the night, the square was lit as brightly as many a daytime on Earth. In the shadows between the moonlight the girls waited. Presently, the soldiers, the mercenaries, the guards came. They carried money, presents, eager smiles, and manifold lusts.

In one shadowed doorway, only the long limber length of one shapely leg showing in moonlight, waited Holly.

"Are you sure?" I whispered to Genal.

"Yes. We have done this before."

"Quiet, you stupid calsanys!" Pugnarses spoke with venom and ill-concealed impatience. His balass stick was gone; now he clutched a cudgel made from homely sturm-wood. Genal also held a cudgel. We watched as the men in their ornate robes, their hair coiffed and perfumed, the rings glittering on their fingers, walked along the arcades and past the doorways of the square, gradually filling it as more and more appeared after the arduous day's tasks. Holly's leg looked almost indecently exposed and alluring, there in that streaming pink moonlight. Two other moons, also at the full, hurtled past low over the crazy rooflines of the warrens.

The men at arms were not wearing their mesh steel now. It would interfere in their delights of love.

One approached Holly. He was tall and saturnine, with a black down-drooping moustache and a mouth like a rast. He wore a gorgeous green robe, much bedecked with silver embroidery. His coin purse chinked as he walked. He had a long dagger belted at his waist.

Holly said: "Do I please you, master?"

His eyes appraised her boldly.

"You please me, wench, by your looks. But can you perform?"

"Come with me, master, and you shall taste delights such as the voluptuous Gyphimedes the immortal mistress herself never vouchsafed the beloved of Grodno."

The man's eyes brightened and his tongue-tip moistened his narrow lips. "You interest me, wench. Two silver oars."

I could guess Holly would be pouting, twisting her hips so as more excitingly to strain the thin material of the shush-chiff, the sarong-like garment worn by girls on festive occasions. "Three silver oars, master," she wheedled.

"Two."

Genal was fidgeting next to me, and Pugnarses rumbled thickly: "May Makku-Grodno take the girl! What does the money matter? Let her make haste!"

Genal said quickly: "She must act her part."

The bargain was struck at two silver oars and two copper oars—those tarnished coins of Magdag with the crossed oars on their reverses, a variety of vapid faces of Magdag overlords on their obverses. The man bent his head to follow Holly into the doorway, with a lascivious chuckle on his lips, his hands already reaching to strip away the shush-chiff. Genal and Pugnarses, one on each side of the door, struck the man over the head and as he collapsed soundlessly forward into my arms I dragged him bodily inside. Not one of us said a word. I stared at Holly in her shush-chiff and, indeed, she was exceedingly beautiful, young and fresh and soft, sweet with the promise of youth.

Then she went to stand once more flaunting her beauty insolently in the pink moonshine, as human bait.

That night, my first at the task, we picked up six men who wished to sample Holly's wares. We bound them and gagged them and took their finery, personal jewelry, money, and weapons. This facet of Holly amazed me; I saw she could act with all the sure purpose of a mature woman. The men would be sent into the warrens by certain paths Holly knew. From there, naked and bound, they would find their way into distant slave gangs over the other side of the building complex. It would be impossible to prove their identities when confronting the immediate response from the overlords and the guards, which was usually a blow to the head. Holly, however, seldom took even that risk. She usually insisted the men be sent to the galleys; who would not tremble at that simple phrase? Sent to the galleys.

When I asked why the hated overlords and guards were not killed out of hand, Genal looked at me as though I were mad.

"What?" he exclaimed. "Send them straight up to Geno-dras, to sit in glory at the right hand of Grodno, before they have suffered here on earth? I want to know they suffer, first, before they die and are received into the Green Glory."

I did not say anything.

What had impressed me as a vital element in the structure of the Eye of the World was that while the slaves believed in the red-sun deity, Zair, in general; the workers, whose allegiance should have wholeheartedly belonged to Grodno, were most lax and loose in their beliefs. This feeling that death would release them to go to their hopes of glory in the green sun was perhaps the strongest religious tenet they tolerated.

The surrounding countryside was terrorized by the mailed men. They took anything they wanted outside the immediate bounds of their city limits and the enormous machine-run, factory-type farms. By galley and by their mounted cavalry, they dominated the northern littoral. There were other cities on the northern shores, but none approached Magdag in size, power, or magnificence.

So far I had seen no zorcas or voves, those magnificent riding animals of Segesthes. The overlords rode a six-legged beast rather like a skittish mule, blunt-headed, wicked-eyed, pricked of ear, with slatey-blue hide covered with a scanty coarse hair that overlords trimmed and oiled. I wondered at their suitability as mounts; the six-legged gait is often awkward and uncomfortable for a rider. The riders did not wield lances, relying on their long swords. I saw little evidence of bows, and those I did see were the standard short, straight bow; neither the reflex compound bow of my Clansmen nor the long English yew bow were in evidence in Magdag. The riding beasts, the sectrixes, seemed to me good sturdy animals, although I doubted their hardiness; they did not, in my estimation, stand enough hands high to give a Clansman all the room he would like in which to swing his ax or broadsword.

More and more I was coming to see Magdag as a great builder's yard. The slaves and the workers, and occasionally the free artificers, lived in their tiny shacks of straw or lathe or mud brick tucked against the sides of the mighty buildings they were constructing or ornamenting. There was great richness in the buildings, masses of gold leaf and encrustation, acres of precious stones, porphyry, chemzite, chalcedony, ivory, kalasbrune, slabs of marble veined and pure, flashing in the suns. Inside the labyrinthine areas where the slaves gathered in the shadows, filth, and the smells there was only mud brick and clay and harsh stone, and miserly quantities of sturm-wood. The imbalances were great and terrible, greater, even, than my own Earth's at the close of the eighteenth century.

Inside these warrens was a kind of no-man's-land. The guards did not care to venture in unless in such force as to smash the slightest opposition. They did so enter, from time to time, to rout out skulkers, for there were many who sought to take sanctuary in the slaves' warrens.

It was Genal who apprised me of the latest plot.

In the maze of alleys and courts linking and separating the hovels and the slave compounds, we walked after a period of a two-day rest. We had disposed of a goodly number of guards, and the reaction was, as usual, brusque. A new guard commander for our gangs, those of Pugnarses and the other slave overseers, had been appointed. He was a man whose meanness was a byword. Already he had had Naghan's woman flogged to death, the bright blood spouting as her back was ripped down to bone, the flesh and blood hanging in striped ringlets of agony. The plan was to kill this overseer, this overlord of the second class, one Wengard, and his whole platoon, and then to make an escape and seize a galley from a harbor—any galley, any harbor.

"I do not like it, Genal," I said.

"Neither do I." He hunched his shoulders as we walked toward the brick works, surrounded by slaves and workers. I was aware that I knew little of the inner conspiracies that must fester continually in a situation like this. There must be gangs, clans, sects, mobsters and criminals, perverts and blackmailers, by the thousand in these sinks. The person who wished to lead this latest revolt was a Fristle, one called Follon. I had no love for Fristles. They were not true men. They had two arms and two legs, true; but their faces were like those of cats, bewhiskered, furred, slit-eyed, and fang-mouthed. Fristles had carried my Delia off to her captivity in Zenicce when I had been transplanted to that beach in far Segesthes.

"There are Chulik guards, now, under Wengard, the overlord of the second class," I said.

"Yes," agreed Genal. "But Fristles are hereditary foes of Chuliks, except when hired as mercenaries by the same employer."

"Who is not a foe of Chuliks?" I said carelessly, not wishing to continue the conversation. I felt sure the Star Lords did not wish me to become embroiled with a plan of rebellion that had almost no chance of succeeding.

"Follon, the Fristle, had told me, now he has asked me outright. Do we join—more particularly, as a stranger here, do you join?"

"No," I said.

I thought that would be an end to it.

All about us the noise, the buzz, the stink, the never-ending toil went on. Work and work and more work, under the lash and the knout, under the balass stick. We worked, we workers and slaves. We worked.

Follon approached me during the single break of the day when the suns stood overhead. His cat-face looked mean, the whiskers stiff and spiked.

"You, Stylor. We have seen you fight. We need you."

There were always fights and scrimmages in the warrens and as a stranger I had had to impress on my unwilling comrades that I was not a man to be trifled with. I had broken in a few heads in the proving of that, and Follon, the Fristle, had not missed that significance.

"No," I said. "You must find help elsewhere."

"We want you, Stylor."

"No."

He puffed himself up at me. He reached up to my chest. His cat-face showed an expression I could clearly read—anger, resentment, blind fury that I had denied what he asked, and, too, fear. Why fear? He thrust at me. I moved back two steps, not a stagger, a deliberate disengagement. He jumped in, hands raking. I sidestepped, and chopped down on the back of his neck. He went on going forward, forward and down. He stayed down.

A whip cracked agonizingly across my back and I turned to stare at Wengard, the overlord of the second class. His mail-clad arm was raised and the whip about to lash down again.

"Cramph! I will not tolerate fighting! Pugnarses! This is your man. . . . Have him disciplined." As Pugnarses, sweating, ran up, Wengard said: "Stripe him with your balass, Pugnarses. No, you calsany, not now! After work, so that he may lie and suffer all night. I will inspect his back. I want to see blood, Pugnarses, blood and bone! And, tomorrow, I want to see him back at work."

The overlord prodded his foot into Follon's prone body.

"Take this stupid calsany away and when he awakes treat him in the same way. You hear, slave?"

"I hear, master," said Pugnarses. I saw his right fist contract on his balass stick, white like tallow, his knuckles like skulls. He dared not tell this mighty overlord that he was not a slave. The whip was poised, ready, hungry.

I rose to my feet and straggled off, prepared to endure a thrashing, of which I have had more than my share in life, rather than do anything that would upset the plans of the Star Lords and so hinder my eventual return to Strombor.

The mighty overlords could not be expected to know what slavery was like. Wengard, now, was serving as a slave-master because he must have committed some misdemeanor. Usually the overlords themselves only came to the workers' and slaves' warrens for sport—blood sport. I felt it would be very good to have Wengard and his ilk for a full day's work in the megaliths of Magdag.

As the twin suns dropped to the horizon, I prepared for my unpleasant interview with Pugnarses. He would not spare me for the fragile friendship we shared with Genal and Holly, for he was ambitious. One day he might, given luck, ruthlessness, and continuing health, become an overseer of overseers himself and wield a whip, clad in a white garment like the overlords themselves, giving his orders to the overseers of the balass. Pugnarses resented the fact that he had not been born an overlord.

Follon waited for me in the lath hut with its straw roof where I expected to find Pugnarses. I put down my clay tablet and laid the wooden implement carefully beside it. I moved gently, cautiously. A Fristle, suddenly appearing at the door, slammed it against the laths. In the sudden dimness I felt a thick net fall and envelop me. I heard a quickly-stifled uproar as Fristles jumped me.

"Pin his legs!" "Smash his head in!" "Kick him in the face!"

I lashed out, but the hampering net blunted my blows.

I saw the gleam of a dagger, a dagger like the one we had taken from the guard who had tried to sample Holly's fresh beauty. I tensed myself and then relaxed, ready to concentrate all my energy on that dagger. The door opened.

"Hold!"

I did not recognize the voice. Someone out of my vision was now giving quick, hissing instructions. I heard fragments. "Would you have him go straight to Genodras, to sit on the right hand of Grodno, in glory? Think, fools! Let him suffer for betraying us. Let him repent and repent again as he labors at the oars. To the galleys with him!"

I did not feel too grateful. Death—what was death to a man such as me? I had gained a thousand years of life by my baptism in the pool in the River Zelph that flows into the lake from which Aphrasöe, the Swinging City, grows. I had quivered at the thought, until I had found Delia of the Blue Mountains, and recognized that twice a thousand years would not be long enough to consume all the love I had for her.

It was my duty not to die while she lived. But, the galleys! I did not think much more. The sack in which they tied me was coarse and stinking and oppressive so that I struggled and gasped to breathe. Ignominiously, I was bundled down the secret slave ways from the warrens to the wharves and jetties of the harbor of Magdag.

After much bumping and stealthy movement I was flung down onto a wooden floor which moved with a swinging, familiar lilt. I was lying on a deck. Once more I was aboard a ship. I felt then the movement of the Star Lords—or the Savanti, those one-time friends of Aphrasöe—a movement I could neither understand nor explain.

CHAPTER SIX

Zorg and I share an onion

The two onions balanced on Zorg's calloused palm were not the same size. One was, to speak in Earthly measurements, something over three inches in diameter, plump and round, its orange-brown outer skins shining, crisp, and flaky. We both knew its insides would be sweet and succulent, tangy and rich. The second onion looked like a slave beside a master: smaller, about two inches in diameter, with hard stringy outer skins already extending up into a growing neck of unpleasant yellow-green. It was scrawny. But it, too, would contain food to sustain us within its unlikely-looking skin.

We studied the onions, Zorg and I, as the fortyswifter *Grace of Grodno* heaved forward on the swell with that blessed quartering breeze filling the sail above us. Sounds of shipboard life rose all about us, with the smells as well. The twin suns of Scorpio blazed mercilessly down on our shaved heads. Our crude, round conical hats fashioned of straw gave pitiful protection. Of course, up on the poop—*Grace of Grodno* was of that class of galley not provided with a quarterdeck—the overlords of Magdag lolled at their ease in deck chairs beneath striped awnings of silk and mashcera, sipping long cool drinks and toying with fresh fruits and juicy meats. Our two naked companions on the bench had already shared their onions between them, onions of the same size.

"The choice is onerous, Stylor," said Zorg of Felteraz.

"Indeed, a weighty problem."

We would receive no more food until breakfast the next morning; we were only reasonably provided with water, and that was simply because *Grace of Grodno*, with her single square sail and arrogantly jutting beak, had caught a favoring breeze. We would make port in Gansk that evening, and sail again the the next morning. The galleys of Magdag would venture on a cruise that would take them across the inner sea out of the sight of land for as much as four days at a stretch, but they did not like that. They preferred to hug the coast.

"If, my friend, we possessed a knife . . ."

Zorg had lost a lot of weight since I had first seen him, as a slave, in the colossal, empty hall of Magdag, dragging the idol of stone with me. The moment I had seen him again, after I had been transferred from the training liburna, I had made it my business to be near him when the oar-masters sorted us into benches. We had been oar companions now for a season—I had lost all count of days. On the inner sea, the Eye of the World, navigation even for galleys is possible for almost all of the season.

Zorg lifted the larger of the onions to his mouth. I simply looked at him. We had come to understand each other in these days. He regarded me with an expression that, for a galley slave, was as near to a reassuring smile as can be. He started to bite.

He bit swiftly and cleanly around the onion, his strong, yellow, uneven teeth chomping like a beaver's. He parted the onion into two not quite equal halves. Without hesitation he handed me the larger of the two.

I took it.

Then I handed him the smaller onion.

"If you value my friendship, Zorg of Felteraz," I said, with a ferociousness I had not intended, "you will eat this onion. Without argument."

"But, Stylor—"

"Eat!"

I do not pretend I enjoyed giving up part of my rations, but this man was clearly not as fit as he had been, or as he should be. And this was strange. It is well-known that if a man can survive as a galley slave for the first week he stands a chance of eventual existence; once he had become, as it were, pickled to the galley slave's life, he can endure unimaginable hardships and indescribable tortures. Once one has proved a galley slave, one can overcome obstacles of monstrous proportions. Zorg had come through the first terrible weeks when men were flogged to death daily at the benches and tossed overboard, when men's hands ran red with blood with no scrap of skin left on their palms or fingers, when they tore crazily at their ankles implacably fastened by the rings and chains, so that the blood and flesh oozed and scraped away to the bone.

The terrors of the galley slaves' lives are well-known in the abstract. I lived through them.

Zorg made that peculiar grimace that in a galley slave passes for a smile and idly, automatically, nipped a nit that crept upon his weather-beaten and salt-crusted skin. The coarse sacks stuffed with straw were alive with vermin. We cursed the nits and all the other bloodsucking parasites, but we endured them because while they lived we had the sacking bundles of straw with their mangy coverings of ponsho skins upon which to fling ourselves. The idea of galley slaves rowing as we were, four to an oar with the whole bodily movement thrust and pulled and flung into the stroke, without some form of bench covering is ludicrous. Our buttocks would have been lacerated within the space of three burs; even the cruel oar-masters of Magdag recognized that. The ponsho skins, which covered the sacks and fell to the decks, were not there because we were loved; they were provided because without them the galley would not function.

I admit, I had become used to the smells—almost.

Life aboard a two-decker beating about in blockade gave one a flying start in enduring discomfort, dampness, stink, and short rations. I enjoyed advantages that Zorg, for all that he was a powerful man and had been galley captain, did not share.

Now his face held a shrunken look that worried me.

Nath, next along on the loom of the oar, burped and cocked an ear. Nath is a common name on Kregen; this Nath was big and had once been burly, for galley slaves tend to fine down. I had wondered how that other Nath, Nath the Thief in far Zenicce, would have fared in the galleys.

"Wind's changing," Nath said, now.

This was bad news to Zorg and to Zolta, the fourth on our oar. As an experienced sailor I had known the wind shift for perhaps ten murs, but I had wished to keep that unpleasant news from Zorg as he finished the onion.

Almost immediately, the silver whistles were heard.

The oar-master took his position in a kind of tabernacle midway in the break of the poop. The whip-deldars ran along the central gangway, ready to lay into the naked backs of the slaves if they were slow in readying themselves. We were not slow. More whistles sounded. A group of sailors handled the sheets, bracing the single sail around. They were an unhandy bunch, and I had time to relish the thought of how my petty officers would like to teach them the ways of the Navy aboard a frigate or a seventy-four. Clumsily, with a great deal of billowing and cracking of sheets, the sail came down. Long before it had been mastered and brailed we were all at the ready, one foot pressed on the stretcher, the other pressed against the back of the bench in front, our arms out, and our calloused hands grasping our oar looms. All the loop-ropes holding the oars clear of the water still outboard, a neat custom of the galley captains of the inner sea, had been removed by the outboard men, in our case Zolta, whose task that was.

Now *Grace of Grodno* rocked before the gentle swell, her forty oars all parallel, in perfect alignment above the water. She must have looked like some great waterwalking beast, light and graceful with her slender lines burgeoning into a richly decorated stern with its upflung gallery, lowering down into the ram and beak low over the water.

Grace of Grodno was a galley that, here in the Eye of the World, men called a four-fortyswifter: forty oars, four men to an oar. The clumsy system sometimes used on Earth of rating a galley by men to a bench was not used in the inner sea. The oars poised, ready. The drum-deldar beat once, a single, admonitory boom. I could see the oar-master as he looked up to where an officer leaned over the poop rail, all white and green and golden finery. No doubt they were savoring a little of our smell back there on the poop now. The officer had a handkerchief to his face. The oar-master lifted his silver whistle, and I collected myself, ready.

The whistle sounded, the drum boomed, all in a practiced series of sounds and orders, and every oar went down as one.

We pulled smoothly through the stroke. The drum-deldar beat out a steady rhythm, a double-beat of his two drums, one tenor and one bass, a smooth steady long-haul stroke. Our backs moved through the rhythm, forward so that our hands and the looms of our oars thrust above the bent backs of the slaves on the benches before us, then a steady—oh, so steady—pull.

Grace of Grodno moved through the water. She moved with the same feeling which had been so strange to me at the time I had stepped aboard that galley in the lake from which the City of Aphrasöe grows. Now, in this smooth inner sea, the galley surged ahead as though on tracks. She scarcely rolled at all, and she drove forward over the calm sea like a monstrous beetle with forty legs.

She was a relatively small galley. Only twenty oars on a

side meant that her length was much below those of the fleet galleys I had seen in the arsenal harbor of Magdag, and, at a guess, I would say she was not above a hundred feet on the waterline. Again at a guess, for I never saw her broadside on from a distance, overall she would not have exceeded a hundred and forty. I admit now that I had been puzzled by these swifters' possession of both ram and beak, thinking them mutually exclusive, but I had learned just how the galleys of the inner sea were fought.

She was, of course, outrageously unseaworthy.

We labored at the oars with a smooth, short, economical stroke that would give us some two knots speed.

I, of course, had no idea what our mission was. I was merely a chained galley slave. As my body went through the unending mechanical motions of rowing, I pondered on that "chained slave" label. Between us, Zorg and I, we had been cautiously and carefully rubbing the link of the chain that bound us to the bench against a metal bracket-strut. Sweat-molded filth crammed into the growing breach concealed against discovery. As we bent forward and flung ourselves backward, over and over again, and the galley drove forward through the calm water, I could not help worry over Zorg.

"Ease up, Zorg," I whispered to him when the whip-deldar had passed, vigilant in his patrolling of the gangway, his whip flicking, seemingly alive, hungry. The galley slaves called the whip "old snake." I knew the expression had been used on Earth. One could easily understand why.

"I—will—bear my part, Stylor—"

"I will push and pull that much more, Zorg." I was annoyed. He was a friend. I was worried about him. Yet he insisted stubbornly on pushing and pulling with the best, all out of his pride. Oh, yes, I knew the pride that burned in my friend Zorg of Felteraz.

"I am Zorg." He spoke in a low mumble. We could speak while rowing this easy stroke. "I am Zorg," he said again as though seeking to hold onto that, and then: "I am Zorg, Krozair! Krozair! I will never yield!"

I did not know what he meant by Krozair. I had not heard the word before. Nath rowed at the oar with a blind convulsion, his lean naked body panting for breath in the hot air. But Zolta looked across with a quick and rhythm-breaking suddenness. His face showed shock. I fought the oar back into rhythm, cursing in a lurid mixture of English, Kregish, and Magdag warren-filth.

We rowed.

I heard a hail.

Looking back toward the poop as I surfaced from each stroke I could see a turmoil up there. The awnings were coming down. That was good. Now their damnable surfaces would not catch wind and slow our progress. Men were running about up there. *Grace of Grodno,* I had been told, was more than a moderately fast galley for a four-fortyswifter, and in our cutting across a gulf in order to reach Gansk we had dropped the nearest land below the horizon.

It seemed to me as I rowed that I had been rowing all my life. Memories were faint around the edges, other worlds and other lives away. Only Delia of the Blue Mountains remained clear and beautiful to me in that time of inexpressible misery. I had been engaged as a galley slave in battles, when the galley of Magdag on which I served had captured a fat merchantman from one of the cities of Zair, and twice we had been involved in a real battle with a galley from Sanurkazz. But, so far, I had not been in action aboard *Grace of Grodno.* I did not know the ways of her captain or her oarmaster, her whip-deldars or her drum-deldar in moments of emergency. Zorg and I had been through a lot together on the calm waters of the Eye of the World. Now, the signs were clear: *Grace of Grodno* was clearing for action.

The drum-deldar increased his beat.

We pulled into it, keeping time, hauling the heavy looms through their prescribed arcs as delimited by the rowing frames guiding and controlling the movements of the extreme inboard ends of the looms. As the inboard man I had the most space to move through, and we were graded downward and outward as to size, where Zolta, the smallest, perched almost over the water on the projecting deck-platform behind the parados.

Soon it became clear, from the way in which the officers, soldiers, and sailors were continually looking aft, that we were being pursued. There would therefore be little chance of the ram being brought into action. As though confirming that a party of sailors appeared on the low foredeck—it was too small to be called a forecastle—and began to rig the forward extension of the beak. I heard shouting from the aftercastle at the extreme aft end of the poop. Soon an officer ran forward and the sailors began to unship the extension, amid a great deal of acrid comment.

Nath, his eyes upturned, his lungs pumping, spat out:

"So the Grodno-gasta thinks he'll fight! Ha!"

Grodno-gasta, I knew, was a blasphemous and extremely indelicate remark.

"Zair rot him!" snarled out Zolta, pulling.

We were now pulling at a back-breaking pace and still the drum-deldar stepped up the rate. Zorg was heaving now, not using his body as a good oarsman, but trying to do the work with his biceps. His face was a color that appalled me, slatey blue-green, something like the hide of a sectrix. He was gasping with a convulsive effort at each stroke.

"Sink me, Zorg!" I said viciously. "Roll with the stroke, you stupid man of Zair!"

He choked and did not have the spittle to hawk. His eyes rolled. He managed to croak out words: "I will never yield! Krozair! My vows—I am—Zorg! Zorg of—of Felteraz. Krozair!" He was rambling now, his body going up and down with the oar, hardly pulling a quarter of his weight. Then he used another name I had not heard before, and I knew that he was no longer with us aboard this foul galley of Magdag but far away: in delirium, yes, but not here with us. "Mayfwy," he said and, again, in a long sobbing groan: "Mayfwy."

He could not escape the observation of the whip-deldar much longer. Nath, Zolta, and I were pulling now with all the dead weight of Zorg hanging on the oar. Sweat reeked down our naked bodies. Then the green conical straw hat fell from Zorg's head and tumbled down.

Bareheaded, Zorg was the object of instant attention.

The whip-deldar lashed him. He laid the whip unerringly across my friend Zorg's back. Old snake talked to him.

Zorg's tanned skin split and blood oozed, then spouted out as the whip fell again and again. I, alongside, was splattered with the blood of my friend as the whip-deldar of Magdag flogged him to death.

"Get back to your oar!" roared the whip-deldar. "Pull!"

But Zorg of Felteraz was past all the pulling he would ever do in this life on this world of Kregen beneath Antares.

The confusion attendant upon freeing a dead slave from his shackles and throwing him overboard and replacing him with one of the oarsmen at the moment luxuriating in a spare capacity and chained deep in the hold, a luxury we all tasted in turn, was as nothing compared with the confusion evident on the poop. As the body of my friend Zorg, all naked and limp, with the blood dripping from his butchered back, was dragged out from the bench and hefted up to be thrown overboard, soldiers ran up to the aftercastle carrying bows. Others manned the ballistae. The sailors were readying their cutlasses. The confusion was abhorrent to me, as a man trained aboard a king's ship, but all my attention was required for the eternal rowing. Pull, pull, pull—and continue to pull. Once again the drum-deldar, under the shrilled commands from the poop, upped the rate.

I did not see Zorg consigned to the deep.

I did not see the splash his mutilated body made as it broke the surface of the water and vanished from mortal men's sight. I knew he believed that, after his death, he would go up to Zim to sit at the right hand of Zair, in all his glory. Suicides did not achieve this resurrection, either to the green or to the red, otherwise many of my fellow galley slaves would have found that shortcut to paradise.

I acted, I believe, out of pure animal instinct, out of hatred, out of sheer lust to kill and kill yet more of those wolves cᶜ Magdag. Yet I was a trained seaman, accustomed to handling ships, cunning in the use of wind and weather, and I knew that wolves of greater power than those of Magdag chased *Grace of Grodno*. If I say that instincts impelled me to foolhardy action that professional expertise would approve, that will perhaps best sum up what I then did.

As Zorg was taken from me, his shackles released, I put all my strength into breaking the last web of metal still joining the rubbed-through link. I surged up with such force that the loom of the oar cracked against the rowing frame. Nath and Zolta looked at me with numb faces, their bodies and arms going through the rowing motions that were ingrained into their muscles.

I felt stiff, tight about muscles abruptly trying to perform some different series of actions from those they had been forced into for hour after hour. The whip-deldar heard the crack of loom against rowing frame and came running, his whip high, his face vicious. I caught the lash in my left hand and jerked it and with my right hand I choked him around the throat. I threw him down among the slaves at the oars.

Then I was on the gangway.

So quick, so sudden, I stood there. I had once before seen a slave break from his oar. He had tried to dive overboard and sailors had caught him and held him, so that, later, the whip-deldar could cut him up with old snake.

I moved to the side, above the gawking faces of the slaves.

"I raced aft down the gangway."

Four soldiers, in mail, their long swords swinging free, ran down the gangway toward me. My movement to the side convinced them I was going to dive and they hesitated, ready to let me go, willing to be rid of a fool slave who might, just might, be picked up by the following ship. Or so I read their hesitation. If I was picked up, the pursuer would have to slow his pursuit. I think they came to the decision that the pursuer would not stop, would not be fobbed off by a screaming face in the water. They started toward me again—and I was on them. My balled fist smashed in the face of the first. He had no time to scream. I grasped his long sword. It hissed in the air. I clove the second through his ventail and he toppled backward, horror on his face, blood staining the mesh.

"Grab him, you fools!" screamed a voice from aft.

I leaped and swung and my blade hewed into the side of the face of the third even as I avoided the fourth's blow. This was more like the sword fighting to which I had been accustomed aboard Earthly ships, boarding in the battle-smoke. It was very little like the rapier and dagger work of Zenicce.

I bunched my left hand into the fourth man, smashed my hilt down into his face, then I cast him from me.

Now the slaves were yelling.

They were making a hideous row, like vosks in swill, snorting and roaring and screaming. I raced aft down the gangway.

The oar-master in his tabernacle saw what I intended.

He leaped up, shrieking: "Bows! Strike him down!"

I hauled myself up one-handed to the tabernacle and even as he tried to clamber out I cut him down. The drum-deldar had even less chance. The passion of my blow rolled his head down along the gangway for several yards before it toppled off into the rowing benches.

Soldiers were milling, running down the ladders from the poop.

So far I had not uttered a word.

Now, as the soldiers came running, I raced before them along the gangway. The first whip-deldar lay dead, but his mates were flogging the slaves on in an attempt, a desperate attempt, to keep the rhythm of the stroke. But the rhythm had been lost with the death of the drum-deldar.

Their whips were no defense against the long sword. Both whip-deldars went down, the one from amidships and the other from the bows. The mail-clad men were roaring now, pouring toward me. I lifted my voice.

"Men!" I roared. "Galley slaves! Stop rowing! Ease oars! The day of judgment is at hand!"

It was a melodramatic way of putting it, yet I knew the type of man I was dealing with in those whip-beaten galley slaves of Magdag. Some banks of oars faltered, the rhythm went wild, and then, because oars must of necessity swing together or they can do nothing, the larboard and the starboard wings of *Grace of Grodno* fluttered uncontrollably and clashed and fell silent. The looms went inboard. The slaves were now making so much noise I felt convinced the men of the pursuing galley, men and galley I had not yet seen, must hear them and take heart and know their time was near.

An arrow feathered into the gangway near me. I started aft again. I had not had a sword in my fist for too long. I am no believer in the joy of battle, the uplifting surge of blood, the way some men speak of their exaltation in battle. I do not enjoy killing; that, at least, the Savanti had had no need to teach me. But now—something about my whole series of experiences since reaching this inner sea, this Eye of the World, impelled me to a stereotyped reaction. Hatred, revulsion, anger, all were there and mixed in my motives. I felt a savage exultation as my long sword bit into the heads and bodies and limbs of my opponents.

I was young then, a sailor with a grievance, and I swung a mean sword. I roared at them, smiting and striking and lopping. It was necessary to strike with great force to cut through the mail, or so to smash it in as to pulverize what lay beneath. Mail-clad men fight slowly when they hack and slash. They must put extra weight and power behind each blow.

Because of my galley slave training, because of that baptism in the sacred pool of lost Aphrasöe, because my arm was nerved by dark impulses of hatred and revenge, I struck each blow with swift force, smiting and smiting the enemies of Zair who had killed my friend Zorg of Felteraz.

I do not know how long it went on. I only know that I felt a wave of resentment, of disappointment, when the galley lurched and rolled, the harsh grating bump from aft shocked us all forward, and men in mail with gleaming long swords poured over the poop. They wore red plumes in their helmets. They struck down with quick and cunning skill and

swamped across *Grace of Grodno*. In the bedlam I heard the
fresh and horrific screams from the galley slaves.

I felt a treacherous lurch beneath my feet and a soggy feel
of the deck.

The galley was sinking. The men of Magdag had opened
her sides in some way, opening them to the sea, willing all to
death in their final defeat.

Now there were no men left of Magdag between me and
the men of Zair, the red-sun deity, the men from the south.

"The galley is sinking," I said, to one who stepped toward
me, his long sword reeking, yet not so befouled with blood as
mine. "The slaves must be freed—now!"

"It will be done," he said. He looked at me. He stood as
tall as I did, broad and limber, with a bronzed open face
with that same set of arrogance to his beak of a nose that
my friend Zorg had possessed. His thick dark moustache was
brushed upward. The men of Magdag wore down-drooping,
hangdog moustaches.

"I am Pur Zenkiren of Sanurkazz, captain of *Lilac Bird*."
On the white loose garment he wore over his mail a great
blazing device coruscated in my eyes. A circle, it seemed, a
hubless spoked wheel within the circle, embroidered with silks
of brilliant orange, yellow, and blue. "And you, a galley
slave, I assume?"

"Yes," I said. I remembered things I had almost forgotten.
"A galley slave. I am the Lord of Strombor."

He looked at me keenly. "Strombor. It seems, I think, I
have heard—but no matter. It is not of the Eye of the
World."

"No. It is not."

Slaves were being cut free from their shackles, were
leaping up, screaming and weeping in their joy, scrambling
over the ornate poop to the beak of *Lilac Bird*. Pur Zenkiren
made a motion with his long sword, all bloody as it was, a
kind of salute.

"You, the Lord of Strombor, a stranger. How is it you
came to be fighting the heretics of Magdag, and taking their
galley?"

The twin suns of Antares were less hot now, the emerald
and the ruby, sinking to the sea horizon. I looked at the long
sword, at the blood, at the dead men, at the slaves in all their
wretched nakedness leaping for joy as they scrambled across
the poop.

"I had a friend," I said. "Zorg of Felteraz."

CHAPTER SEVEN

A blow makes and breaks

If I seem to you to have passed somewhat lightly over my experiences working in the building complexes of Magdag or to have been less than open in what I have said about my life as a galley slave on the swifters of Magdag, I feel I owe no explanation. Of misery and pain and despair we all know there is enough and to spare, both on our own Earth and on the world of Kregen that I made my own. The long periods I spent under duress passed. That is all. Like black clouds passing away before the face of Zim, the times of agony and humiliation passed.

The hatred I bore the men of Magdag was perfectly natural, given the circumstances of my birth and upbringing, for the Navy does not tolerate weaklings and my training had been harsh and uncompromising. Only in later years have I attained to any little maturity of outlook I may possess, and this, I confess freely, has been brought about in large measure by the liberating influences breaking out on this Earth, for Kregen remains as savage, demanding, and merciless as always.

I have experienced great joy in my life, and Delia of Delphond has been my great and consoling power of the spirit; I owe most of what humanity I possess to her. Now, released from mind-killing and body-exhausting toil, I was free once again and I can remember with what wonder and the light of fresh eyes I looked about me on the deck of *Lilac Bird* as *Grace of Grodno* sank, bubbling, beneath the blue waters of the Eye of the World.

No, it is not necessary to detail my feelings about the men of Magdag, the men of Grodno. If I say that little Wincie, a cherry-lipped, impish-eyed, tousle-headed slip of a girl of whom I was very fond, had been killed in a most barbarous fashion, it conveys little. Her task was to bring the skins of water for the brick making and to slake our thirsts; the

mailed men on one of their sporting sorties had caught her
and had, as you twentieth century moralists would phrase it,
gang-raped her. These are words. The reality in agony, blood,
and filth is a part of the mosaic of life. It does not need to be
dwelled on to make my position—the young man I then was,
harsh, relentless, vicious to those I hated, malignant in my
cherished feelings of injustice—clear enough to the dullest of
minds.

Now they had flogged to death my friend, Zorg of Felteraz.

Not all the slaves had come weeping with joy aboard the
swifter from Holy Sanurkazz. Some had wailed and resisted.
These were prisoners of Magdag, men sentenced to the galleys for some crime and with the eventual prospect of freedom before them. Now they would become the galley slaves
of their hereditary enemies. Life was stark and brutal on the
inner sea.

Lilac Bird interested me. She was a larger galley than
Grace of Grodno, although not of the largest size that
plowed these waters. I gathered her speed had given her captain, Pur Zenkiren, some concern, as she was new and he had
had high hopes of her. She was a seven-six-hundredswifter.
Simply, this means she had a hundred oars, arranged in two
banks with seven men on the upper bank at each oar and six
on the lower, two banks of twenty-five oars a side. I thought
her length insufficient in proportion to her beam, given the
ridiculous shapes of galleys, anyway; her draft was still too
deep, caused by the weights, than was desirable for the
swiftest of galleys. I caught myself. Here I was, starting to
think like a sailor again.

"You are feeling fit in yourself, my Lord of Strombor?"
Pur Zenkiren spoke pleasantly as we sat in his plain after
quarters, with the arms in their racks, the charts upon the table, the wine glasses and bottle between us. They did not use
beckets or swinging tables; they wouldn't venture out if a
storm was brewing.

"Fit, thank you, Pur Zenkiren. I owe you my liberty—I
had some concern that you might return me, a stranger to
the benches."

He smiled. His face was weather-beaten, his eyes dark and
penetrating, and that arrogant beak nose lifted at times so
that, for a heartbreaking moment, I would catch that glimpse
of Zorg. Zenkiren, like Zorg, had a mass of black curly hair,
shining and oiled and remarkably romantic, I have no doubt.

"We followers of Zair have a respect for a man, my Lord of Strombor."

A single chart, of remarkably poor quality, hopeless accuracy, and miniscule scale, had been found in the locker, which showed Strombor. The whole coastlines outside the inner sea were incorrect, but the names were marked down: Loh, Vallia, Pandahem, Segesthes, with Zenicce marked and, alongside in a panel, the names of the twenty-four Houses of Zenicce, both noble and lay. The fascinating thing here was that Strombor was marked and Esztercari was not, proving the map to have been drawn well over a hundred and fifty years before.

"We have a little contact with the outside world, mainly with Vallia and Donengil, but we are an inward-looking people. The main effort to which we are all dedicated is defiance and resistance to the power of Grodno, no matter when, how, and where such a resistance shall be made."

I looked at him. He spoke as though out of rote. Then he smiled at me again, lifted his glass, and said: "To the ice floes of Sicce with Magdag and all her evil spawn!"

"I'll drink to that," I said, and did so.

They had given me a decent white loincloth and I had washed and rubbed scented oils on my body, and I had eaten real food again. Now, sitting drinking with the captain of the swifter, I felt human once more—or, I reminded myself, as human as I would ever feel while the canker of Grodno and Magdag continued to exist.

My feelings were made very plain to Zenkiren, who had sized me up to his satisfaction, as he thought.

The many parallels of the red-green situation in the Eye of the World to that old battle between Esztercari and Strombor had occurred to me; although I found greater contrast and interest in the Catholic and Islamic conflicts of the late Renaissance, or the bitterness between Guelf and Ghibelline. I was aware, too, that the greater malice seemed always to exist between those whose beliefs had diverged from a single origin. The people of the sunset, the old original inhabitants of the Eye of the World, had built well and industriously to produce the Grand Canal and the Dam of Days, that terrifying structure I had not yet seen. They had also built fine cities, some ruined and lost, some ruined and partially rebuilt, now inhabited by the newer men who had split from the old red-green comradeship.

"Those vile cramphs of Magdag," Zenkiren said to me as

we voyaged back to Sanurkazz. "We know how they build.
They are obsessed by building, diseased by it."

"It is destroying their culture, their life," I said.

"Yes! They think to find favor in the sight of their evil
master, the false deity Grodno the Green, by every act of
building, every new construction of monstrous proportions.
They bleed their countryside dry for workers and wealth. So,
then they must raid and ravage us in order to replenish their
stock."

"I saw a farm, a massive affair, very well-run and produc-
ing—"

"Oh, yes!" Zenkiren waved a dismissive arm. "Of course!
They have millions to feed; they must produce food, as we
must. But they raid us continually and take our young men
and our girls and children for their consuming buildings."

"You raid them."

"Yes! It is the glory of Zair laid upon us." He looked at
me and hesitated; it surprised me, for he was a fine captain
and a man who knew his mind. "You were the friend of Zorg
of Felteraz. I have heard from Zolta of that. You are a
Lord. I think—" Again he hesitated, and then, in a slower
and softer voice, asked: "Did Zorg speak to you of the Krozairs of Zy?"

"No," I said. "He used the word Krozair when he was
dying. He seemed—proud, then."

Zenkiren changed the flow of conversation, then, and we
spoke of many things as *Lilac Bird* rowed steadily toward the
south. She was followed by two other swifters, smaller galleys
in this swift raiding squadron under Zenkiren's command.
They had snapped up three plump merchantmen as well sinking *Grace of Grodno*, and the merchantmen wallowed along
aft.

In all honesty I must admit I did not even think it strange
that Zenkiren should take my word that I was the Lord of
Strombor. I was beginning to adopt the attitudes of mind of
the leader of a House of Zenicce, and my years as Vovedeer
and Zorcander with the Clansmen had given me the air of
habitual authority. But I believe Zenkiren would not have
cared had I been the lowliest of foot soldiers, for he did everything merely because he knew that I had been the friend
of Zorg of Felteraz and had avenged his death.

I was convinced the word Krozair linked these attitudes. I
had seen, as *Grace of Grodno* finally sank, the air bubbling
out and the timbers breaking free and shooting up, a white

dove circling *Lilac Bird*. That dove heartened me. Could it be, I wondered, that the Savanti were taking a hand again? Could they be confirming my continued existence on Kregen even though I had been forced away from Magdag? I looked for the Gdoinye, the scarlet and golden raptor; I did not see it.

Zenkiren had been taking a considerable risk in sailing so close to the northern shore. He had been on the lookout for choice tidbits in the way of Magdaggian merchantmen and the fortyswifter had been a delectable item to snap up. We did not know why she had been enroute to Gansk, and perhaps we never would learn. Zenkiren's concern had been for *Lilac Bird*'s disturbing lack of speed. Only my intervention with the consequent interruption in the pulling of the fortyswifter had given him the chance to overhaul her, and then the Sanurkazzan galley had reached up so swiftly there had been no need to use the ballistae mounted in her bows.

The ballista used on the ships of the Eye of the World was called a varter, and it was a true ballista, in that its propulsive energy came from two half-bows whose butts were clamped in perpendicular thongs twisted many times. The cord was drawn by a simple windlass. The varter could be adapted to shoot arrows, or bolts, large iron-tipped monstrous balks of timber, or to hurl stones. It could achieve a considerable degree of accuracy.

Every sixth day on ships of Sanurkazz the religious observances connected with Zair were solemnly undertaken with due rites and prayers. Religion, I had thought, was the sop for the masses, along with bloodthirsty broadsheets detailing the latest murders and hangings, cockfights, prizefights, and the occasional tankard of ale at the local alehouse. Religion kept the masses in order. These men of Sanurkazz, however, well though I might mock them in the privacy of my own thoughts, were very splendid in their best clothes, the ship-priest in his vestments, the silver and gold vessels, the blazing embroidery of the banners and flags, the shrilling notes of the silver and ebony trumpets, all conspiring to seduce any solid man into an euphoric haze of belief.

Naturally, the day on which the rites of Zair were performed was not the same day as that on which Grodno was similarly honored.

I say similarly; I had seen the religious services of the men of Magdag, and they were different in a way that, looking back, I can see was no different at all. Then, I considered them depraved and evil.

It seems obvious that there was only one color which the men of Magdag could paint the hulls of their swifters. The ancient pirates of Greece, who roamed the Aegean, used to paint their hulls green. The men of Sanurkazz had struck a compromise. Green was of some use as a camouflage color; not much, a little. Red would have been some degrees more visible; so the galleys of the men of Zair of the southern shore of the inner sea were painted blue.

They carried three sets of sails in more or less regular use: white for daytime cruising, black for night sailing, and blue for raiding.

On this voyage back to Holy Sanurkazz, a voyage which was something in the nature of a victory triumph, we wore white sails.

Magdag stood upon the northern shore of the inner sea over to the western end; her power and law ran for many dwaburs toward the east until it tended to diminish a little as cities with their own marine wished to flex their own muscles of independence. All, however, were in some way tributary to Magdag, and all, naturally, were partisans of the green.

Holy Sanurkazz stood upon the southern shore of the inner sea over toward the eastern end, at the narrow neck of one of the dependent seas that extended southward. Her hegemony stretched in somewhat different ways from her opponent's toward the west, where cities flourished which grew steadily weaker and less assured the farther west they had been sited. All, however, owed a single burning allegiance to the red.

It seemed clear that the strategy dominating the inner sea would be that of raiding to keep the opponent occupied, and a series of direct and violent blows against the chief hostile city. With either Magdag or Sanurkazz reduced, the other cities of the losing side would, like children deprived of parents, quickly succumb. This was a strategy that had not found favor with either the men of Magdag or Sanurkazz. The answer was obvious enough and human enough not to surprise me. Booty was for the taking upon the seas, and to strike against a smaller city was infinitely safer than any direct assault against the master citadel.

Stretching my legs on the tiny extent of quarterdeck boasted by *Lilac Bird*, I saw Zolta below me thoroughly enjoying himself on the central gangway. He strode up and down, clad like myself in a clean white loincloth, flourishing a whip and every now and then laying into the galley slaves. We were bucking a nasty little wind, and I had cocked my eyes at the clouds more than once.

"Hai, Zolta!" I called down.

He stared back and up, his face brown and cheerful, his black eyes glittering. He cracked the whip with a snap.

"I am collecting interest, Stylor!" he shouted up.

The drum-deldar quickened his beat. The bass and the tenor drums boomed closer together. On the ships of Zair the drum-deldar sits forward of the rowers, in the belief, I gathered, that the sounds would carry more speedily to the oarsmen on the benches. Above the heads of this top bank of oarsmen a light fighting platform ran around above the bulwarks of the galley where fighting-men could stand in action. Below them, the lower bank of oarsmen were tugging at their shorter and more sharply angled oars. With seven men to a loom, monstrous oars could be wielded. Zolta, with his borrowed whip, intended to see the oars were moved, and sharply. The whip-deldar, from whom Zolta had so unofficially taken over, was standing talking to the oar-master in his tabernacle just below me, and laughing at the antics of Zolta.

So my friends who owed allegiance to the red-sun deity, Zair, used slaves too. Could I have expected anything else? I did know that slavery was practiced mostly aboard their swifters. In their cities normal citizens carried out work, in a way that made sense to an Earthman with a European heritage, and the few slaves were mostly for personal body service.

I looked out over the larboard beam and the clouds there lowered, more black and ominous than they had been half a bur before. I had no wish to interfere with Zenkiren in his handling of his ship. Aft of us the two trailing galleys plunged heavily, and spume broke and burst from their prows. The merchantmen were riding the seas more easily and I saw they had reduced canvas.

Zenkiren stepped out on deck.

The oar-master popped up his little ladder from the tabernacle with its solidly-bolted door. He gestured to larboard.

"I see, Nath," said Zenkiren. "We must weather this out."

This Nath, again, was another of that common name, and not my Nath the Thief, or my oar-mate Nath, who was spending his time playing any one of the many gambling games of Kregen with the released slaves below decks.

Lilac Bird was beginning to roll now in a devilishly uncomfortable corkscrew fashion. Long and thin galleys are no sea boats. Some of the oars faltered as white water broke. The oar-master dived back to his place as the drum-deldar thumped a slower rate, and the whip-deldar jumped along the central gangway below the parados and took the whip from Zolta.

We were in for a blow.

Storms, hurricanes, typhoons, cyclones—gales of all descriptions are no news to me. The gale that overtook us now was such as to give me no cause for alarm at first. Why, snug aboard a seventy-four, or even a thirty-eight frigate, on blockade, we would scarcely have bothered over this blow. However, the swifters of the inland sea were primitive fighting machines, not the sophisticated sailing machines on Nelson's Navy, and *Lilac Bird* behaved like a bitch of the sea. She twisted, she hogged, she sagged, she pitched and yawed and rolled and when she did roll she sent thrills through me I'd forgotten existed.

We smashed ten oars before they were all safely inboard and stowed. That operation—I had had to carry it out myself as a galley slave—is a miserable proceeding. Then covers were dragged out by the sailors and lashed over all the openings in the upperworks. *Lilac Bird* stuck her nose down and heaved like a rooting ferret. I snatched a glance aft and saw the two galleys like matchsticks in the sea, foaming up and down, great spouts of white water crashing upward from their slim bows.

The merchantmen were out of sight. The clouds lowered down and the sky grew black; rain began to fall. That cheered me up a little, but the way this broomstick of a craft was behaving was enough to alarm any sailor. And I had considered she should be longer!

The two rudder-deldars were yelling for help and reliefs rushed high upon the poop to grasp the rudder handles, to control the two paddle-shaped rudders, one on each quarter. Even as they reached the poop the galley rolled and squiggled in her snakelike fashion. To a groaning of timbers and sheets of spray flying inboard the starboard rudder snapped across.

Lilac Bird lurched to starboard, her larboard rudder almost out of the water. She spun around and water and wind smote her without mercy. Zenkiren had been standing near me, shouting to his men. As his ship lurched it caught him unexpectedly so that he staggered, tottered across the deck, and hit his head hard against the break of the poop. He dropped to the deck, senseless.

His second in command, a certain Rophren, jumped up, his face an unhealthy color. He stood shaking.

Now, through the sleeting smash of the spray and the whine of the wind, we could hear, clear and close and ominous, the roaring sound of great waves battering rocks.

"It is all finished!" shouted Rophren. "We must jump for it—we must abandon the swifter!"

I went up to him quickly. I hit him alongside the jaw and I did not bother to catch him as he fell.

The galley heaved up and down beneath me as I ran back.

"Keep on that rudder!" I shouted at the deldars there. "Hold her when she comes around."

Then I ran forward, pushing past the spray-drenched whip-deldars who stared upon me with frightened, puzzled faces. At the main mast I collared some of the sailors skulking there and kicked them into hoisting a scrap of the sail, the yard braced hard up diagonally across the deck. Wind filled that bit of sail at once, pouting it out, hard and drumming. But the galley responded, impossible sea boat though she was. The foremast yard I had likewise braced hard around. We were drifting away to leeward like a bit of driftwood. Down there, iron-fanged rocks awaited us. Now, through the gloom, I could just make out the spout and leap of spray.

I had a moment of doubt that we could weather that fanged pile of rock.

We were being carried broadside on downwind.

"Keep that rudder hard down!" I bellowed into the wind.

Slowly, slowly, we were forereaching on the rocks. But, I thought, too slowly, too slowly.

Spray stung my eyes and I brushed it impatiently away.

I dared not hoist any more canvas; the galley would simply spring away like an arrow and impale herself on the rocks if she did not simply roll over in the first few moments before her head came around. Water broke over her in torrential sheets.

I clung on and hoped.

Rophren had regained consciousness. He had a group of

officers with him as he approached me. Their faces showed the fear of the sea corroding within them, the hatred of me.

"You—the Lord of Strombor! You are under arrest!" Rophren spoke flatly, his fear shrieking at the end into his words so that he stammered over them. "We are all doomed—because you stopped me giving the order! We could all have jumped when I said and been saved—now we are too close to the rocks! Cramph! You have killed us all!"

A youngster with a florid face and close-set eyes whipped out his long sword.

"He won't go under arrest! For I shall cut him down—now!"

The long sword glimmered silver in the spray, high over my head. It slashed down.

CHAPTER EIGHT

Nath, Zolta, and I carouse in Sanurkazz

I moved sideways and I kicked that florid-faced young man where I had kicked Cydones Esztercari, neatly, making him double up and retch all over the sea-wet deck. I took the long sword away. I held it so that Rophren and his friends could see it.

"Countermand a single order I have given," I said, "and you die."

Their hands bunched on their sword hilts. They were proud, arrogant men, used to command. They lurched on the decks as the galley surged and bucked and fought the sea. I stood there, limber and straight, balanced, and the sword in my fist maintained a steady arc upon them.

Whether they would have charged me, desperate in their ill-founded belief that I was consigning them all to a watery grave, whether they would have remained, like chained leems, snarling and impotent, I do not know. I rather suspect the latter, for I have been told that when I, Dray Prescot, challenge a man with a sword in my fist I present a most daunting and unhealthy spectacle.

As they stood there, wet, miserable, and frightened, facing the boiling sea or the bright menace of my sword, a sharp hail lifted from the bows.

Up there Nath, my Nath of the galley bench, perched. He pointed and waved a dripping arm.

"Clear, Stylor!" he screamed. "We're clear!"

We looked, those men like chained leems, and I. The rocks were moving astern of us, their spouting white-fanged venom dropping astern as we pulled away. Slowly, struggling for every inch, *Lilac Bird* labored her way past that cruel point of rock and so weathered the cape and we could run more comfortably into the gulf beyond.

After that it was merely a matter of a routine court of inquiry when Zenkiren regained consciousness. Rophren was placed under arrest. The florid-faced young man, Hezron of High Heysh, also was placed under arrest; but in his presence I spoke for him, knowing this had been his first cruise as an officer aboard a swifter and this his first storm.

"The dangers of the sea vary in proportion as one comes to know them," I said. "I do not hold it against Hezron that his untutored fear impelled him to seek to kill me. Perhaps he may hold it against me that I kicked him between wind and water."

Zenkiren did not smile; but I was watching his face as he sat in the seat of judgment at his table, with the other officers present and the glowering, pasty-faced Rophren between two men-at-arms, and I thought he might have smiled at another time. Zenkiren was a jolly man who loved a good belly laugh despite his ascetic brilliance.

"What do you say to that, Hezron?"

Hezron of High Heysh lifted his head. He was a boy who was used to throwing his weight about, that was clear, a member of a rich and powerful family in Sanurkazz.

"I do not forget an injury," he said, and his words splintered in the cabin as *Lilac Bird* pulled toward the harbor. "I shall hold it against you that you demeaned me, that you dared lay a hand on me. I, Hezron of High Heysh. You will not forget that lightly, barbarian."

I looked at him. I had heard the opprobrious epithet barbarian applied to me, as a stranger from the outer seas, more than once, but never like this, never with so much venom. I thought of the galleys of the inner sea, I thought of their fighting qualities, and I wondered. Those ships of Zenicce, which city was not popular on the outer oceans, and the wide-ranging fleets of Vallia, were they fashioned by barbarians? Was the gorgeous enclave city of Zenicce barbarous? If it was, it was of a form and style of barbarity these swiftermen of the Eye of the World could not understand.

"If you wish to make an issue of that," I said, and I know I spoke in a harsh and barbaric voice, "you are welcome to meet me at any time with weapons in our hands."

"That is enough of that!" said Zenkiren. He looked annoyed. "Only through the courage and skill of the Lord of Strombor was *Lilac Bird* saved." He made a face. "Both our consorts were lost." This was true. Their timbers were washed up over the days that followed, with dead bodies. The slaves, where they floated ashore on balks of timber, were still chained to those timbers.

Rophren was remanded to await judgment by the court of the high admiral. That was what, in effect, he was, although his Kregish title ran for five lines of purple prose.

Hezron of High Heysh was reprimanded, and then released, on the authority of Pur Zenkiren, and at my behest. It made no difference to Hezron's attitude to me. I knew I would have to guard my back where he was concerned.

We ran into the outer harbor of Holy Sanurkazz.

I have, as I have said, seen many cities, and I was looking forward to the view of the chief city of the followers of Zair. I expected—looking back, it is foolish, I can see, to expect anything until the reality is there before you, living and real.

Sanurkazz had been sited on the narrow neck of land stretching between the inner sea and the smaller dependent sea, the Sea of Marshes, which formed a kind of blunt arrowhead, the two sharp faces washed by the waters and the base walled off by a girdling wall of six curtains. There were many buildings, some of noble proportions and in a kind of columnar architecture I found pleasant enough. A great deal of warm yellow stone was used that was quarried some few dwaburs along the shore. The tiled roofs were red. Much lush vegetation grew riotously among the houses and along the avenues and streets. There were also many flat-walled roofs made into bright gardens, and water mills pumped water to flow into fountains that tinkled tirelessly throughout the city. The markets were exuberant, noisily filled with the clink of coins, the sounds of calsanys, the cries of vendors. In the streets of the crafts there was the eternal noise of the craftsmen's hammers as they beat out bronze, gold, or silver, or the whir of wheels as they fashioned the pots with the bold red designs, or worked the leather which glistened with strength and suppleness and which was famed throughout the inner sea.

Oh, yes, Sanurkazz was a marvelous city, filled with life, ardor, and animation. The harbors were cunningly sited so as to obtain perfect protection from the weather and from any corsair attack by sea. The arsenals were cleverly placed so as to be mutually protected. The domes and spires of the temples pierced the brilliant air

Oh, yes, Sanurkazz was delightful. It was a city in which to be alive. Magdag was a city of colossuses, of towering buildings marching endlessly into the plain, of work, toil, and a demanding discipline, machinelike, obsessed. Sanurkazz was a city of individuals.

But—there was not a single central fact about Sanurkazz. It was a collection of individuals. It charmed. It had marvelous byways, courts, and tree-shaded bowers where flowers bloomed in brilliance and perfume; it had marvelous inns, pot houses, and roistering spots. I enjoyed myself in Sanurkazz. But I sensed that it lacked that obsessive single-minded purpose of Magdag.

The conflict between red and green was not a clear-cut contest between good and bad. Although at that time I was willing to credit all evil to Magdag, I believe I do not flatter myself if I say that I was capable of perceiving that there were grave flaws in Sanurkazz. It was an intensely human place. I suppose the best way to sum up Holy Sanurkazz would be to say that it roistered in the sun. Carousing was a devotedly followed occupation. Then, every sixth day, the whole city gave itself over to the intensely religious observances connected with the worship of Zair, the red-sun deity.

The women of Sanurkazz were a luscious lot, full-breasted, lithe, sensuous of lip and saucy of eye. To them the idea that a woman should veil herself before venturing on the streets would have smacked of perversion. With Zenkiren's promise that he would employ me aboard *Lilac Bird*—in a capacity on which we would agree—I had money to jingle in my purse, a white apron to wear, and a long sword at my side slung from a belt and harness fashioned from that wonderful Sanurkazz leather.

Out on the fertile fields south of the city and alongside the Sea of Marshes agriculture proceeded on the basis of small farming, with estates of the nobles dotting the countryside. Beyond them, further south, the plains began and here herds of chunkrah roamed. I promised myself I would ride out one day and spend some time with the chunkrah and think of my Clansmen of the Great Plains of Segesthes. Southward again and the climate grew drier and the deserts extended, bleak and orange and harsh. I understood that beyond the deserts lay the coastal lands of Donengil, but almost invariably these would be reached by ship through the Great Canal. Donengil, I guessed, would have a climate very much like the West Indies, on a vaster scale.

Industry of an essential hand-worked kind existed on a surprisingly large scale. There were iron works, and bronze works, manufactories for the production of swords and the supple mesh steel, mining and logging and weaving, all the necessary facilities to maintain a city-state like Sanurkazz I visited the extensive forests, and saw lenk and sturm growing, saw the cedars and the pines on the uplands to the southwest, saw the way in which the shipwrights selected timbers from the living tree, and placed forms around them so that they would grow into the required shapes for keel arches, or stern-posts, or any other of the necessary ship shapes.

The people of Kregen are not all in the same stage of evolutionary industrial or social or political growth, of course. Steam bending of wood was known: indeed, for the building of galleys such as *Lilac Bird,* it would be essential. The ancients of Earth without knowledge of steam bending were forced to use green wood with the sap in so that they could bend the timbers to shape. The wood warped and very soon the ships leaked and became useless. The galleys of the Greeks were essentially light craft, with one man to an oar, designed to ram The Romans with the corvus, the studded gangplank for boarding, attempted to bring land-fighting techniques to the sea, but their ships were still slightly built. With Earth's Renaissance and the galleys of the Catholic powers against those of the Muslims, the galley reached a new development. It is hardly correct to say, as so many do, that these last galleys were the direct descendants of those of ancient Greece and Rome.

With one man to one oar, as was universal among the ancients, with the trireme's sets of seats in threes, slanting back toward the stern, with oars of from about fifteen feet in length to about eight feet, with the thranites, the zygites, and the thalamites pulling those oars, with their everlasting baling caused through warping timbers consequent on the use of green wood, and with all their early effort concentrated on quick ramming, rolling the sinking galley off the ram and a smart backwater, the ancient Greek triremes must have been finely tuned instruments. The confusion attendant upon a single oarsman losing his stroke must have worried the trierarch as much as anything else. One man to one oar set a very definite upper limit to the power it was possible to transmit. These sailors of the Eye of the World had gone for the later system, the arrangement *alla scaloccio;* but, with a daring I found admirable, had concentrated their propulsive power into two or three banks. While technically correct to call *Lilac Bird* a bireme, and the other large galleys of the inner sea triremes, I shall stick to what the Kregans themselves called them, swifters.

Wind scoops of a pattern I was familiar with directed fresh air below decks, and many gratings and openings gave free ingress for ventilation. Despite that, the lower rowing deck, where the thalamites sat and sweated, presented a spectacle of hell on Kregen I had no wish to suffer again. If I have not made it clear that for Zorg, Nath, Zolta, and I, fresh out of the thalamite deck of a Magdag swifter, the open pulling benches of *Grace of Grodno* came as a taste of reprieve, I can assure you this was so.

At that time and for some time to come, I was still unsatisfied that the best arrangements for oarsmen had been found.

With my head full of galleys and swifters and triremes I accompanied Nath and Zolta to their favorite drinking haunt, The Fleeced Ponsho—Kregans sometimes have a warped sense of humor—where buxom Sisi apparently was prepared to favor these two unlikely cutthroats without overpayment merely because they happened to have escaped from the Magdag galleys.

"With one man one oar," Zolta was saying, rubbing his chin where his black beard was growing enough to itch, "even with the apostis—for which we must give credit to the Archbolds of Zair—"

"Huh!" interrupted Nath, as we swung into the low doorway of the tavern, out of the pink moonlight from the two second moons of Kregen. "Those rasts of Grodno-gasta claim the credit for inventing the apostis!"

"May Zair rot them!" rumbled Zolta. He pitched his body onto a bench and yelled for Sisi. "Anyway, friend Strombor"—they had taken to calling me that, now, and both could not really stomach the "lord" bit—"as I was saying before Nath opened his black-fanged wine-spout—Sisi! Hurry up, you lecher's delight! I'm as dry as the Southern Desert! As I was saying, one man one oar, even with the apostis, is fine for small handy craft. I'd not care to be aboard when a hundred-and-eightyswifter got on her tail! Ho! She'd be hoicked clear out of the water!"

They still had to convince me.

Sisi's arrival with three leather tankards brimming with wine from Zond, rich and dark and potent, silenced our argument as we quaffed. Then Nath belched and leaned back, brushing the back of his hand across his lips.

"Mother Zinzu the Blessed! I needed that!"

We talked and drank and argued, and got into a gambling game with some ponsho farmers up from the country and with Nath's uncanny ability to manipulate the dice we were doing very well indeed, when a fight broke out—there always seemed to be fights following Nath's dice manipulation. Laughing and roaring and throwing tousle-headed ponsho farmers from us, left and right, we roistered from the tavern. When I say that Zolta being the smallest of those four of us who had labored on the oar took the outboard, do not infer he was a small man. He could pick up his groundling and hurl him into the bar display with the best.

Sisi came yelling and running, the bodice above her red gown billowing with her outraged anger, but Zolta swept her up in his arms and bestowed on her a wet and bristly kiss and then we went whooping out of The Fleeced Ponsho. The mobiles, the Sanurkazz equivalent to a police force, fat and jolly men with swords at their sides rusted into their sheathes, hallooed into the flower-draped little square before the tavern as we went dancing out at the other side Nath had a bottle of wine in his hand and he was laughing and dancing, and Zolta was grinning a great big foolish grin and obviously thinking of Sisi. I had to laugh at my two ruffianly companions But we had pulled an oar together in the galleys. That made us comrades with inseparable bonds. We had been four Now we were three. I believe my laugh was no laugh a civilized man would recognize.

We scampered up the moon-drenched alley.

"We must find another tavern, and that right soon," declared Zolta. "I am primed."

"And what of Sisi, oh man of little faith?" demanded Nath He pulled the cork out of the bottle with a single jerk.

"She will keep, fat and juicy. I am primed, I tell you, Nath, you nit that crawls upon a calsany."

"As to that—" said Nath, and then paused to upend the bottle and down four hefty slugs· glug, glug, glug—and glug. "Nits are of a size more suitable to he who pulls nearest the parados—yes?"

He yelped as Zolta's toe caught him, and then they were both roaring and yelling and running up the alley, the bottle brandished in Nath's hand, and the great contagious roaring laughter welling up from Zolta to inflame the fire. I sighed. They were ruffians, true, but they were oar comrades.

From the direction of The Fleeced Ponsho came the measured tread of booted feet. There was a ring about those footsteps, four men at least, and clad in mail. Men in Sanurkazz did not wear mail with the same habitual ferocity as the men of Magdag. The mobiles only wore half-mail. Mind you, they were so fat and indolent a lot, preferring a bottle of wine to a fracas any time, that I was surprised they'd even arrived when they did.

The footsteps approached and I stepped back into the shadows of a balcony from which great blossoms glowed, their inner petals shut, their outer petals open to the moonlight.

"The rast went this way," a grating voice said. I remained very still. I did not even make an attempt to free the long sword at my side. The time would come for that.

"Hark at those two cramphs—" Nath and Zolta were certainly making a hullabaloo enough to awaken the whole district. "We had best hurry."

Four men in mail pressed on along the alleyway. They entered a patch of the pink moonlight that moved only slowly with the gentle orbital movement of the two second moons. Their faces showed pink blobs, barred by ferocious upthrust moustaches. The mail glittered where it was not fully covered by the loose-fitting white surcoats. Those surcoats looked odd, and then I saw that they were bereft of the usual sizable badge, worn breast and back, that marked a man for his allegiances.

I think I knew then what all this was about. But I wanted to know for sure. After all, I, Dray Prescot, had more important things to do on Kregen than to engage in a petty feud with a spoiled boy, no matter that he might be the scion of a wealthy and noble family.

The men's swords glittered in the moonlight.

They would have passed me by, hidden in the shadows beneath the balcony. I remember there was a sweet scented odor on the air from the great moon-drinking blooms.

I stepped out into the alleyway.

The long sword lay still in the scabbard.

"You wanted to speak with me?"

It was a challenge.

"You are he whom men call the Lord of Strombor?"

"I am."

"Then you are a dead man."

The fight did not last long. They were fair swordsmen, nothing of note, nothing that my wild Clansmen could not have dealt with. Hap Loder, for example, would have been yelling for a drink as he finished them off, with all his panache.

When I returned to *Lilac Bird* I said to Zenkiren: "I wish to see the father of Hezron."

"Oh?"

We understood each other a little better now, Zenkiren and I. I had asked Zolta what Krozair might mean, and he had shuffled and hedged and then said to ask Zenkiren. His reply had been, simply: "Wait."

When I had pressed him, he said: "It is an Order. It is not something discussed lightly in taprooms." He gestured around his cabin, so plain, so severe, and I had not understood.

Now he looked at me and put a finger to his lips as I told him what had occurred in the alley outside The Fleeced Ponsho.

"This might be serious, my Lord of Strombor. Harknel of High Heysh, Hezron's father, is a powerful man, wealthy and influential. There are intrigues in Sanurkazz, as you may well believe."

I made an impatient movement. Zenkiren spoke more forcefully.

"The boy hired killers and they bungled the job. If you tell the father he will have to deny all knowledge of it, and then discipline his son—for failing, mind, for failing! After that, you will have not that young puppy Hezron out for your blood, but old Harknel himself. Think on, Strombor—and, there is something else."

"I have thought," I said instantly. I couldn't have assassination threats hanging over me if I had work to do for the Star Lords—or the Savanti—or, and more especially, if I was to find my way out of the Eye of the World back to Vallia or Strombor and to my Delia of Delphond. "I will see whoever it takes to have this puppy restrained. That is all."

He pursed his lips. He tried to be fair, did Pur Zenkiren, captain of *Lilac Bird*. He held up a piece of paper—paper of a kind I did not recognize, and my instant alertness relaxed.

"I have had a letter, Strombor. I would like you to go on a little journey—to Felteraz."

"*Felteraz!*"

"Yes, my Lord of Strombor. You are to see my Lady Mayfwy. The Lady Mayfwy—wife of Zorg of Felteraz."

CHAPTER NINE

Of Mayfwy and of swifters

Two disgusting specimens of some abhorrent species of water vermin were hoisted aboard next morning, swinging groaning and complaining over *Lilac Bird*'s parados to be dumped all squishy and green of face onto the deck.

The mobiles in their gaudy clothes and rusty swords who had brought them home stood on the jetty, guffawing, their hands on their hips, their heads thrown back, emptying their stalwart lungs into the early morning suns-shine. Both the suns of Kregen were close together. The genial sounds of work in the harbor floated up, cries and calls, the clink of tools, the slop of water, the screams of gulls. The lighthouse men were going off watch, rubbing their eyes and yawning. The tall pharos reared up from the far end of the jetty past the first of the seaward defense walls, its immense lantern mirrors dark and motionless. Down by the fishmarket the catch was being landed and the wives were arguing and fighting and more than one silvery-scaled fat fish went *slap!* across the cheeks of a beldame. The scene was one I could half close my eyes and absorb and imagine I was back in Plymouth—well, almost.

Zolta and Nath lay on the deck, two pitiful objects.

Sharntaz, the new second in command, rolled across to inspect them with the toe of his boot.

I, Dray Prescot, who seldom laugh, felt the strange bubbling inside me, straining my ribs. Nath held his head and groaned. Zolta held his stomach and moaned. As objects of pity they aroused only the most violent hilarity in the rough seafolk of Sanurkazz.

When Zenkiren appeared and everyone immediately straightened up ready for morning inspection, he cast a single glance at the two culprits, who attempted to stand up, their faces the color of that interesting cheese sometimes discovered abandoned in the buildings of Magdag.

"You two," he said. He jerked a hand. "With the Lord of Strombor. *Move!*"

"Aye, Captain," they stuttered, and shambled off after me.

It was hardly fair on them, but I knew they would not forgive me if I traveled to Felteraz without them. As I had explained to Zenkiren, they were oar comrades of Zorg also.

We made the journey in a two-wheeled cart drawn by a docile ass, a somewhat different variety from that of the Plains of Segesthes but with the same patient obstinacy, and as I handled the reins those two lay in the back and groaned with every jolt of the wheels.

"My head! Mother Zinzu the Blessed! For a little wine to moisten these cracked lips!"

"You drank it all last night," said Zolta disagreeably.

"And that wench you found me! Aie! How she—"

"You have no stomach for the finer arts, Nath, and that is the truth, by Zim-Zair."

"Ha! Since when have you used Krozair oaths, my fat tallowed sea snake?"

Then we were all silent, for a space, for we remembered our friend Zorg of Felteraz, to whose widow we now traveled.

The way was not far but we did not hurry in the warm sunshine. The weather continued fine and mild. For Zolta and Nath this was a holiday as well as a pilgrimage; for me it was a digression from my set course I had to make, a task laid on me, a task I knew without a single hesitation Delia of the Blue Mountains would approve and applaud.

Felteraz, a town and an estate and a small fishing harbor, lay a little over three dwaburs to the east and we had had to be ferried over the neck of the Sea of Marshes to pick up our asscart. The gut there was about a mile or so broad and no bridges spanned it, but the shining water was always alive with small craft, oared wherries, pulling barges, dinghies, ferries, and the occasional stately passage of a swifter, every oar in line and rising and falling as one to the beat of the drum-deldar.

Now we ambled along the dusty path, for the suns had quickly dried the overnight dew. We passed cultivated fields, and small farms and a tiny village or two nestled into the rocks. Here there could be habitation near the shore. For the frowning walls of the citadel of Sanurkazz to the west and the much lesser citadel of Felteraz to the east provided protection and a powerful deterrent to a swift raiding descent on the coast. In general the coasts of the inner sea, the Eye of the World, lie barren beneath the suns.

I wondered what Mayfwy would be like. Zorg had never mentioned her, save that once, when he had been unable any longer to keep bottled within him the passions of his life, for he had been dying. He had said "Krozair" and "Mayfwy" in a breath, a dying breath. I had formed an image of her, of a serene and calm grand dame, straight, with the management of the estate and the overlordship of the town and harbor and citadel a burden she was capable of bearing with dignity and composure, a charge she accepted with all the loyalty I had come to know and admire in Zorg, her husband.

We stopped to eat in one of the villages, and Nath quickly bargained for a bottle of Zond wine, and Zolta had an apple-cheeked girl perched on his knee and screaming with laughter in almost no time at all. I ate bread, soft, fluffy bread torn in chunks from the long loaves of Kregen, and smeared with honey from the innkeeper's hives. A heaping dish of palines in the center of the table completed Nath's hangover cure; there is nothing as sovereign as palines to pick a man up from the floor.

There are many things I know I have forgotten in my long life. I sincerely believe I shall never forget that ambling ride on an asscart from Sanurkazz to Felteraz along the dusty coast road of the Eye of the World with the warm sunshine golden and glorious upon us, streaming in opaline radiance upon the vineyards and orange groves, and upon the browned and smiling faces of the people we passed. It is a simple memory, but a long one. And those two lusty rogues, Nath and Zolta, rollicked and sang in the cart as we rolled creaking and lurching along the road.

Felteraz came in sight. I shall say little about the place. The town was charming, high-banked along the terraced side of a hill, trending up to where a great dike cut off the frowning mass of the citadel. I have seen the incomparable view along the brilliant cliffs of Sorrento. Felteraz is something like that. The harbor lay cinctured by a solid granite wall and there was also a lighthouse as there was in Sanurkazz. From the high loft of the citadel I could look out and down along those cliffs which the setting suns crimsoned and opaled in breathtaking radiance, smothered in profuse vegetation, with blooms of gorgeous color and scents of delight breaking the patterns of greenery and rock.

We rolled along behind our ass up to the drawbridge over

the dike, and the bridge was down and a friendly man-at-arms clad in mail let us through. His white surcoat bore a symbol I was to come to know well: two galley oars, crossed, divided upright by a long sword, so that the whole looked something like the letter X with a center upright. The symbol was stitched in red and gold, surrounded by a lenk-leaf border. The man-at-arms lifted his long sword in salute as we passed, and, gravely, I acknowledged it.

A smiling maid in a white apron, with naked flashing legs, with a spritely eye that sized up Zolta in a moment, led us into a spacious antechamber hung with tapestry and with solid tables and chairs positioned about. She was gone only five minutes or so and I knew Zenkiren had sent a message, that we were expected.

Mayfwy, widow to Zorg of Felteraz, entered the room.

I knew what I had expected. A grand dame, solid, filled with the virtues of her exalted office, wearing stiff robes, brocade, girdled with a golden belt from which hung suspended bunches of iron keys of her responsibilities as chatelaine.

Of all the inward expectation, Mayfwy possessed only the glittering golden belt.

From the belt, the chatelaine itself, hung a silver key.

Mayfwy danced lightly into the room, smiling, brimming over with joy and goodwill. She was young, incredibly young to be what she was. Her mass of dark and curly hair glistened with health and oils and ministrations. Her pert face with its saucy eyes appraised us. Her small and sensuous mouth broke into a smile as she advanced, more sedately, her hand extended.

"My Lord of Strombor. I am heartily pleased to welcome you to Felteraz." She beamed on Zolta and Nath. "And to Nath and Zolta, my dear husband's friends, and therefore my friends. You are heartily welcome." She laughed, rushing on, giving us no time to speak. "Come. You must be hungry—surely you must be thirsty? Nath, deny it if you can! And you, Zolta, the name of the morsel who showed you in is Sinkle."

She went dancing out on her satin slippers and we, like three calsanys, followed her onto a terrace from which the whole breathtaking view of the cliffs and the bay and the harbor below the town spread out below us. I could spare time later to see the view. I studied this girl, this impish sprite, this Mayfwy, who was a widow.

She wore white, a sheer white linen dress that was held in

place over her shoulders by golden pins encrusted with rubies. Her golden belt circled her waist and hung low in the front and to one side, emphasizing the long curves of her. Her figure was lithe and feminine and seductive in an artless way, as though no matter what she did she could never fail to be attractive. In her curled dark hair posies of small forget-me-nots clustered.

I have little idea of what we talked about, there on that sun-drenched terrace over the blue sea. Nath took himself off to organize a wine delivery system, and Zolta was taken off by Sinkle, who had the grace to giggle as she led him out.

"Zorg," I said, and plunged brusquely and brutally into an account of our lives as slaves. She quieted down, and listened attentively. She did not cry, and as I talked and felt the response flowing so gently from her, I knew she had cried all the tears she could shed. Captivity and slavery had worn Zorg down. This elfin sprite had once been his match. Her dark days of agony had passed when news came that Zorg's galley had been captured. "He was sent to the galleys as a punishment for breaking the heads of those evil men of Magdag. They sought to discipline him. I tell you, Mayfwy, Zorg's spirit was never broken." And then I told her of what Zorg had said as he died, but I did not tell her of the manner of his death.

"He was a proud man, my Lord of Strombor. Proud. I thank you for your goodness in coming to see me." She gestured, a half helpless little movement of one slender naked arm. She wore no jewelry apart from those blazing rubies in the golden pins clasping the shoulders of her deeply-cut gown. The scent of her perfume came very sweetly as she moved.

I thought of the Princess Natema Cydones, of the Noble House of Esztercari, in far Zenicce, and then I did not think of Natema, who must by now be married to my friend Prince Varden Wanek of the Noble House of Eward, for some considerable time.

"You are not drinking your wine, my Lord of Strombor."

I reached for the crystal goblet.

Truth to tell I always preferred the rich and fragrant Kregan tea I had become used to on the Plains of Segesthes with my Clansmen, but this Felteraz wine was light, golden, and sweet, and cloyed not unpleasantly on the tongue.

"I drink to your eternal happiness, my Lady of Felteraz."

It was polite, a formula; it was also clumsy.

Her face moved toward me, her eyes immense and luminous, dark with remembered pain. "Ah! My Lord of Strombor!"

I rose and walked to the marble balustrade hanging above the tremendous view. I could see three galleys, hundred-swifters, tucked in the inner harbor, their yards and masts struck down, their awnings up, their oar ports leathered over. Gulls wheeled over the sheer drop. The perfume of the flowers was overpowering.

We took time, Nath and Zolta and me, to make ourselves as respectable as three ruffianly fighting-men might for the lavish meal Mayfwy provided that evening. The dishes passed before us, served on platters of beaten gold—which always let the food go cold too fast for a real gourmet—and the goblets of wine consumed were beyond counting. Mayfwy laughed and my two companions roared and sang and told stories that brought a sparkle to my Lady of Felteraz's eyes. Zorg was dead. He now sat in glory on the right hand of Zair in the paradise of Zim. He would not begrudge his old oar comrades some fun and relish from life, nor would he begrudge the girl he had loved the same human needs. We had seen Zorg's and Mayfwy's son and daughter: a fine, upright youngster with the features we had come to recognize in Zorg, and a winning little girl who at first was shy until Zolta perched her on his shoulders and pretended to be a sectrix, the while she belabored him with a stick, at which Nath cried out: "That's the idea, my little darling! Beat him like a calsany! He can only improve!"

The evening meal which in truth was more like a banquet—and I fancied, not without a twinge of shame, a banquet in our honor—passed. Also present were the guard commander and a number of the chief men of the estates and their ladies, all good kindly folk with country ways that came as refreshing as a cool westerly after days of sweltering in southerlies.

I was left at last with Mayfwy in a small retiring room, with only three rose-colored lamps for light, with a soft sofa on which she half reclined, her linen dress changed for one in much the same style but created all from shimmering silk, with a side table on which delicate wines waited our attention.

"Now, my Lord of Strombor," she said to me, her smooth and elfin face serious, that sensuous little mouth trying to be firm, her hands clasped. "I want you to tell me the truth about Zorg. I can stand it. But I must know the truth!"

I felt genuine distress.

How could I explain to her what her man had endured?

Such a thing was barely possible.

I could feel my heart thumping. The wine rose to cloud my vision and coiled thickly in my head. The rosy light of the lamps shed gleams on her curled gleaming hair. Her silken dress clung here and there to her body. She half reclined and gazed at me, and her ripe red mouth trembled so that I could think of nothing save obeying her commands; and yet, to speak of what I knew of the horrors of a Magdaggian galley to this girl?

"My Lord of Strombor," she said softly, and now her breathing was as unsteady as mine. She leaned toward me, her lips half parted, yet clinging still, her eyelids half closed, her breast rising and falling. "Please—my Lord?"

I leaned toward her.*

The Magdaggian hundredswifter had turned now, reached around, her oars a smother of foam in the sea. Again a hurtling mass of rock from her aft varter skimmed over our heads. Men were yelling as arrows feathered into them. The Magdag galley turned, her oars churning, and still Zolta had not sorted out the horrible confusion on our rowing benches amidships.

"Throw them overboard, if you have to, Zolta!" I roared at him. A man at my side screamed and started back with an arrow pierced clean through his eye. "Cut them loose! Get the oars into action!" The hundredswifter was swinging around and her ugly bronze beak was building a comb of white water as she picked up speed.

In only minutes that bronze rostrum would smash into us, her beak would rend over our parados and men would come leaping like sea-leem down among us. My thinned crew couldn't stop that strength in boarding.

Zolta's sword flashed and flashed again as he cut down the frenzied slaves. Nath was there, down from his place at our

* This is the point where at least one cassette is missing, as I have written in *A Note on the Tapes from Africa* at the beginning of this volume. It is clear from internal evidence that Prescot achieved command of a four-sixtyswifter and the next consecutive cassette picks up his story when he had spent probably three, at the least, seasons as a galley captain on the inner sea. What is lost we do not know, but from our knowledge of Dray Prescot I think it evident it was lurid, violent, and vividly colored in the extreme.

A.B.A.

forward varters. The whip-deldars were unchaining the dead
slaves. The mass of rock from the Magdaggian varter had
pulped their naked bodies like nits beneath a thumbnail.

Slaves toppled over the sides. The splashes as they hit were
lost in the uproar. As in the many fights I had been in, some
of which I have mentioned, on the Eye of the World, once
again I was struck by the absence of the smashing concussion
of gunfire, the choking clouds of smoke. I could see, all right.
I could hear. Both senses brought me tales of destruction.

Now our after varter could come into action and the men
there let fly and at once began their frenzied efforts to wind
up the windlass. The ballista was cocked again. The hundredswifter was bearing down on us now, gathering speed, the
bronze ram cutting the water, the metal gleaming and bright.
Where the strengthening wales along the sides met forward at
the proembolion the Magdaggians usually covered the junc-
tion with a sectrix head of bronze. Above that and beneath
the beak the wales met in a bronze risslaca-head, a mythical
lizard monster. After the ram had pierced and crushed us below water, the proembolion would push us back off the ram
and upright so that the boarders could leap down from their
gangways along the beak.

"Hurry it up, Zolta!" I roared.

My decks were covered with dead men. Arrows stood everywhere. My own archers were shooting, but I could not see
the results of their handiwork past the erected palisade across
the low foredeck of the hundredswifter. Her twin banks of
oars rose and fell now in a quicker beat. Each blade hit the
water as one, in two straight and parallel lines, churning her
forward like a runaway train on tracks. I yelled at Nath
again and he charged back up to the forward varter and
hounded his men there into making a final fling.

My sword was in my fist.

If we were captured it would be the galleys of Magdag for
us. I had tasted the freedom of the inner sea. I would not
willingly go back to slavery again.

Zolta was beating all the fresh slaves we had up from the
hold, herding them onto the benches. Here was one time
when a single-banked swifter had advantages. Four slaves to
an oar, then huddled down, lifting the looms, preparing for
the stroke.

Even then the whip-deldars were chaining them down. I
nodded. That was good. The oarsmen must respond at once
to every order. If they were unchained they would be unset-

tled, thinking of seizing the chance to jump overboard. More
of my men fell on the gangways as arrows flew down.

Zolta waved his sword. His face was as wrathful as a winter
storm.

"Clear," he bellowed. "Clear, Captain!"

I yelled down to the oar-master, but old Rizil was up to the
job and at once his silver whistle shrilled, the drum-deldar
smashed out the first booming beat, the bass and the tenor
drumming in turn. The oars swooped down, hauled water,
feathered and lifted in that short but incredibly powerful motion of oars arranged *alla scaloccio*. I felt *Zorg* leap through
the water.

All our artillery was shooting as we turned, and then the
after varter fell silent and it was up to Nath as we swung
around, bringing our bow against that of the green galley.

Bronze ram against bronze ram, now, we hurtled across
the narrowing space of water.

The foe was a hundredswifter, two banked with probably
five or six men to an oar. *Zorg* was a sixtyswifter, single-
banked, with four men to an oar. We would be slugged solidly backward at the point of impact.

Both captains, that man I fought and I, knew what to do
in this situation.

Amid the shrill of wounded men, the clang of the ballistae,
and the plunging swoop of the iron birds of the air, we both
stood as I stood, on the quarterdeck, waiting, judging, estimat-
ing, ready to choose the exact time.

But—which way would he go?

He would surely try to ram. As surely he would know I
would seek to avoid collision and seek to shave down his side,
smashing his cat head, rend away his whole double-bank of
oars. But—which side, larboard or starboard?

I found my face twisting and realized I must be smiling at
that Magdaggian captain's dilemma. He wished to strike me;
then he must make the decision. I must needs turn first; he
would think. Yes, he surely must think that.

Zolta was at my side, his sword bloody, panting.

"If they set foot aboard, Captain, they'll have to wade
over my blood!"

"Yes, Zolta," I said.

My men were crowding forward now, their white surcoats
with that brave blazon of Felteraz heartening us all, their
long swords ready. They crouched like leems, ready. I spoke
quietly to the rudder-deldars.

I had observed a slight incline in our passage, a slender movement with some current and the gentle breeze.

"When I give the order," I told the rudder-deldars, hard-voiced, "turn instantly to starboard. To starboard. When you hear my order. Understood?"

"Yes, Captain," they said, sturdily handling their rudders with a skill I had thrashed into them. "We hear."

"Come on, Zolta," I said. I spoke with a false cheeriness. "Let us go forward. Our blades are dry and thirsty."

"By Zair the all-merciful!" said Zolta. "No Grodno-gasta will stop me enjoying a maiden tonight on Isteria!"

Now the hundredswifter was half-hidden before us by our own palisade stretching across the foredeck aft of the outreaching beak. We ran forward and waved a quick encouragement to Nath, who was keeping his two varters on the bows clanging away with a speed and precision his crews never reached in all the practice I made them sweat through.

I was in command of my own ship; I had been in command now long enough just to have reached a time when organization was beginning to go as I wanted; no mangy Grodno-worshiping sea-leem would cheat me of that now!

Then Nath, high on the varter platform, let out a shrilling shriek of triumph.

"May Mother Zinzu the Blessed be praised! Their drum-deldar lies like a squashed paline!"

Immediately the beat of the hundredswifter's oars faltered. Even as the thought: *Lack of training!* flashed through my mind I turned and, funneling my hands, yelled aft: "*Now!*"

Zorg swung viciously to starboard.

Our larboard side oars went in with a speed that clearly told of the slaves' knowledge of what would happen if they were caught with their blades extended. I saw the cruel beak of the Magdag galley lurch away. It opened out a glimpse of her bows where the varter crew labored at the windlass. I saw the cat head disappear beneath our beak and felt the jolting crunch as our bronze-clad proembolion, fashioned into the head of a charging chunkrah, ripped it away.

Then we were roaring down the larboard side of the galley, tearing away the oars in a vast and horrible splintering of wood, shaving her side as clean as a Magdaggian harbor barber shaves the head of a slave.

I knew what was happening to those two banks of slaves aboard the hundredswifter. They were men of Zair, fellows, comrades: they would understand what we were doing now, and regret it, and feel the bitterness, but their acrid hate would be for Magdag.

We shot past the upflung stern of the galley and not a single mailed man of Magdag had got aboard us.

After that we lay off on our oars and shot the galley to pieces.

When we boarded, the shambles, blood, and filth had no power to sicken me. After that it was like any other successful action on the inner sea.

Of the eight hundred slaves aboard some three hundred and twenty-nine were either dead or so badly wounded, crushed, as to surely die. Of the Magdaggians we were able to chain to our oar benches a paltry twenty-two. But we outfitted the captured hundredswifter and, with all our reserve of oars used up and many splintered together, we set course for Holy Sanurkazz.

I did all that was necessary in the burial of the slaves at sea. Our decks were scrubbed, our wounded cared for, the rescued slaves happy, now, to labor for just a little while longer at the oars to take us into home waters—and this time with the threat of the whip on their naked backs removed.

We sailed past the pharos over by the outer wall of the sea defenses of Sanurkazz. Zolta had, indeed, enjoyed his maiden on the island of Isteria, where we had passed the night. How often I have spent in that snug anchorage, the last before Sanurkazz herself, a night thinking of my return to Felteraz!

The people of Zair welcomed our return, as they always welcomed the return of a successful venture against Magdag. The four fat merchantmen we had taken would provide me with a substantial increase to my fortune. I had my eye on a gown all of gold and silver thread, silk lined, that I felt sure Mayfwy would admire. And, too, after this Zenkiren could no longer keep from me the command of a double-banked swifter, a hundred-and-twentyswifter! She would be called *Zorg*, of course, the moment I assumed command.

I knew the very ship. She had been reaching completion as we had set sail. Now, she must be ready, brand-new from the shipwrights and fitters, lying waiting for me in the arsenal. Zo, the new king, a man whom I quite liked, would surely not refuse a request from Zenkiren that one of his sea captains should take the command. The high admiral might grumble and Harknel of High Heysh would be sure to interfere and try to prevent me from any success, but intrigue

"We shot the galley to pieces."

would be met with intrigue. I, too, now had powerful friends in Holy Sanurkazz.

Was I not, after all, the Lord of Strombor, the most successful corsair captain of the Eye of the World?

The formalities were quickly over. The freed slaves, with many expressions of thanks, went to recuperate in Sanurkazz.

My crew was paid off and roaring for a well-earned leave. All the flags of gold, silver, and scarlet floated in the bright air above Sanurkazz and carpets of brilliant color and weave hung from hundreds of balconies smothered in flowers. My agent, wily old Shallan, with his wisp of beard, lined cheeks, and merry eyes, who would charge fifteen percent on a loan and chuckle with merriment as he did so, would see to the disposal of the prizes after the required dues had been paid to Zo, the king, the high admiral, Zenkiren, and to Felteraz.

I sat in the stern sheets of my personal barge, with a crew of sixteen free men to row, Zolta at my side, Zolta's girl acting as drum-deldar, and Nath steering a precarious course as he upended a bottle at the rudder, as we rounded the curve of coast from Sanurkazz to Felteraz. As we glided into the harbor I contrasted this arrival with that first time when we had rolled up roaring on the asscart.

Zenkiren was waiting for me in a tall cool room of tapestries and solid furniture with another man, a man who might have served as a model of what Zenkiren would be like in another hundred years. Mayfwy kissed me on the cheek as her maids brought in wine in chased silver goblets.

"Mayfwy!" I said. Then, "I have a cedar wood chest for you—"

"Dray!" she said, her eyes dancing, her cheeks flushed with my return. "Another present!"

"As I recall," said Zenkiren dryly, "he can never keep his hands off Magdag gold and silver. If he didn't bring you a present I would think my Lord of Strombor had sailed a lonely sea."

"As for you, Zenkiren," I said, unwrapping the blue-etched and gold-mounted Fristle scimitar I had picked up off the deck of that damned Magdag pirate, "I thought this toy might amuse you."

"It is magnificent!" said Zenkiren, running his fingers along the curved blade. "I thank you."

"And now," he said, and a note of solemn seriousness entered his voice, "I wish to present you." He turned to the other man, who had remained calm and cool, his old strong-featured face composed, his simple white apron and tunic immaculate, the long sword at his side scabbarded in the fighting-man's style.

"May I present the Lord of Strombor." He turned then to me. "I have the honor to present to you, my Lord of Strombor, Pur Zazz, Grand Archbold of the Krozairs of Zy."

CHAPTER TEN

The Krozairs of Zy
point the path

I can remember, even now, vividly, unforgettably, the zephyr of anticipation that blew through my whole being.

In the seasons I had been hunting with the corsairs of Sanurkazz I had heard a hint dropped here, a casual snatch of conversation there, and I had picked up information that must have been the sum total, or nearly that, of what the ordinary idle, happy, careless folk of Sanurkazz knew of the Krozairs of Zy.

Now this tall, aloof, calm-faced man was here, in the familiar room of the citadel of Felteraz, at the express desire, as it seemed to me, of Zenkiren—and he was the Grand Archbold of the Krozairs!

What followed must have been very familiar to him, for he had been master of the Order for a very long time. From hints I picked up I gathered that Zenkiren himself was in line for the succession, that my friend Zenkiren would become Grand Archbold. Pur Zazz sized me up with a cold and level stare. Instinctively I straightened up and squared those inordinately broad shoulders of mine. He looked me over. I felt that he was stripping my flesh away, was paring my very self down to the essence beneath. I had been roistering and going pirating on the inner sea, I had been living life to the full, I had been amassing wealth, and I had made friends. All that seemed to me in that moment to be petty, a mere preliminary to what this man would require of me.

If I do not go too deeply into what happened to me in the year that followed on that interview it is because I am bound by vows of silence I do not wish to break, even to an audience four hundred light-years distant from the scenes of that rigorous training and selection and adherence to the principles of dedication to Zair and to the Krozairs of Zy.

The Order maintained an island stronghold in the narrowing strait between the inner sea and the Sea of Swords, that other smaller dependent sea opening off southward from the Eye of the World. Like the Sea of Marshes it covered an extensive area, but it lay westward, something less than halfway along the curved southern shore. The island had once been a volcano, but through the geological aeons its crater had smoothed and filled, the subterranean fires stilled, and fresh water had found its way up to rill out in pleasant springs. The outer jagged scarps rose harsh and rocky beneath the suns; within a habitation had been built very little less harsh. The Order took its vows seriously. They kept themselves aloof from other orders of lesser chivalry like The Red Brethren of Lizz; they were dedicated to the succor of destitute people of Zair, to the greater glory of Zim-Zair, and to the implacable resistance to Grodno the Green and all his works.

After the novice had served his novitiate he was ranked Krozair, given the titles and insignia of his station, a man fit to stand in the forefront of the ranks of Zim-Zair in the eternal struggle against the heretic. Only men of worth were ever approached. Many refused, for the disciplines were harsh. Many fell by the wayside and never reached into the inner knowledge.

Once a candidate had become a Krozair, he was entitled, as other orders also conferred the privilege, of prefixing his name with the honorific Pur. Pur was not a rank or a title: it was a badge of chivalry and honor, a pledge that the man holding it was a true Krozair. Then the newly-fledged Krozair might choose a number of paths that opened before him. If he chose to become a contemplative, that was his privilege. If he chose to become a Bold, one of the select brethren who manned the fortress isle of Zy and other of the citadels maintained by the Order throughout the red sections of the inner sea, he would be welcomed. Should he desire to return to the ordinary ways of life, he might do that also, for the Order recognized its mission in the world. But a stricture was laid upon that man, that proved Krozair.

Whenever he received the summons to join the Krozairs, wherever they happened to be in need of his aid, then, wherever he happened to be, and whenever it might occur in his life, he was bound by all that he held most holy and dear to hasten as fast as sectrix or swifter might take him to join his brothers of the Order.

"There have been a number of famous and immortal calls in the past, Pur Dray," Pur Zenkiren told me one time as we came from the salle d'armes where we had been knocking the stuffing out of each other with morning stars. "I have been privileged to answer one such summons, some thirty years ago, when the devils of Magdag came knocking on the very doors of Zy itself. From all over the inner sea the brothers gathered." He laughed, a faraway look in his bright eyes. "I tell you, Pur Dray: we had quite a fight of it until the Order gathered and the long swords sang above the hated green."

I had been on Zy long enough to answer, with sincere meaning: "I pray that the summons will come again, and soon, Pur Zenkiren, for the Order to go up against Magdag itself."

He made a face. "Unlikely." He smiled and clapped me on the shoulder. "We are few. Finding men, as it is phrased in the Discipline, of the right caliber, is difficult. We have our eye on men as soon as they don sword and coat of mail. We are a lazy sun-loving lot, we men of Sanurkazz."

"Agreed."

The disciplines were strenuous, difficult, and extremely demanding. The use of weapons had become of itself almost a religion. Sword practice was carried out as a religious observance. Every move was sanctified by religious ardor. Like the Samurai, we dedicated our wills and our bodies to the pursuit of perfection, the facing of an opponent without seeing him as though he were there. We tried to make our opponents transparent, as though they were far off. We could sense a blow, the direction of a cut, the movement of a slash, by an intuitive process beyond reason, allied to our sixth sense. We could move into a parry almost before our foe instigated his attack.

Always, even as a young seaman aboard a seventy-four, I was accounted a good cutlass man. I have spoken of the need for such physical prowess, such good healthy cut-and-thrust, to enable me to survive when I first entered Kregen. Since then I have been in many situations where swordsmanship was vital, and I have been accounted a good man with a blade. But I freely admit that I learned from the disciplines of Zy a dexterity in swordplay that turned me into a different kind of swordsman entirely.

Only in my own inner feelings about the superiority of the point to the edge could I teach the Krozairs much; and the knowledge was unnecessary, for they fought armored men in mesh iron, where the thrust from a sword would be stopped, where the way to dispose of your man was to slash his head off, or lop a limb, or break in his ribs. The disciplines were, in their way, too far advanced for the style of sword fighting practiced on the inner sea. Breathing, isometrics, arduous and prolonged exercises, continuous dedication, long hours of contemplation, hours of drawing on the will and making of the will itself a single central instrument whereby a man might know himself and thus see his enemy as transparent and removed, a foe he could outwit and outmaneuver and eventually triumph over, endless hours of instruction and devotion—all these were my daily portion during that year on the Krozairs' lair, the isle of Zy.

I will not speak of the mysticism.

Then came the day when the Grand Archbold put me through the final ceremonies, and, purified, uplifted, I was pronounced a fit Krozair, worthy to hold the honor of Pur prefixed to my name.

"And now, Pur Dray, what will you do?"

I believe they knew what my decision would be. The Order maintained its own small fleet of galleys, and I had now made up my mind that I would aim for the command of the finest of these. This would take time. In the meanwhile, I intended to return to Felteraz, to a swifter command under the aegis of Zenkiren, who was now commodore in the king's fleet, and to my previous life. I did not want to give up Felteraz.

Any thoughts of becoming a contemplative, or one who actually tended the succored, was, I knew, to my shame, perhaps, not for me. Equally I did not wish to become a Bold, even though this was a sure way to the Grand Archbold's position. But Zenkiren, a roving brother, was to become Grand Archbold. And, perhaps, the greatest reason for my decision to go again into the inner sea—I had almost said outside world, thinking of my young self in those days, so gullible, so (if Zair will pardon) so green—was that I had never forgotten the Star Lords and the Savanti. I knew they still had plans for me. I knew they would manipulate me whenever it suited them.

And—my Delia, my Delia of the Blue Mountains.

Could I forget her?

"I have sent for *Zorg*," said Zenkiren to me as we stood on one of the lookout posts near the crest of one of the long steep slopes of the island. A surprise.

"It has meant a lot to me, Zenkiren, to know that he was here, in these halls, these chapels, these salles d'armes. I sometimes think I can sense his presence here, as we perform the same observances as he performed."

"They have been observed by the Order, not here, necessarily, but in our many abodes, for hundreds of years. And they will go on, through the years, being thus observed."

When *Zorg* made landfall and nosed under the colossal rock arch that led into the inner harbor under the island, I was waiting. I donned my white surcoat with its circled emblem with the hubless wheel within. I saw Nath and Zolta on the beak, perched like gulls on a rock face, ready to jump ashore at the first practical moment. As it was, Nath jumped too soon and would have fallen with a splash had I not hauled him up.

They were all grins and grimaces, dancing around me, prodding me to see if I could still withstand a gut-punch, like in the old days. To them the idea that I was now a Krozair, and they must call me Pur—on top of the "lord" bit they had been unable to swallow—came as ludicrous nonsense with which I thoroughly agreed.

"Nath! Zolta! You disgusting ruffians! Why, Nath, your gut is so swelled with wine a season on the benches would trim you down to man-size again! And you, Zolta—I could scabbard my long sword in those pouches under your eyes!"

"Stylor!" they crowed and we wrestled affectionately.

Zenkiren stood to one side, his arms folded and one hand stroking his chin. The Grand Archbold, Purr Zazz, made a sound that might have been "harrumph" if that silly way of speaking had penetrated here. There were five other newly-fledged Krozairs, and we were all to go back together on *Zorg*, which was now under the command of Sharntaz. They, too, didn't quite know what to make of these two bearded rapscallions in the dedicated, austere enclave of Zy, even if the two specimens of hardy and iconoclastic inner sea sailors were only standing on the outer jetty wall.

But the essential dignity and purpose and a breath of that mystery overawed even Nath and Zolta eventually, so that they quieted down. The laymen kept to the outer courts, those opening off the harbor, of course; only Krozairs and lay brothers, the so-called Zimen, were allowed past the iron doors into the interior of the island. Not all of Zy was austere and given over to the pursuit of the inner light; there was great beauty there, for the Krozairs of Zy believed that

Zair was just as approachable through beauty as through devotion and dedication in war.

When the time came for our departure, Zenkiren told me he would be staying on in Zy for a time.

"Pur Zazz is old. There are many weighty matters to be discussed, chapter by chapter, langue by langue, in council. You will come to these in your turn, Pur Dray, one of these fine days."

I knew that the Order was in general maintained by Krozair contributions from all the free cities of Zair along the southern shore, and they therefore would have their say in council. Back along the Sea of Swords lay large salt pans, as there were off the Sea of Marshes, and Zy gathered much of its revenue from the salt as did Sanurkazz. But without the continuous support of the brothers of the Order scattered throughout the Zair portions of the Eye of the World, the Krozairs of Zy would be in parlous state.

Sharntaz greeted me with a kindly word and the necessary formality as one captain going aboard another's vessel, and also with the sign—I hesitate to call it a secret sign, it was so obvious and lucid a greeting—that identified a Krozair brother.

He smiled. "I have no idea what swifter you will be given, Pur Dray. But I rather imagine you will want to call her *Zorg*."

"That is my intention."

"So be it. We now stand on the swifter *Lagaz-el-Buzro*.

I nodded. "Also, I shall take those two useless hands, Nath and Zolta."

He chuckled. "And very welcome to them you are, for their drinking and their wenching. But useless? I would rather have a crew like them than one composed of the spoiled brats of Sanurkazz nobility."

I nodded again. I agreed. There was no need of more words.

Zorg that was now *Lagaz-el-Buzro* pushed off. Everything that had to be done had been done. I was going back to report to the high admiral, with a strong recommendation from Zenkiren, and my future in the Eye of the World looked bright. Also, I wanted to see Mayfwy again, and the children, Zorg and Fwymay.

We drew into Sanurkazz. I reported to the high admiral who did not like me and knew the feeling was reciprocated

But Zo, the king, was disposed toward me, for I had never caused him any offense, and, besides, I had brought him during the course of my last season's activities more gold, jewels, and the precious commodities that are the lifeblood of the inner sea's trading than any other of his captains.

I got my ship.

I have already given some explanation of the controversy then raging in the inner sea over the relative merits of what were called, for convenience, the long keel and the short keel theories.* Long keels, that is, a long narrow swifter, are necessary for speed. But the short keel men, those who argued for the same oar-power packed tighter, claimed that a shorter craft for the same beam might lose a knot or so of speed but gave immeasurably greater maneuverability and turning capacity. I had not yet made up my mind. Zo, the king, appointed me to a five-hundredswifter of the short keel construction. Immediately I set about devising ways of improving the speed of my new *Zorg*. I had two banks of twenty-five oars a side. I carried six hundred slaves, allowing me a reasonable turnover in use and rest periods.

"I thank you, Light of Zim," I said formally. "Rest assured. I shall bring you in a tail of accursed Magdag broad ships and swifters." It was a rote speech, but I meant it with all my heart.

I went raiding on the Eye of the World.

The seasons slipped by; Felteraz remained as beautiful as ever. Nath grew ever more corpulent. Zolta had a number of narrow escapes from the form of marriage that would have clipped his wings. We sailed and we pulled and we crisscrossed the inner sea with burning wrecks and floating corpses; the totals of our prizes steadily mounted as we pulled in past the pharos of Sanurkazz.

Clever distribution of the weights was always the problem in trimming a swifter. A galley that depends on oar propulsion must possess a shallow draft, yet we were packing as many as a thousand or twelve hundred oarsmen in, besides the crew, soldiers, and varters. Sometimes shipwrights went to dangerous lengths to conserve weight. Although all the enormous deadweight of the guns aboard a ship of the line

---

* Clearly, here, Prescot is referring to passages in the lost cassettes. This is a great pity, for any light he can shed on galley propulsion and crewing is of the greatest academic interest to scholars.

A.B.A.

did not have to be carried, the weights were still considerable. *Victory*'s longest deck measures a hundred and eighty-six feet in length, and the width is fifty-two feet. She is built of wood. A swifter of that length would measure something like twenty feet beam. The differences make for cranky, unwieldly, and extremely unseaworthy craft. But then, no galley could live in a sea that *Victory*, or her sisters of my old Navy, could sail with ease.

Galleys are useless on the open ocean. I know.

I had seen the Spaniards out of Cartagena wallowing as we flashed past with our royals set.

I could never sail back home to Strombor in Zenicce, or to Vallia, that island hub of an ocean empire, aboard a galley.

Equally, I would not relish the journey aboard a broad ship, what the ancients also called a round ship, of the inner sea.

All my growing fortune, my success, the luxury with which I might surround myself if I so wished, the good friends I was making—to my continual surprise, for I think I have indicated sufficiently that I am a loner in life—meant little. I felt more and more restless as the long days of raiding, cruising, and carousing passed. I hungered for something I was not clearly conscious of desiring.

That cunning and politely vicious man, the noble Harknel of High Heysh, continued his attempts at persecution, but I held him off, contemptuously, almost with boredom. He did not pose the kind of problem I was in the mood to deal with. Because he had not been born with the all-important Z either in his name or his place of abode, by which he was known, his resentment of that further embittered him. He had seen that his son possessed the Z in his name. I had found, not without amusement, that my name was taken as Prezcot. It had helped. A man had to have the antecedents or the newly-won, right to name either himself or his son with the Z. I often wondered what Zolta's history was, but he would never tell me. Nath, now, was the son of an illiterate ponsho farmer, who had taken to the sea in revolt against fleeces, dips, and eternal flock-tending.

At the beginning of a new raiding season, when the twin suns of Scorpio were so close they appeared almost to touch as they rose in the sky, we had returned from our first cruise, happy and successful. Isteria had witnessed some carousing the night before and we had left a trail of mayhem at our many ports of call. I had taken my last cruise aboard this swifter, and was due to shift to a new six-six-hundred-and-twentyswifter, one built on long keel lines, as an experiment. She would be *Zorg,* of course.

Nath wore a bandage around his head.

A Magdag oar blade had welted him nastily during our last fight and he could still hear the bells of Beng-Kishi ringing in his head.

"He's all right," scoffed Zolta. "He wouldn't know it if the tower of Zim-Zair fell on him. He has the skull of a vosk."

Vosks notoriously had exceptionally thick skull bones, so I laughed, and said: "Maybe, Zolta. He should be thankful. He kept the varters going all through—"

"Vosk skull!" said Zolta, and then Nath threw a wet mop at him and I took myself off to my aft state room. It is not seemly for the captain of a king's swifter to be seen romping with the crew. But again that nag of dissatisfaction came to me.

I have mentioned the single occasion on which I attempted to alleviate the lot of the slaves aboard my galley, and of how they rose as one man and attempted to cut the throats of all my crew.* Both red and green kept slaves: the red only for gallery work and a few personal body servants, the green for every aspect of menial labor they required. I had conceived it that my duty lay with the men of Zair—and I heartily loathed and hated the men of Magdag—but also I tried to remember that perhaps the Savanti had sent me here to the Eye of the World to do something positive about this abhorrent slavery. If they had, if the Star Lords also had their own requirements, I must obey, but I would do so with the clear understanding that I would make for Vallia or Zenicce just as soon as I could.

The Proconia, those fair-haired people who dominated all the eastern shoreline of the inner sea, were involved in another of their internecine wars. As I have said, we always kept out of it, for we had enough to do with Magdag. This time Magdag herself had taken a hand in an attempt to dominate the only area of the Eye of the World where neither Grodno nor Zair were worshipped.† My new *Zorg* was direct-

---

* Further information lost to us from Prescot's narrative in the missing cassettes.

A.B.A.

† Idem.

A.B.A.

ed to join a squadron outfitted for an expedition toward the east. This would be entirely new sea for me. I found a fresh interest in life again and Mayfwy had had made for me a new coat of mail of a fineness almost as supple as the mail worn by that mailed man in the Princess Natema's alcove. That mesh steel had come from Havilfar, I had learned. The mesh of the inner sea was practical, lumpy, and unsophisticated by contrast.

The Victorian antiquaries who, to do them justice, revived an interest in Medieval artifacts, persisted in their odd usage, a quite erroneous nomenclature, of "chain" mail for the mesh iron coat, or hauberk, for far too long. One even still sees this silly word used of a coat of mail. I sat, I remember, in the stern sheets of my barge, feeling the iron links between my fingers, and thinking deep and powerful thoughts of nothing at all as we rowed back from Felteraz to Sanurkazz. The suns, very close together, were sinking into the sea ahead of us. The water shimmered and sparkled with the most wonderful colors. We drowned in sparkling light. The lighthouse men were climbing up the winding stairs to the pharos. A few fishing craft were sailing out. Some birds flitted against the cliffs. The glow of lamps and torches were lighting all over the city.

Perhaps I was dull, tired, maybe, stale. Whatever the cause I was scarcely aware of the abrupt rush of men with dark cloaks swathed over their mail. We had just touched and bow oar had hauled us in with his boat hook and I, as was proper, was first out of the boat onto the steps. The men smashed into us in a fierce and silent onslaught. At once Nath's long sword cleared his sheath and he was fighting for his life. Zolta, cursing, hurled himself into the fray. My men tumbled up from the barge.

We would have had a hard time of it; maybe I would not have survived, had it not been for two men who appeared unexpectedly at the side of the jetty. I heard two whirring thuds, and as two men pitched screaming to the stones of the jetty I knew I was again seeing and hearing the terchick, the balanced throwing knife of Segesthes, in action.

Both victims had been struck in the face where their mail did not protect them.

Zolta was yelling like a crazy man. My long sword cleared its scabbard in time to cut down the attacker who pounced on me like a mad graint. I could see the two newcomers and they were going to their work with a will. Swords flashed in the dying light. Men yelled and bodies made heavy splashes as they toppled from the stones. The attackers had been caught flat-footed by that unexpected flank onslaught; and as more of my men came racing up the stairs, green and slippery with weed, Zolta, Nath, and I with reinforcements drove them off. We had been lucky; without those two on the flank, they might have overwhelmed us by sheer numbers. Nath was puffing with his mouth open, his bulk heaving.

Zolta, to my surprise, was not making rude comments. He was looking at the newcomers.

"By Zim-Zair!" he said, in wonder. "Is that a sword? Or is it a toothpick?"

I knew, then.

A light, arrogant, and yet pleasant voice answered.

"They don't like it through their eyes, friend. They don't like it."

The man who bent to retrieve his terchick from the bloodied face of a dead man wore buff clothes, short to the thigh and belted in; his legs were encased in long black boots. However, the item that truly identified him for me was the jaunty broad-brimmed hat, with the gay feather, and with those two strange slots cut in the brim above his forehead.

He straightened, the cleaned terchick in his hand. In a single rapid motion it vanished into the sheath behind his neck.

"The little Deldar," he said, "has his uses, like the Hikdar," and he slapped the long left-handed dagger at his right side. "And the Jiktar, my toothpick, as you so disrespectfully called the queen of weapons."

His rapier was long, thin, and elegant, rather too ornate about the hilt, and there were spots of blood about the hilt he had not cleaned off.

Nath and Zolta were over their surprise, now. They had seafared long enough around the inner sea to have learned of the men of Vallia.

The other Vallian, who was older and stouter and whose square-cut face showed a trace of displeasure as he slapped his rapier hilt, said a few words beneath his breath that halted his young companion in his tracks.

The older man scanned us in that streaming dying light, with the dead men and the blood between us. He took a step forward. He did not remove his hat, whose feather was black.

"Which of you," he said in a harsh voice, at once metallic and flat, "is the man known as Dray Prescot?"

CHAPTER ELEVEN

"Remberee, Pur Dray! Remberee!"

I was going home.

I was going home to a place I had never seen.

What was this Vallia like? This Vallia of the island empire, of the fabled opulence: the ocean-spanning shipping, the fleets of airboats, the wealth and power and beauty. What did it mean to me apart from my Delia, Delia of Delphond, Delia of the Blue Mountains?

I did not forget that my Delia was known as the Princess Majestrix of Vallia.

Tharu of Vindelka, Kov, the older of the two Vallians, treated me with a grim distant courtesy that puzzled me. He was icily polite. When I asked him about Delia's father, the emperor of Vallia, he rubbed a reflective thumbnail along a narrow scar on his jaw. "He is a mighty man, sudden, all-powerful unpredictable. His word is law."

Tharu had made all the arrangements. Vomanus, his aide, was volatile in his enthusiasm for life with a fetching kind of swaggering arrogance. I gathered from Zolta that Vomanus had a love of love also, for my two rascals, Nath and Zolta, took Vomanus out on the town as a kind of way of saying thank you. Tharu of Vindelka ripped into Vomanus on the following morning. I had insisted that they stay at my villa in the best part of Sanurkazz, and I heard the grim rumbling tones rolling on remorselessly, and the dispirited replies from Vomanus, who badly needed a hatful of palines.

We got down to business that very first morning.

Delia, Princess of Vallia had returned home immediately after an exhaustive search of the enclave of Strombor, all the rest of Zenicce that could be searched by parties of allied Houses, the Eward, the Reinmans, the Wickens, and the speediest airboats' messages and inquiries to the Clansmen of

Felschraung and Longuelm. Of course I could not be found.
By that time I was trying to explain why I was walking naked on a beach in Portugal, some four hundred light-years
away.

"Now that we have found you, my Lord of Strombor,"
said Tharu in his metallic voice, "we will sail at once for Pattelonia on the southeast coast of Proconia. I have an airboat
waiting there. You know whereof I speak."

I nodded. I could feel my pulses jumping, the blood surging through my veins. Delia had gone home to Vallia and
had started a search operation to find me that had turned her
world upside down.

She had known—for how could she not so well understand?—that a mystery surrounded me. I had not told her of
my origin, although I fully intended to. But she had shared
with me that eerie experience of being flung in a gesture of
contemptuous dismissal out of the sacred pool of baptism in
far Aphrasöe, to find herself running on a beach in Segesthes.
She must have reasoned that something similar had occurred
again, and this time to me alone. So she had set herself to
finding me. I heard from young Vomanus of the efforts that
had been undertaken. He was very apologetic that he and
Tharu had missed me before. I gathered that they had
searched Magdag but in all that festering confusion of slaves
and workers the discovery of a single man, who bore a name
different from the one they sought, was well-nigh impossible
and had defeated them. Chance had dictated that they had
visited Sanurkazz when I was away at Zy. They had thought
they had at last found the man their princess had instructed
them to find, and they awaited my arrival, for they would
not venture to the Grand Archboldship of the Order. They
were thanked by me for waiting; they had almost certainly
saved our necks.

"A message must be got back to Vallia as soon as is practicable," said Tharu. "Then the Princess Majestrix may
graciously consent to recalling all the hundreds of other en-
voys she has sent chasing all over the world in search of
you."

I didn't much care for his tone.

I saw Vomanus casting an anxious look between us, and as
I was conscious of my position vis-à-vis Vallia, I thought it
expedient to say nothing. I told Nath and Zolta to take care
of Vomanus: I thought he was a friend.

The coldness of Tharu of Vindelka's attitude quickly made

itself understandable as I talked with the Vallians. There, as everywhere, it seemed, intrigues flourished. There were parties of various shades of political opinion, for religion in Vallia was undergoing some kind of psychic upheaval and no one seemed anxious to talk on the subject, and the emperor was acting with his usual autocratic hauteur. I would have to face that man, Delia's father, and tell him that I intended to marry his daughter no matter what he said or did. Tharu raged with anger that his party had not made the vital match with Delia, and he was forced to bottle all that frustrated resentment, for he acted under the orders, as he put it, of the Majestrix that no man may disobey. At that Vomanus pointed out that many men did disobey, and Tharu retired into that hard cold shell. He didn't like me. He considered not only had he lost the chance to marry off his favorite son or nephew to Delia but that Delia was marrying far below her station.

He was right, of course.

A broad ship had been found by Shallan, my agent, that was sailing to Pattelonia with supplies for the upcoming expedition. I had a nasty interview with Zo, the king, and quite unable to explain why I was suddenly leaving my command, Sanurkazz, and him, I went out in what was in reality disgrace. It did not matter. I was shaking the water of the inner sea from my boots.

I will not dwell on the interview with Mayfwy. She had heard the news and had been crying, but she dried her tears and put up a brave front. I kissed her gently, kissed Fwymay, who was turning into a beauty like her mother, clasped hands with young Zorg.

The problem of Harknel of High Heysh I must, perforce, leave unfinished. My natural inclinations after his last attempt to kill me on the jetty had been to take my men, march to his villa and burn it to the ground, and to hell with the high admiral and Zo, the king. Those jolly fat men of the mobiles would no doubt have gathered round, bottles in hand, and might conceivably have helped toss a torch or two.

But I could not do it. I could not risk a vile retribution from Harknel upon Felteraz. Felteraz was important. Very. I had to leave all this ferment in mid-boil. But I was glad to go. I understood what canker had been eating away at me as I went corsairing on the Eye of the World.

Nath and Zolta were a problem—a pair of problems.

I asked them to stay with Mayfwy. She would have need of their long swords.

"What, Stylor? Leave you now, our oar comrade! Never!"

Tharu of Vindelka grumbled, but agreed that there would be room on the airboat for the two. Vomanus was openly delighted.

"Anyway," said Zolta, "the Krozairs will never let harm befall Felteraz. And the king will also protect the citadel, for it holds his eastern flank. Do not fret, old vosk head."

My good-bye to Pur Zazz, the Grand Archbold of the Krozairs of Zy was formal, and then warmly fraternal. He did not seem at all perturbed that I was traveling better than a thousand dwaburs away.

"When the Krozairs have need of you, Pur Dray, and the brothers receive the summons, no matter where you are, I know you will come."

I gripped the hilt of my long sword. I nodded. It was true.

"You will be traveling beyond Proconia, which commands all the eastern seaboard of the Eye of the World and extends her varied powers as far to the east as The Stratemsk. Those mountains are said to have no summits, they extend clear to the orange glory of Zim, and form a pathway for the spirit to the majesty of Zair." He smiled and poured me more wine. "That is nonsense, of course, Pur Dray. But it tells eloquently of the fear and veneration in which men hold the Mountains of The Stratemsk."

I was aware, of course, that educated men knew that both the green and the red suns were suns and not thinking beings. But many of the illiterate folk of all shades of opinion held that the suns in their majesties were entities in their own rights quite apart from being the abode of the deities of Grodno and Zair. Astronomy was a strange art, on Kregen, twisted by its special circumstances into byways unknown to astronomers on Earth. The astrological lore and amazingly accurate predictions achieved by the wizards of Loh astonished even me at a later date.

"Over the mountains you are going where no man can say." Pur Zazz was as cultured and refined and intelligent a man as the inner sea might produce. Now he said: "Men say that beyond the mountains, in the hostile territory, there are whole tribes who fly on the backs of great beasts of the air." He smiled at me again, not ironically, but with the seriousness these subjects merited in an oar-powered geography. "I would welcome news, Pur Dray, of your adventures, and the sights you encounter."

"I will regard that as a first charge upon me, Pur Zazz."

When I left him, straight and commanding in his white tunic and apron, with that blazing emblem of the hubless wheel within the circle upon his breast, and the long sword belted in the fighting-man's way at his side, I half knew, then, I would never see him again.

"Remberee, Pur Dray."

"Remberee, Pur Zazz."

Saying good-bye to Zenkiren was not as easy. But I told him that a message to Strombor would always find me, and my vows to return would remain for as long as I lived.

I did not say that if the Star Lords or the Savanti decided otherwise I might not be in a position to return.

"Remberee, Pur Dray, Lord of Strombor."

"Remberee, Pur Zenkiren."

We clasped hands the final time, and I went down to my barge.

Nath and Zolta, very subdued, saw to getting us under way.

The hurt looks on the faces of my friends, looks they had tried to conceal, would haunt me for a very long time to come.

Two men had arrived from another world, another place across the outer oceans, mysterious and strange and with nothing to do with the Eye of the World, and I had upped and run panting like a dog running to its master. Who was this strange remote Princess Majestrix who called the foremost corsair captain of the inner sea? This is what they were saying.

But—they did not know Delia, my Delia of Delphond.

The broad ship sailed like a bathtub. I endured. I would far rather have preferred to make this little voyage into seas I had never scoured before aboard a swifter, but I was no longer in the employment of the king, no longer in his service.

The Magdaggian caught us as the twin suns, very close together, were sinking in the west and setting long shadows across the placid sea. She pulled toward us, all oars in neat parallel lines, churning the sea, and we could not escape.

"By Zantristar!" I yelled, hauling out my long sword. "They won't take us without a fight!"

The sailors were running, milling. Nath and Zolta, their long swords flaming brands in the dying light, tried to beat them into a resistance. But the merchantman stood no chance She carried perhaps thirty crew, with little stomach for a fight they knew they could not win. They were launching a longboat and clearly they anticipated rowing to a nearby island, where we had intended to lay up for the night, and from which the Magdag corsair, lying in wait, had pulled with such sudden ferocity.

"My orders, from the Princess Majestrix herself," Tharu told me in his flat voice, "are to bring you safely back to Vallia. Put up your sword."

"You fool!" I said. "I am Pur Dray, the Lord of Strombor, the man the heretics from Magdag will give most to have in their clutches. There is no captivity for me!"

"It is a fight you cannot win," said Vomanus. He was fingering his rapier, and the look on his lean reckless face told me he would dearly love to join in.

"We are neutral." Tharu spoke impatiently, abruptly. "The barbarians from Magdag would not dare to harm us. They may kill all their enemies from Sanurkazz, but they will not touch me, nor Vomanus here—nor you, Dray Prescot."

"Why?"

The galley's long bronze ram curled the seas away in a long creaming bow wave that roiled down her sides where her oars flashed down and up, down and up, like the white wings of a gull. She was a hundred-and-twentyswifter, double-banked, fast. I could see the men on her beak ready to board us and others at her bow varters. Her sails had been furled, but her single mast had not been struck.

Tharu of Vindelka moved to the rail so that I turned to face him. Nath and Zolta below were frantic in their despairing efforts to rouse the crew. Vomanus walked quietly aft. The longboat was in the water and an oar splintered against the broad ship's side in the panicky haste.

"They will not take you, Dray Prescot."

"Why? What will it matter to them that I know the Princess Delia of Delphond? That my every thought is of her? I have never seen Delphond, Tharu, nor the Blue Mountains. But I regard them as my home."

He let that square, hard face of his relax. I did not think he was smiling.

"My duty is clear, Dray Prescot, who is intended to be Prince of Delphond." A grimace clouded his face with his inner resentments. "Rather, I think you had best be a Chuktar—no, on reflection, the dignity of a Kov is better suited. It will impress the Magdaggians more. I am, you should know, a Kov myself, although of a somewhat more ancient lineage."

I stared at him. I as yet did not know quite what he was talking about or where he was driving. Then I heard a light scrape of foot on the deck to my rear. I am quick. The blow almost missed. But it sledged down on the back of my head and dazed me and drove me down, and the second blow put out the lights.

When I regained consciousness I was aboard a Magdag swifter and I was dressed in the buff coat and black boots of a Vallian, a rapier swinging at my side was complemented by a dagger, and I was, so I gathered, an honored guest of Magdag. My name, I was told by Tharu, was Drak, the Kov of Delphond.

CHAPTER TWELVE

The Princess Susheeng meets Drak, Kov of Delphond

Because the vessels of the inner sea almost invariably put either into port or were dragged up onto a convenient beach at night they were seldom provided with bunks or hammocks. I was lying on a kind of hard wooden settle covered with a ponsho fleece dyed green.

Green.

It is difficult for me, even now, to recollect anything coherent out of my thoughts then.

Suffice it to say that I simply lay there for a space while the whirling thoughts crowded, mocking and vicious, through my still-dazed head. My skull rang with the blow.

Tharu, Kov of Vindelka, leaned over me so that his stiff beard bristled against my cheek.

"Remember who you are, Drak, Kov of Delphond! It is our heads as well as yours that depend on your memory."

"I have a good memory," I said. I spoke dryly. I was thinking of Nath and Zolta. "I remember faces and names and what people say."

"Good."

He straightened up and I could see a little of the cabin, that of the first lieutenant as I judged, having some skill in reading the infinitesimal touches that mark rank from rank upon the sea—any sea—and despising the lot of them.

"Wait." I caught his sleeve. He thought I wanted assistance to rise and began to draw haughtily away, but I looked him in the eye. Vomanus came into view, his lively face now sadly apprehensive. "Tharu—Delphond I understand, and Kov, because you told me. But Drak? Where did that come from?"

Tharu's square face darkened and he cast a malevolent glance up toward Vomanus.

Vomanus said: "I called you that, Dray—ah, Drak—as the first name that popped into my head."

"Once this young fool had named you, I could do nothing less than accept it. The Magdaggians are not fools."

It seemed that Vomanus was lying, judging by his face.

Tharu went on speaking as I let him go and levered myself up. My head rang like those bells of Beng-Kishi.

"Drak was the name of the emperor's father when he ascended the throne. Also it is the name of a being half-legendary, half-historical, part human, part god, that we may read of in the old myths, those from the *Canticles of the Rose City*, at least three thousand years old." He spoke impatiently, a cultured man telling a peasant.

Well, and wasn't he right?

I stood up.

Beng-Kishi clanged a trifle less discordantly.

"You've done it now," I told them. "If these devils from Magdag find out who I am, they'll fry you over a fire, chip you into kindling, and feed you to the chanks." Vomanus looked a trifle sick. Mention of the chanks, the sharks of the seas of Kregen, made me think of Nath and Zolta again.

"We saw them pulling for the shore in the longboat," said Vomanus, swallowing.

"They either drowned or were saved," said Tharu. "It is no matter. They were unimportant."

He made a mistake, saying that to me, their oar comrade.

I brushed past him and, ducking my head, went out onto the deck. We were drawn up in the lee of the island; fires blazed as the watches kept a vigilant lookout. The stars of the Kregan night sky blazed down, forming those convoluted patterns the wizards of Loh can read and understand, or so they say. A cooling breeze blew and stirred the leaves ashore. Sentries stood on the quarterdeck and I caught the flash of gold as an officer moved. Only two of the lesser moons were up, and they would soon be gone in their helter-skelter hurtling around the planet.

The thought of conversation with a man of Magdag was nauseating to me. I looked hungrily out to the shore. Perhaps Nath and Zolta were out there, waiting to pounce. But what chance would we stand, three against a swifter crew? I knew an arrow would feather into me if I dived overboard; I decided that I would chance that. I would dive and swim to the island, and the devil take the chanks. If I was to walk the length of the central gangway and try to jump down to the beach I would be stopped. I knew the habits of Magdag captains, as I knew those of Sanurkazz. I knew what I would do were I the swifter captain.

Vomanus joined me, and then a Magdaggian Hikdar, who turned out to be the man whose cabin we had taken. He didn't seem to show his annoyance. I made an excuse, and went below again. The stink of the slaves and their eternal and infernal moaning and clanking of shackles and fetters made me irritable.

I believe, now, looking back, that I had not lost my nerve. There have been times in my life when I have followed a course of action that the casual onlooker would feel smacks of cowardice. I answer to no one, of course, for my actions—except to Delia. If I got myself killed, Delia would be alone, and more and more I was coming to the conclusion that she would need me by her side in the days to come. There were great forces moving implacably and with incredible cunning, somewhere. . . .

We sailed with the rising sun and headed west.

The news was bad. Pattelonia, the city of the Proconia where the flier had been left, had been raided and left in flames. The men of Sanurkazz had suffered a defeat. This swifter, *My Lady of Garles,* a five-five-hundred-and-twentyswifter, had sustained some damage and lost some oarsmen. She had been entrusted with dispatches for the admiralty in Magdag and her smart capture of the old broad ship on which we had been traveling had come as a pleasant diversionary tidbit. Tharu, bowing to the inevitable, had consented to be taken back to Magdag. Without a flier, travel across The Stratemsk and over the hostile lands beyond to the place where we could pick up a ship for Vallia, Port Tavetus, was impossible. Ergo, we must go to Magdag and wait for a ship from Vallia, which was due, so Tharu told me, sometime soon.

The impression I gained was that Tharu, Kov or not, was mighty grateful not to have to fly back over The Stratemsk and that weary length of hostile territory to the Vallian empire port city. The realization made me tremble. I acknowledged something I had not even allowed myself to think from the moment I had arrived, naked and despairing, on the beach of that Portuguese shore.

I felt a profound sense of thankfulness and gratitude. My Delia still loved me! How often I had almost allowed myself to think that she had forgotten me! I knew how unworthy I was, and how I had dismayed and disappointed her in our brief dealings. But she had not forgotten me. She had summoned the strength of her island empire, the only important area of land on this planet that was under the sway of one government, to search for me and seek me out and bring me home to her. Also I felt a strange kind of humbleness in my pride. How puffed up I was, how vaunting in my ambitions, how comical in my aspirations!

Delia's orders had sent this harsh, proud noble, the Kov of Vindelka, to seek me, had caused him to fly over uncharted realms of savages and mythical beings, to risk a neck he must consider the next most-important neck in the whole world. I had him summed up now. He was a king's man. In this case, an emperor's man. For the emperor of Vallia he had an obsessive drive to duty, and that extended to the emperor's daughter, and, *faute de mieux*, to the daughter's betrothed, much though he might dislike and feel contempt for her choice.

If I had been a vain man, a proud man in the evil sense of pride, how I would have rocked with glee!

As it was, and I would ask you to believe me in this, I felt like falling to my knees and thanking the god of my childhood, and also throw in a kind word or two to Zair, the red-sun deity, just to be on the safe side. With that comically impious thought I knew that I was finding my old self again.

While medicine and surgery and knowledge of the proper care for the sick were in a state far advanced of what I had been used to on Earth, the doctors of Kregen were a bunch one did well to give a wide berth to. They had not and still have not, reached anywhere near the recent achievements of Earthly medicine and surgery—in the matter of heart transplants, for instance. They leaned heavily on herbal drugs, which could obtain seemingly miraculous cures, and their surgery also had developed techniques of acupuncture I found nothing short of miraculous. It was nothing for a patient undergoing a serious operation with his head, or his insides, exposed to the knife—his earlobes or the web between his thumb and first finger quilted with needles—to be given a mouthful of palines to munch, and to keep up a bright conversation with the surgeon. I admit, the first time I saw that, I had a vivid mental picture of the cockpits I was used to, with the aprons caked with blood, their saws, their tubs of boiling tar.

So I did not have the slightest desire to consult a doctor

when I began to feel a little of that impatient drive to go to Vallia making me feverish. Since that dip in the sacred pool of baptism in the River Zelph in far Aphrasöe I had never had a day's illness. I did not intend to succumb now.

Pulling into Magdag was, as you may readily imagine, a disorienting experience for me, ex-Magdag galley slave.

My first impression was that the walls did not rear as I remembered them. This came because of the low freeboard, a necessity on an efficient galley, bringing my oarsman's viewpoint down much below that where I now stood on the quarterdeck.

Magdag reared her piles of stone heavily into the bright air. Gulls wheeled and shrieked, but with all my Krozair training I heard them only as croaking magbirds against the tuneful sounds of our own gulls in Sanurkazz. Flags and banners floated on the breeze. The twin suns shone mingled upon the smooth water. *My Lady of Garles* pulled steadily in past the outer breakwater, past the forts with their bristling varters, past the inner breakwater with the forts where always a Sacred Guard, composed on five days of the week of Chuliks and on the sixth of young and high-spirited Magdag nobles, were ready to vent their warrior-like high spirits on anything weak and unable to resist that might come their way. Many a fisherman went back to his quarters with a broken head and his fish baskets full of holes and cuts, having been used by the Magdag nobles for sword targets in their fun.

We rounded to in an inner basin, one of the many harbors of Magdag into which I had never previously been.

Vallia kept no consuls in the cities of the inner sea, presumably, I thought at the time, so as not to become embroiled in the politics of the area. The Vallians are above all, even above their warlike proclivities, a trading nation. But Tharu was quickly able to arrange accommodation for us, through a contact, in what I regarded as a senselessly luxurious palace.

His comment was frosty.

"You are now moving in areas somewhat removed from your usual purlieus." I liked that word even when he used it, but I had gone past the period of wanting to bait this Tharu for all he said in his pompous aristocratic way. If all the nobles of Vallia were like him I was in for a boring or headily exciting time, depending on how much I was prepared to put up with them. "I am a Kov of Vallia—as are you, for my sins—and we demand style in our living. Anything less than this would be unthinkable; in itself it is barely good enough, as I have told Glycas in no uncertain terms."

"Glycas?"

We slaves of Magdag knew little of the upper crust.

"A most powerful force, a man who has the king's ear. We are renting this palace from him—" If he was about to say words to the effect that I should be careful how I comported myself in case I damaged the furnishings, he thought better of it.

Vomanus had taken off his buff coat with a sigh of relief and now wore only a white silk shirt with his breeches and black boots, a shirt, however, whose overlong sleeves were wristed by a mass of ruffles which he liked to flourish up and down his brown and muscular arms as he gesticulated in his talk.

"The place is well enough, Tharu," he said.

Tharu glared at him, but let the matter drop.

We were all anxious to leave and return to Vallia, and soon news came that a Vallian ship had been signaled. I guessed the Todalpheme of Akhram would have a hand in that business.

We passed the days in walking about the city, patronizing wineshops and taverns in the evening, watching the dancing girls and the various varieties of sports available. The girls were slaves, dancing girls clad in bangles, beads, and precious little else. They were totally unlike the girls who danced so gaily for us among the wagon circles of my Clansmen.

I was back in the snuffle of slavery, with beasts half-human, half-animal for guards, and I didn't like any of it.

I scarcely used the suite of rooms assigned to me in the palace rented from Glycas. When I had been taken unconscious aboard *My Lady of Garles* with a glib explanation, Tharu, with his accustomed harsh authority, had quickly persuaded the Magdag captain to take aboard our baggage also. Tharu's own iron-bound chests stood in his rooms. So it was that, with the exception of deviced clothing, I had all that I had brought from Sanurkazz—silks and furs, jewels, coins, weapons, my own long sword, and the coat of mail Mayfwy had had made for me. I could clearly see the danger these represented. They were soaked with the traditions of Zair. They would make me a marked man if discovered.

So I had them hidden away beneath my bed, the three bronze-bound chests of lenken planks a nail in thickness. Then I took pains to explain to my Magdaggian hosts how I had picked up a long sword and a coat of mail as mementoes of a pleasant visit to their city, and when comments were made that the hauberk was unmistakably of Sanurkazzian cut I forced myself to laugh and said that no doubt this was the booty of a prize made to the greater glory of Grodno. That pleased those men of the green sun.

Mind you, it was refreshing once more to stroll about with a long rapier at my side.

Glycas was a dark-visaged man on the threshold of middle age, which on Kregen meant he must be turning a hundred or so, and his black hair was still crisp and fashionably cut, his hands and arms white, his fingers loaded with rings. But he was not a fop. His long sword was hilted plainly, with a bone grop that I, personally, would not have tolerated but which I knew was much favored on the inner sea. He was short and squarely built and he possessed a temper that had made him notorious. He was, truly, a dangerous man.

His sister, the princess Susheeng—plus a score of other pretentious names denoting her exalted rank and the broad acres of her estates, the thousands of slaves she owned—was lithe, lovely, and dark-haired, with eyes that tried to devour me with amorous glances from the moment we met. I was forced to contrast her with the gay reckless simplicity of Mayfwy, and had to acknowledge the animal vitality of this woman, her burning gaze, the intensity of the passion with which she took anything she wanted. All her noble honorifics amused me, through their pomposity. I realized afresh how lightly my Delia carried all the ringing brave titles to which she was heir, how subtly and how surely, with what courtesy and quiet gravity—shot through with her own elfin irony at life—she fitted the role of Princess Majestrix of Vallia.

The Princess Susheeng made a dead set at me. I was aware of this, and it annoyed me, through the complications that inevitably must ensue. Vomanus openly envied what he called my good fortune. Tharu, with a darker vision, contained his own resentment and annoyance.

I told her, one day as we stood on the third-level ramparts overlooking one of the harbors that opened out below the palace in which we were lodging, that I was looking forward earnestly to returning home.

"But, my Kov of Delphond, what has your vaulted Vallia to offer you that you cannot find in far greater quantity and quality here in Sacred Magdag?"

I winced, covered that lapse, and said: "I am homesick, Susheeng. Surely you understand that?"

With incongruous pride, she said: "I have traveled not for one single mur outside the lands of Magdag!"

I made some empty reply. That a person would boast of that kind of chauvinism appalled me.

"Well, Princess," I said, and saying it realized how incautious I was, "I intend to return home as soon as possible."

The woman nauseated me.

I had my mind on other women. Put this Princess Susheeng in the starkness of the gray slave breechclout, teach her the humility that is the only sure path to serenity, and she would turn out well. Slaves had no chance to reach to anything beyond their slavery, except those who escaped physically, by running or by death, and the humility a slave learns is corrosive and corrupting; but this girl might profit from it, if she knew she was to learn by her experience.

I wanted to travel to Vallia—and at once.

She saw all that in me; she saw my utter rejection of her.

The next day Vomanus and I were wandering through one of the high-class jewelry streets, a kind of open-air market, when we bumped into the Princess Susheeng with her body of retainers, blank-faced Chulik guards and a group of swaggering popinjay show-off Magdag nobility all fawning on her. She treated them all like dirt, of course.

"And what is that trinket you are buying, Kov Drak?"

She used the familiar tone of address to infuriate her attendants, of course.

I held up the jewelry. It was a beautiful piece of cut chemzite, blazing in the suns' light. It was work of Sanurkazz style and skill.

"I think it a pleasant piece," I said.

"It is of Zair," she said, her mouth drawn down. "It and all like it should be broken up and refashioned into more seemly work of Grodno."

"Maybe. But it is here." I forced myself to go on. "No doubt it is the booty of some successful swifter captain."

She smiled at me. Her mouth was ripely red, a trifle too large, soft, and rapacious with overfed passion.

"And is it for me, a parting gift, Kov Drak?"

"No," I said. I spoke too sharply. "I intend to take it to Vallia as a keepsake of the Eye of the World." That was half of the truth, as you will readily perceive.

She pouted, and laughed gaily, as at a joke, and made

some flighty and, in truth, slighting, remark, so as to retain
her composure before her toadies. Then she walked swiftly
from the market to her sectrix, which she rode well enough,
I grant you.

I know, now, that that scene saved my life.

That evening the Vallian ship was sighted rounding the
point. She would tie up in Magdag this night. So far I had
not set eyes on a ship of Vallia, for they were rare enough in
the inner sea, tending to make armadas of their voyages to
take advantage of the prevailing seasonal winds, and I had
always been raiding when they had called at Sanurkazz. I had
once tried to set course to intercept a Vallian I knew to be
due off Isteria; however, for a reason that I did not then
comprehend, I missed her.

I looked forward to the encounter.

Vomanus took himself off to the harbor to greet the Vallian captain, and then he was back cursing and swearing, to
saddle up a sectrix and ride off to a more distant anchorage
to which the Vallian vessel had unaccountably been assigned
by the port captain. I shouted some jovial remark after him.
I had wanted to ride myself, but Tharu had sternly vetoed
that.

"A Kov does not ride down to the jetty to greet the mere
captain of a ship," he said, and that was that.

I had gathered that a Kov was what we on this Earth
would call a duke; the information depressed me. I had often
found that empty titles mean nothing, and that intermediary
ranks are stifling and frustrating.

There is a board game played a great deal on Kregen called
Jikaida. As the name implies it has to do with combat. The
squared board is, in shape, like an elongated chessboard,
and with a touch of Halma about the moves, as one army of
Jikaida men clash with the others. If you expect the colors of
the men to be red and green, you are wrong. They are blue
and yellow, or white and black. The red and the green, it
seems, are reserved for real battle. So to take my mind off
waiting, Tharu and I settled to a game of Jikaida.

I make it a practice whenever it is practicable never to sit
with my back to a door.

When the door to our room smashed open and the mailed
men burst in, their faces covered with red scarves, I jumped
up. Tharu, whose back was to the door, was knocked flying
across the table. Jikaida men went flying in a shower of blue
and yellow. The table tangled my legs. My rapier was lying

on the floor at my side, casually in reach but scabbarded—
for this was a great city and who would expect attack within
a palace?—and by the time I had the blade free a poniard
stuck its tip into my throat and a single move would mean
my instant death.

At that moment I felt that I was growing old—I, Dray
Prescot, who had bathed in the sacred pool of Aphrasöe and
would live a thousand years!

I was trussed up like a vosk and between two of the burly
thugs was carried like a roll of carpet out and through a
secret passage behind a full-length portrait of some arrogant
Magdag swifter captain in the midst of a hypothetical destruction of a Sanurkazz fleet. Naturally, I had had no idea of
the passage's existence. Far below I was carried out and flung
into a dung cart which reminded me of the galley slaves'
benches. We bumped along cobbles. I had had no sight of my
attackers. I could hear no sound from them. I was gagged, and
so I did not expect to hear from Tharu.

They threw me down in a stone cellar where green slime
ran on the walls. I looked at their red scarves concealing
their faces. Only their eyes, bright and quick, like rasts', shining at me over the red cloths, were visible.

Afterward I learned I spent five days in that cellar, bound
loosely but sufficiently to prevent escape, fed on slops, without exercise and with a bucket for toilet purposes, and with
two men on guard at all times. Tharu was not with me.

On the sixth day I was rescued. My guards stood up with a
casual air as mailed men entered; then they stiffened and although I could not see their faces I could imagine the sudden
terror there as they scrabbled to draw their weapons. The
newcomers cut them down without mercy, even though the
last man attempted to surrender. As he sank onto the floor,
his blood oozing from the deep gash smashed through his
mail, his killer snatched up the red scarf.

He held it up, and spat on it.

"See!" he cried. "It is the work of those vile heretics of
Sanurkazz! The stinking vosks of Zair have done this—"

He bent quickly and slashed my bonds free. Others of his
men helped me rise. "But now you are safe, Kov of Delphond!"

CHAPTER THIRTEEN

I return to the megaliths

"My Lord Kov," said Glycas to me, formally. "I make the most profound apologies. It is unthinkable that such indignities should happen to an honored guest in Magdag. But—" He spread his hands. His dark eyes were most bright upon me. "These are troublous times. The vermin of the red swarm everywhere—"

"Drak should be thankful we saved his life," said the Princess Susheeng. She lolled in a hammock-type chair of silk and fringing tassels of gold thread; one of her arms was thrown back over her head, drawing up her body into a sensuous curve. "Those sea-leem of Sanurkazz will all be destroyed and put down one day. But I am happy that we saved you from them, Drak."

The high balcony overlooking the harbor received a cooling breeze for which we were grateful, the heat being excessive at this time. Magdag, being north of Sanurkazz, is somewhat cooler, but neither bask in the strong bracing breezes that sweep in over the Sunset Sea to cool Zenicce, far to the east. A long and powerful warm current, the so-called Zim-Stream, sweeps up from the south past the coasts of Donengil, the southernmost portion of Turismond. Driving in an arc toward the northeast it pushes in a clearly demarcated line of differently colored water through the Cyphren Sea between Turismond and Loh and so washes all the western and southern shores of Vallia. Its southern branch retains enough energy on occasions to reach Zenicce on the western coast of Segesthes.

"I do thank you," I said. Then, holding myself tightly under control, I said: "It seems they took everything I possess."

Glycas nodded. "Everything you had with you. Strange things, I have no doubt."

"From Vallia," said Susheeng.

I quivered alert.

"Drak should be thankful we saved his life," said the
Princess Susheeng.

"Hardly any," I said, offhandedly. "I have been collecting curios from the Eye of the World, artifacts of Magdag—and of Sanurkazz."

"Ah—of course," said Glycas, in a silky murmur I didn't trust.

"Had your Vallian ship captain not taken his ship to so distant a berth, no doubt your gallant companion, Vomanus, would have been here." Vomanus had been enraged to a purple fury when he had at last seen me safe. Tharu, that harsh, stern man, Kov of Vindelka, had not been seen since the attack. Everyone considered him to be dead. I felt that if he was not dead, then he might look upon that state as something to be desired if he had been sent to the rowing benches of a Magdag galley.

"These stupid uprisings continue to occur," Glycas said smoothly. "The slaves on the buildings to the greater glory of Grodno seek to invoke the vile heretical worship of Zair, the misbegotten one. We shall make inquiries and punish the guilty."

"And meanwhile?"

The Princess Susheeng rose like a graceful and deadly leem from the hammock-chair. She smiled on me and her red lips were moistly sensuous. "Oh, we shall, of course, accept entire responsibility for you, my dear Drak, until another Vallian ship calls."

"It will not be wise for you to continue on in this palace, alone," said Glycas briskly. "We hope you will do us the honor of taking apartments in our own palace—it is the Emerald Eye Palace, after all. Only the king, above whom no man dare seek to lift himself, has a finer palace in all Magdag."

"So be it," I said, accepting the inevitable. Then I had the wit to add: "I thank you most sincerely."

So it was that I moved in with Glycas and his rapacious sister Susheeng into the Emerald Eye Palace. The place was large, ornate, not particularly comfortable, noisy—and it had been built with slave labor.

At every opportunity I would clear out of the place and stroll about the city. Although Vallia was my objective, I still looked at the defenses of the city with the eye of a raiding Krozair from Sanurkazz. Glycas had insisted that I take with me an escort of half a dozen Chuliks. I had protested, but the manner of his insistence indicated that he would not have me say no. I thought of that scorpion I had seen on the rocks of the Grand Canal; that was how this man Glycas appeared to me, quick, sudden, and deadly.

The city smoldered under the lambent fires of the twin suns. I walked about the paved streets and avenues, studied the architecture, patronized a few drinking dens and amusement arcades. I even forced myself to look in on a small arena where groups of drug-inflamed slaves fought each other for the shrieking enjoyment of the Magdag nobility. Sickened, I left. Sectrix racing, I thought, might tempt me. But horse racing as it is practiced on Earth has never appealed to me—the degradation of man and beast and the motives thus revealed do no credit to Homo sapiens—and the men of Magdag had evolved no different method. I yearned, then, for the free ranging races with my Clansmen as we sped over the Great Plains, joyous in the race, astride our zorcas or voves.

So it was natural that, saddling up a sectrix and with my bodyguard similarly mounted, I rode out from the Magdag city gate on the landward side and headed for the megalithic complex of obsessive building.

On several occasions I had spoken to architects, often at one of the many intimate dinner parties Susheeng delighted in arranging, hurling shrill abuse at her slaves as they scurried about doing the actual work of preparation. These scented and elaborately coifed men had assured me that the buildings were essential for the soul and spirit of Magdag. Only through this continual erection of stupendous monuments of stone and brick could Magdag find a purpose in life. I heard talk of the Great Death, of the time of dying, and now I knew this to mean the period of eclipse, when the green sun was eclipsed by the red. This astronomical event would in the very nature of things have a tremendous significance for the men who worshiped the green-sun deity Grodno. It would, in truth, be a death. When the green sun passed before the red, and being smaller it did not thus create an eclipse but rather a transit, was the time for the Magdaggians to break out in another of their surges of violence and upheavals of conquest. During those times the men of Zair looked to their defenses, sharpened their swords, and sailed the inner sea in strength.

What the men of Magdag did during the green sun's eclipse, during the time of the Great Death, I was to learn.

. . .

The massive buildings were as I remembered them.

I felt my heart move with pity and anger as I saw the slaves in their thousands laboring beneath the suns.

Progress had been made on the buildings that I recalled as being half finished. I saw gang overseers lashing on the slaves to faster and faster work. The Chuliks would not let me approach too close. They had their long swords half unsheathed. They were not happy. I could smell the tension on the hot air.

"They are behind their schedules," I was told by a rast-faced guard commander, an overlord of the second class. He was the first I had met since my second arrival in Magdag. I had been moving in the company of overlords of the first class and of nobles—Zair forgive me.

"The time of the Great Death approaches," he said. He seemed happy to spend the time talking to a noble. "We must have at least one new hall finished by then."

"Assuredly," I said.

He nodded with his own driving conviction. "We will," he said. He held a whip and ran the thongs through his blunt fingers. "We will."

Choked by the redolent memories of the slaves and workers, with sudden brilliant images of Genal, Holly, and Pugnarses in my mind, I looked over the fantastic scene. I could see it with a new eye, now, from a different perspective. The place swarmed with men and women. In their gray garments, or naked, they moved over the buildings on their scaffolds like a confused army of insects. Huge masses of stone were hoisted into the air as the shrieked commands of the whip-masters cut through the air as their whips cut through the sweating skins of the slaves. The piles of bricks grew under the sun, and were carried away by endless streams of slave children. The shouts, the bedlam, the smoke of dust and chips that hung over everything, the stinks of the thousands of people, rose like an evil miasma. This was what Babel might have been; although here everyone could understand his neighbor. This convulsion of perverted energy smoked to high heaven upon the plain of Magdag, there on my adopted world of Kregen.

Making it my business to inspect every part of the work, I visited places I had never seen before. There were the smiths, working miracles of beauty in scrolled iron and brass. There were the masons cutting stone to delicate perfection. The artists painted their frescoes, their friezes, working with the sure speed that had painted this figure in this position in these col-

ors a hundred times before. A strict and formal routine held
the decoration into ritual patterns. Inside some of the lofty
halls with their plethora of columns and innumerable images
and paintings, I sometimes felt I had reentered the hall I had
left only moments before.

The production lines stunned me with their expertise set up
or the development of some of the artifacts used. Earth did
not reach that state of expertise until the automobile assembly line indicated what mechanical effectiveness might be obtained from this breaking-down of function into separate
work-quanta.

Men in long lines labored to produce, for example, barrel
after barrel of the iron nails used in fixing wooden fasciae.
They worked with a kind of numb professionalism, slaves
chained to their benches, the only sounds the eternal clinking
of the hammers, the bellow of the forges.

I saw the way masses of slaves were yoked to the gigantic
stones ferried down from the mountains of the interior. They
could sort themselves out into their gangs and tail onto ropes
and haul away under the lash with a skill I remembered.

Down by the sludgy banks of the sluggish stream that bore
the ferried stone from the interior—a blackish-gray basaltic
stone and quite unlike the yellow stone used in the construction of the city's noble houses—I saw the wide extent of the
kitchens. Holly had cooked for the workers on a small scale,
by the gang. The slaves had mass cooking. The place stank
and crawled with flies and vermin. Down by the river, which
ran red here, I saw immense piles of bones, and tall stacks of
vosk skulls, too thick and strong to be easily disposed of. The
rubbish dumps stretched, it seemed, for miles. Pollution,
something I had hardly expected to experience on Kregen,
had come to Magdag with a vengeance.

My Chulik guards made no effort to show me the warrens,
and I had enough sense to know I could never enter there
dressed as I was and with a mere six Chuliks. Glycas had invited me to what he termed a hunting party. When I had
gathered that this meant that a group of his friends would be
riding, mailed and with long swords in their hands, into the
warrens to chase, and cut down and rape what fell in their
path, I declined, pleading a fever.

My life had become, again as it had so often done in the
past, intolerable to me.

Something must be done, something could be done, and if
I, Dray Prescot, thought anything at all of myself and what I

was here for at the express command of the Star Lords, then
I would have to do it.

I would have to do it.

I wanted to do it.

The Princess Susheeng was becoming tiresome. My door
was kept locked at night, but she scratched on it two or three
times. I knew it was her, for I could smell her perfume, thick
and odoriferous and liberally applied. I fancied she would be-
gin a more obvious attack soon and, remembering the Princess Natema, I put in hand a little scheme. Away inland, to
the north, beyond the chain of factory farms similar to that
one where I had been captured by the men of Magdag, lay
broad pastures, lush plains covered with head-high grasses.
Here big game hunts were a pastime I might welcome. I recalled with a pang the Savanti, and of how Maspero had
apologized for the atavistic behavior of himself and his
friends as they had led me out on a graint hunt that would
lead, if any danger and harm there was, to them alone.

Away beyond the plains of Turismond lay lands that were
colder and colder until at last they vanished beneath the mist
and ice. So the Magdaggians said. They never cared to venture there, seldom went other than a few dwaburs into the
plains. They were essentially an inward-looking people: the
Eye of the World aptly named for them.

Arrangements for my expedition were made and Vomanus,
who I thought had a permanent girl waiting for him in some
palace or other of the city, was dug out to accompany me. I
managed to avoid asking either Glycas or his sister. We had
a few Chulik guards, a safari of slaves for porterage, and
mounted aboard our sectrixes we set off. Very quickly I lost
the safari. I had told Vomanus to carry on as though expect-
ing to meet me out on the plains. I dumped the sectrix and
my gear, and donned the gray breechclout I had stolen from
a slave of the palace. I crept by night into the workers' areas
by the buildings.

I was not home, but I felt a queasy sensation of homely
familiarity grip me. At that point I almost called the whole
stupid venture off. But I went on. This, I remember thinking,
is a part and parcel of what the Star Lords wish me to accomplish.

As the familiar odor of the warrens rose about me and I
saw again that crazy skyline of tumbling walls and leaning
towers, the sacking-draped flat roofs where the workers
would lie out in the heat of the night, the dark mouths of al-

leys where the streaming pink moonlight fell aslant the dust
and the cobbles, I had to restrain myself from picking up my
heels and running. Even then I could not be sure which way
I would run.

The old familiar hovel looked the same.

A worker who had found a bottle of Dopa lay propped
against the wall snoring lustily. I could hear the restless
sounds of thousands of people all about me, people crammed
into hovels compressed into narrow streets of tumbledown
buildings. I pushed open the familiar door. Genal sat up on
his sacking bed, blinking like an owl.

"Who—?" He squinted in the parallelogram of pink moonlight. "No—Stylor? *Stylor!*"

I moved in fast and gripped his hand.

"Lahal, Genal. You are well?"

He looked at me, swallowed, closed his mouth.

"Lahal, Stylor." Suddenly he jumped up and ran across the
packed earth floor with its bit of sacking carpet, knocking
over an earthenware pot on the way. He bent over another
pallet that I had not noticed. He shook the sleeper.

"Pugnarses—wake up, wake up! It is Stylor, returned from
the green radiance of Genodras!"

I chilled.

Pugnarses awoke in a foul temper, cursing by Grakki-
Grodno, the sky deity of beasts of haulage, and looked blear-
ily at me. He tumbled up from the pallet. His shaggy hair
and eyebrows, his malevolent look, all coalesced and I put
out my hand to cover my feelings, and I said: "Lahal, Pugnarses."

"Lahal, Stylor."

I felt out of place. They both stood looking at me as
though I were a ghost. In a way, I was.

But they were both acting in a natural way, both cursing
by and calling on Grodno, the green-sun deity of Genodras.

What, I wondered then with a dizzying feeling of helplessness, would Pur Zenkiren, or Pur Zazz, make of this situation?

I pulled myself together.

"I cannot stay long," I said. "And I cannot venture outside
the warren."

Genal said, at once, hotly: "You may stay here as long as
you wish, Stylor. Here, you are safe."

He bent and picked up a gray tunic. I saw the green and
black badges of a worker overseer, he of the balass stick. "I

wield the balass now, as well as Pugnarses. We can offer you help, Stylor." He eyed me keenly, looking at my shoulders and biceps. "Was it the galleys?"

"Aye, Genal, it was."

"And you escaped!" Pugnarses whistled. I suspected he was annoyed that Genal had aspired to the balass while he, Pugnarses, still stayed as a worker overseer, and had not yet reached his coveted ambition, the white loincloth and the whip of the overseer of overseers.

"What of Follon the Fristle?" I asked. It would be as well at first to let these two believe what they willed.

Pugnarses let rip with a disgusting sound. Genal made a face and an obscene sign. I had forgotten the manners of slaves; this was a salutary reminder. I had best not forget.

. . .

"He, too, is of the balass. He gave information about an escape—when you disappeared—he was rewarded."

"I'm glad you had the sense not to become involved, Genal."

"But we will rise, one day—"

"Yes," I said.

Their heads lifted as I spoke.

"And—Holly?"

Their reactions were interesting. Both cast a swift look at each other, then away, and their faces went blank.

"She is well, Stylor," said Genal.

"She is more fair than all the painted women of the palaces of Magdag," said Pugnarses with some vehemence.

So that was how it was.

I had not come to the slave and worker warrens to see Holly, although I hoped I would see her soon. I had to establish an identity with these men. Already they believed I was an escaped galley slave, coming to them for help. That was a start.

"I may have to ask your help in concealing me," I said. "From time to time. For I have great plans." I broke off. A slim shadow broke the parallelogram of pink moonlight. Soon, that moonlight would silver as the night wore on, but the shadow now hesitating in the doorway was surrounded by a pink halo.

A low voice breathed a single word.

"*Stylor!*"

Holly was still incredibly lovely. She had matured, but I knew those innocent lines of naïveté concealed an iron resolve. Beside her the Princess Susheeng was an overblown, raddled bloom of autumn.

"Lahal, Holly—" I began.

But she rushed toward me and flung her arms about my neck. Her slender lissome body pressed all nakedly to mine. Her lips, hot and moist and overpowering with a passionate ardor that shocked through me, crushed down on my mouth. And as she kissed me with such abandon I saw over her shoulder the faces of Genal and Pugnarses, staring at me, stricken.

CHAPTER FOURTEEN

The plans of Stylor

Life thereafter became exciting and interesting and extraordinarily rewarding.

I spent many nights out among the warrens. After I had rejoined the safari and had then returned after a quick hunting trip to Magdag with a few leem as trophies, I arranged a cache near the warrens, adjacent to the river, where I could reach by sectrix easily from the Emerald Eye Palace. I had a cache there of weapons, clothes, and money. I would ride out from the palace without the Chulik escort, having disposed of them by a straight deception, change into my gray breechclout, and glide silently into the maze of alleyways and courts. Long before dawn I would return.

On the sixth day I could often manage to spend the entire time with the slaves and workers, as Glycas and Susheeng were devoted in their observations of the rites of worship owing to Grodno. Particularly at this time, when the time of the Great Death approached, everyone of Magdag was punctilious in their religious life.

The business of Follon the Fristle was completed in a strange way that turned out to my advantage.

To say that all Fristles looked alike to me would not be true. I could recognize individuals when necessary. One evening as the last of the suns vanished in the sky and the Maiden with the Many Smiles sailed clear above clouds I rode down to the river and hitched my sectrix to a tree branch. Away beyond the bank the warrens stretched, orange in that ruddy reflected light, and I took heart from that.

In only a few moments I had stashed my Vallian gear, wrapped the gray breechclout around me, drawing the ends up between my legs and tucking them in. In the belt that held the clout was a sharp and gently-curving knife snug in its sheath. As I padded toward the first sprawling line of shacks and mud-brick dwellings, I heard a scream, muffled but close.

Screams were common in the slave warrens of Magdag.

Then, forcing itself on my attention, a struggle reeled out into the moonlight: two Fristles locked together. It took me a moment or two to decide that this was a male Fristle attempting to rape a female. She couldn't scream anymore for the man had his arm locked around her throat. I could see her slit eyes, painfully twisted, and the way the blunted fangs of her mouth champed against her thin dark lips.

Then I saw the male Fristle was Follon.

I recognized him well enough.

I loped over and took him around the throat. Fristles habitually wear a kind of leather jack, brass-studded. Those employed by Magdag had dyed theirs green. It was with some considerable force that I kicked that green color. Follon tried to yell and my fingers clamped on his windpipe. He couldn't get his curved scimitar-like sword out. I bore down on him.

The female Fristle sagged to the ground, whimpering. She wore no clothes. Her body, with its light dusting of fur, gleamed golden in the pink rays of moonlight. Another Fristle, older, with a dun-colored hide, slipped to the fallen female's side, held her head, and began to croon strange half-hissing, half-sobbing words in native Fristle. Then:

"He would have used my Sheemiff, and discarded her, killed her!"

It suddenly became easy to think of these half-human, half-cat people in fully human terms. The old woman glared up with a lift of her narrow chin and her slit eyes blazed red. The girl Fristle moaned again. I saw blood on the fur of her legs.

Follon gave a tremendous wrench, but I held him and leaned back and then, as Zair is my witness, whether it was his own lunge, or my impassioned grip, or my subconscious desire, I do not know.

But, audibly, I heard his backbone snap.

I had been given a thousand years of life without consultation or request and now I could see a long, dark, and exceedingly narrow tunnel before me, delimiting a life in which it seemed my fate would go on facing up to the consequences not only of my own actions but also the reverberations from the natures of other peoples and other beings. It was in the nature of that scorpion to try to kill me; it was in my nature to defend myself. What was natural about this Fristle trying to rape a young girl of his own kind, and was it natural for me to prevent him? I think it was then, as I let the dead limp form of Follon slip through my hands to the ground, that I first began to sense the dim and awful doom that overhung me. I was doomed. Oh, yes, everyone is doomed in the sense that everyone will eventually die. But I began then to feel the clinging strands of a doom outside of time and space drawing about me, and with every step I took, every decision I made, I would merely encompass my own destruction the more securely.

I cursed the Star Lords, then, hating them and all their works.

Follon's body had to be disposed of and so I carried him down to the river that flowed so sluggishly through its retaining banks of granite through Magdag to the sea. Here the banks were of mud, and in the shadow of a toppling tower of vosk skulls, I hoisted the dead Fristle, ready to cast him into the flood.

The old Fristle woman, with a cry, darted forward. She made her intentions plain. I stopped most of the mutilation, but she divested the body of all its clothes and money and she took the curved sword.

"These I will keep," she said, looking up at me. She was crouched, bent with age. "My Sheemiff is yours for the asking, for you are a great Jikai."

I shuddered, and the two women Fristles eyed me speculatively. Jikai! How often, lately, had that great word been debased!

With some formal rote of acknowledgment, I bade them farewell and took myself off. Truth to tell, the sleek furred body of the girl Fristle, with its human outlines, stirred me. I half ran through the pink-tinged shadows into the warren.

As I had asked during my last visit, the Prophet had been found. Now he was waiting for me.

It seems fairly clear that Delia's loving actions in setting her whole empire in action to seek me out had upset the plans of the Star Lords. I had no way of knowing just what problems Delia had overcome in instigating this search: Tharu would not broach the subject and Vomanus shied away from it. He was a good and likely lad and, with a little discipline of the sort that gives a man an eye to survival, would turn out well. But the Star Lords—for, as I have said, I had by this time convinced myself that my presence this time in Magdag was of their fashioning—had drawn me here from Earth, four hundred light-years away, and here must lie the labors to which I must put my hands.

What those labors were blazed painfully obviously to me.

The Prophet looked just the same, with his white hair and beard fierce in his righteous rebellious ardor.

"The workers will rise, Stylor," he said in his rolling sonorous voice. "Too long have we suffered. The time is ripe and we know the secrets of the overlords' hearts." He stared at the assembled workers with an exalted look, an expression of dazed fanaticism on his face, drawing the gaunt lines into sharper and more hungry wedges of skin and muscle.

"We know!" said Genal, with a reflection of that dedicated fanaticism uplifting him.

"Yes, we know the time," said Pugnarses, and the hunger on his face glared bleakly out upon the gathering of those men and half-men who would lead the revolt.

We made plans. I listened. They had accepted me as one who had proved himself, and when I had promised to secure them weapons as proof of my intentions, I was a brother rebel.

But the talk consisted of high-flown sentiments, of passion, hatred, and anger, of long detailed descriptions of what the rebels would do to the overlords once they had them in their power. I fretted.

At last I stood up. They fell silent.

"You chatter," I told them. They reacted angrily to this but I quieted them. "You talk of chaining the overlords in the gangs and making them haul stone, and of the whips you will wield. Have you forgotten? The overlords wear mail, and they carry long swords! They are trained fighting men. What are you?"

Genal leaped to his feet, his dark face flushed and furious.

"We are workers, slaves, but we can fight—"

"I can bring you swords, spears, some coats of mail, but not enough. *How,* my gallant Genal, will you fight the overlords?"

Such were the dark torments, the passions of frustration twisting in that hovel as I faced them with the truth, that they had no time or energy to spare to wonder—then—where I would find weapons for them. I had brought food, so as not to be a burden on them, and already half a dozen long swords lay hidden in a pit beneath straw, closely wrapped in oiled sacks, below the beaten earth of Genal's and Pugnarses' hovel.

The talk buzzed, coiling, endlessly repeating itself. I let them talk this out. They had to face the truth of themselves.

At last, a silence fell. Pugnarses was knotting his fists together, and every now and again he would smash his fist into the earth of the floor. Genal, I saw, was close to tears, but he did not break down. He was looking at me. I saw that look. I knew the time for hard facts was near. Bolan, a giant man with a head that gleamed all naked and shining in the light, grunted. He had been shaved as a slave once, and his hair had never grown back. He could lift stone blocks that took three other men to shift.

"What do you say, Stylor?" he asked me directly, without artifice, like a charging chunkrah. "You have only dismay and doom for us—can you prophesy to any more effect?"

"Yes, Stylor," cried Genal and one or two of the others. "Tell us a plan." I noticed that Pugnarses did not join in.

Well, he would confirm and conform, for this was the only way he could achieve his heart's desire as to an overlordship.

I told them.

There was nothing clever about the plan. It's only dreamers who believe they can develop something so entirely new that the suns of Kregen have not shone down on it before—always excepting, of course, the men of science and art.

"The merits of the plan are obvious," I said eventually. "And its drawbacks, too. It will take longer than we would wish."

Pugnarses started up. "Long! Yes, too long! Give us the weapons and we will kill the overlords and all their beast guards!"

"But, Pugnarses," Bolan said, rubbing his naked skull, "Stylor has just told us, and I believe what he says is true. You cannot beat the overlords and the mercenaries by a mob of workers and slaves with a few swords and balass sticks!"

"You must train," I said, and I put force into my words. "We will forge an army from the workers and slaves of Magdag so that slavery can be abolished from Magdag."

They nodded, still only half convinced. I enlarged on what I wanted to do, and I admit that it is all elementary and obvious, but to a man who slaves in the sun the thought of a single extra day under the lash between him and freedom is intolerable.

"Give me your help and backing; bestow on me your authority so that I may so order and organize that the workers will rise as a strong and keen weapon." I stared challengingly at them. I was beginning to feel alive again, and the shame of that reawakening as to its means may not be mitigated as to its ends; but it is in my nature to rise to a challenge and to strike down first he who would seek to kill me.

"I will fashion you a cadre of men who will use the weapons I shall bring, and the weapons we will make. I want production of certain weapons that I shall designate, and no others. I value freedom and liberty more than most men, for I have been deprived of freedom—in ways you cannot comprehend—but if I tell you that a galley slave knows about slavery, you will not argue with me, I know." I was jumbled, garbled in what I said, but I convinced them. I obtained total authority over the fashioning of this military weapon from the slaves. I had to. I could see this struggle only in military terms, now; for that was the only way to keep a sense of sanity and proportion. I wanted a small well-trained little army that could blitzkrieg the overlords so that the great mass of slaves and workers might follow and devour the struck-down carcass.

Sentiment had gone. I had seen the misery of the slaves; I had experienced it. I knew of the aspirations of the laborers and artificers—and I was well aware of possible conflicts of interest between slave and worker. I was born, you will recall, in 1775 and this year, I venture to believe, has a certain significance on Earth. On Kregen there were more complex antagonisms even than those surrounding, say, the combatants and theorists caught up in the French Revolution. I determined now to look at the revolt of the slaves of Magdag in purely military terms. Then, I would see that they turned their successful rebellion into a true revolution. That, as I conceived it, was what the Star Lords desired.

Also—my Krozairs of Zy and all of Sanurkazz would benefit.

In the days and nights that followed I took greater and greater risks in sneaking out of the Emerald Eye Palace. I would climb out of my high window and use the ropy vines of the ivy-like plants that clothed the walls to clamber down and so over the wall and astride the waiting sectrix. Vomanus, of course, had to be a party to my mysterious disappearances, and he sweated out many a sleepless night waiting for my return. He thought I had a girl somewhere in the city. While cursing me for my stupidity in not sipping from the flower under my lips, he had a grudging admiration for my foolhardiness in taking wing to sip elsewhere.

The cadre began to train with wooden staves. I had them cut to a modest twelve-foot length. A number of soldiers slaving on the buildings were spirited away by Holly, who used her underground route to good purpose, and these men were only too happy to join us. Their vacancies had to be explained. A death of a slave was a common event in Magdag, and even though the overlords were aware, as Glycas often complained to me, that there were slaves hiding in the workers' warrens, the expeditions to rout them out had to be undertaken with due military care. Glycas loved to ride into the outskirts of the ghetto warrens. He and his sectrix-mounted friends would cut down the workers and slaves not clever enough to run at the first sounds. I suppose between them they killed a thousand or so slaves a season; this was a number scarcely missed in the hundreds of thousands who labored on the buildings of Magdag.

Then the overlords would ride out in their mail and their glory and raid adjacent cities who owed them suzerainty. They had a jolly old life of it, the overlords of Magdag.

The slave soldiers we took in were sworn to secrecy with vows that made their hair curl and their bowels turn to water. They were set to work to drill and discipline the volunteer workers. I personally scrutinized every man at this stage. The soldiers—men of Zair mostly, but there was a sprinkling of the fair-haired men of Proconia, and a number of Ochs, Fristles, Rapas—could make little of the twelve-foot staves. They called them staves, thinking that their function. I did not disillusion them at this stage. That would come later, and as staves they would also serve a purpose.

Soon a small group gathered around me, men I ventured to think would stick to the last.

"You have an overlord of Magdag charging down on you," I said to them as we sat around the hovel, on the beaten-earth floor in the flickering light of the candle. "He is clad in mail. He sits upon a sectrix, which means he towers over you, on foot. And he is bringing his damned great long sword down to cleave your skull to your neck bones." I stared at them, these dozen or so men on whom I must rely. "I don't want the answer, 'Run,' when I ask you the question, 'What do you do?'" We weren't past the joking stage yet. Genal, for sure, would have said "Run."

They coughed and shuffled, and Bolan said viciously: "Leap on the sectrix's back and jab your dagger into the vosk's eyes."

"Fine. How do you get past the sword?"

We argued on. I saw that Genal had the right idea when he said sturdily: "Throw something—a rope weighted with lead—around the sectrix's legs." He laughed nastily. "That should bring the overlord to earth."

"Fine. You'll have to get close to do that with any accuracy. The overlords will be in squadrons and platoons. The ones following will cut you down—"

"So?"

I spread my hands. "Talking in military terms there are two methods of dealing with armored men, and these overlords wear hauberks of mesh iron, link mail. Some wear leg mesh; most do not. Some wear solid helmets; some rely on their coif. There are still two main methods of dealing with them, of dismounting them."

"Kill them," grunted Bolan.

"Yes. You can drive a relatively small hole through the mail, or you can bash a great wedge of it in, cutting it or not according to the opposed strengths." I thrust my rigidly outstretched forefinger at Bolan. He flinched back, but not by very much. He would be a useful man. "To punch a hole you need an arrow, a dart, a javelin or—" I hesitated, found Maspero's genetic language pill had failed me, and so used the English word. "Or a pike."

I opened out my other three fingers rigidly alongside the first finger and I slashed down in a quasi-karate blow at Bolan. This time he did not move a muscle—but, of course, he blinked. "To slash a man's guts in half you need a long sword, an ax, a—" Again the pill failed me in the exact meaning I required. I went on: "You can bash with a mace or, if you have the requisite skill, with a morning star." Again I used English for the elusive words. "To slash, you can also use a species of bill, a halberd, a glaive, a fauchard. And these weapons are those on which we will concentrate our producton."

We spent the rest of that session going over and over the weapons which, to these men, were new.

Just before it was time for me to leave, and these men had no idea where I went when I disappeared from their sight in the warrens, I put the final indignity to them.

I have mentioned that the men of Segesthes considered the shield as the cowards' article, a weak, treacherous, miserable item of warfare, one to which they would not deign to give the name of weapon. They had never seen an offensively-used shield. So I took a break and then, when we had drunk a little wine, I said: "Finally, the production lines will make shields."

I quieted them. The men of the inner sea, also, disregarded shields. Only Ochs used shields, a tiny round targe clasped in one of their six limbs with which they attempted to counter aggression. Men derided the Ochs for their little shields. I spent some time arguing; finally I said: "It is settled. When I give you the patterns for the pikes, the glaives, and halberds, you will also receive patterns for shields. These will be manufactured. It is ended for now." I stood up, looking down on them.

"I will see you tomorrow night. Remberee." I left them.

CHAPTER FIFTEEN

Vomanus takes a message to Delia of the Blue Mountains

The Princess Susheeng of Magdag was a vibrant, alluring, sensual creature. There was no doubt of that at all. It was all too clearly apparent as she reclined on a low divan covered in ornate green silk, the lighter green of the silks partially covering her white body seductive in their flowing curves and hidden shadows. Poor Vomanus in his buff coat and black boots looked gauche and out of place; essentially I felt the same way, no matter that I wore a lounging robe of that detested green. I had felt it politic to do so; now, clearly, it had been a mistake. The intimate little supper party was over and now Susheeng was devising ways of getting rid of Vomanus. I was countering them with a suaveness I had to admire in myself.

"Oh, Vomanus, my pet," said Susheeng in a dripping-honey voice. "I wish to speak with Drak alone."

She could have said, simply: "Vomanus, clear out." Since she had not, it was obvious that her brother Glycas' warning of the importance of Vallia had got through to her.

Vomanus, casting me a dirty look, rose and, with a graceful farewell speech, left. Susheeng turned her bright eyes on me. Her breast rose and fell beneath the scrap of green silk.

"Why do you always avoid me, Drak? Time after time I seek you out—and you are not there. Why?"

I was astonished. This proud and haughty woman, a beauty in any man's eyes, was in effect begging me. She leaned gracefully toward me, and the green silk moved again tumultuously.

"I keep myself busy, Princess."

"You do not like me!"

"Of course I do!"

"Well, then. . . ? If you knew how lonely I am. Glycas is

151

forever busy about matters of state. The campaign in Proconia does not go well." I had to keep from shouting aloud my joy. She went on, slumping back now, her feelings of neglect beginning to stir different emotions. "All he can talk about are the pirates from Sanurkazz. Everyone is wondering when that arch pirate, that evil devil's spawn, that cramph, the Lord of Strombor, will strike again. He cost me a cool three merchantmen last season. Money of mine, lost to me, in his filthy hands. This Pur Dray, this Lord of Strombor, why, he is a worse Krozair than that mangy Pur Zenkiren."

I felt drunk.

I had quaffed but little wine, for I had to keep my wits about me. But—this was how the enemies I had sworn to oppose talked about me, about Zenkiren, about the Krozairs of Zy! I felt suddenly strong and liberated, rejoicing in the powers that Sanurkazz extended across the Eye of the World.

"I feel sorry for you, Princess," I said. "But I believe you also raid the men of the southern shore. Is this not so?"

"Of course! They deserve it; they are rasts before Grodno."

Then, shaking those creamy shoulders, she reached for her goblet and drank deeply. Her face was more flushed than usual. I thought of Natema. I tensed myself, ready for what might come. There would be no ghetto warrens for me this night.

The work of preparations was going well, and already the production lines were turning out long, beautifully shaped shafts of pikes and halberds, and the smiths were forging the heads to fit. Grindstones were being stolen and if a Rapa guard was found with his throat slit, wasn't that what they hired themselves out to expect?

"My dear Drak," said Susheeng. "I swear you are thinking of something else."

A naturally gallant man might have mumbled that no man could think of anything in the presence of Susheeng except her; that way lay dragons. I said: "Yes."

"Oh?" Her eyebrows lifted. That cruel look flashed over her face.

"I was thinking how strange it is that neither you nor your brother, the noble Glycas, are married."

Her breath caught in her throat. "You—would—?"

"Not me, Princess Susheeng." I took a breath. "I am spoken for in Vallia."

"*Ah!*"

I thought that would finish the matter. She had known that my urgent desire to return to Vallia—as she thought of it as a return—had cooled lately. She had thought it was on her account and now she knew otherwise. I made a big mistake then.

The next night I was able to slip into the warrens with the pattern I had worked out for the shields. They were large, rectangular, curved into a semi-cylinder, and I insisted that they be built to withstand an arrow from the short straight bows of the overlords' mercenary guards. If this meant they must be backed with metal, then the metal must be stolen from the building sites where it was being fashioned into masks and wall-coverings to the greater glory of Grodno. I overrode all obstacles. The weight of the shields thus produced, I said, was not important. I had in mind their use as a kind of pavise. I showed how they might be used in the testudo. I got through to my men in command.

Susheeng was waiting for me as I climbed back in through my window.

"I have been waiting for you all night, Drak."

I kept my composure.

"I was restless, Susheeng. I have been walking—to clear my head."

"You lie!" She flamed at me then, passionately. "You lie! You have a girl out there in the city, a whore for whom you deny me! I'll kill her, I'll kill her!"

"No, no, Princess! There is no other girl in Magdag."

"You swear by Grodno that what you say is true?"

I'd swear anything by Grodno; false deities mean nothing. But there was no girl—and then I thought of Holly. I said, harshly and with an acrid contempt: "I do not need to swear, Princess. There is no other girl in Magdag."

"I do not believe you! Swear, you rast! Swear!"

She lifted her white hand on which the green rings flashed. I caught her wrist and so for a space we stood, locked, looking into each other's eyes. Then she moaned softly and sagged against me, all the rigidity gone from her body. She leaned into me and I could feel her softness. "Tell me true, Drak. There is no other?"

"There is no other, Princess."

"Well, then—am I not beautiful? Am I not desirable? Am I not fair above all other women in Magdag?"

What had Natema said, and what had I said, when I

thought Delia was dead? Now I was by that span of years more mature.

"You are indeed the finest flower of Magdag, Susheeng," I said, and felt shame at the vicious irony of my words.

A crisp knock at the door followed by a Vomanus who concealed his chagrin at sight of Susheeng, who was smoothing down her hair now, effectively chopped off that scene.

When Susheeng had left with a long lingering glance at me, Vomanus said enviously: "Well, you lecherous old devil! So you managed it in the end!

"Not so, good Vomanus." I looked at him, and I found he ranked favorably with those other young men who had followed me to death. "And aren't you supposed to treat a Kov with some kind of respect, hey, young lad?"

He laughed delightedly.

"Of course. But I told poor old Tharu not to tell you who I was, and I don't intend that you should find out now. Just take it from me, Drak, my friend, Kovs are Kovs and Kovs to me."

I glowered at him from under lowered eyelids and he, despite that he had known me for a little while now, started back and I knew I wore that corrosive look of pure authority and domination on my ugly face that I despair so much of.

"And are you going to tell me you aspire to the Princess Delia yourself, good Vomanus? That I am a rival?"

"Drak—Dray! What are you saying?"

I never apologize. I turned from him. Then: "Vomanus—I thank you for your help and comradeship. But I fancy that she-leem Susheeng will set spies on me. I am going to have to disappear."

"What!"

"There is work waiting for my hand. I love the Princess Delia as no man ever loved a woman before in all this world of Kregen, aye! and all of Earth—" He stared then, thinking me going off my head, I shouldn't wonder. "But before I can return to her and clasp her in my arms again I must discharge the obligations laid on me. A Vallian ship was signaled last night—you did not know?" For he had started and his face had lighted up. "Listen carefully, Vomanus. I take a great comfort from your comradeship and your ready wit and help—now, hear me out! I want you to return on the ship, go to Delia, and tell her I am well and dying for her and that I shall return just as soon as certain business has been conducted here. She will understand, I know. I know she will!"

"But, Drak—I dare not return without you!"

"Dare not? When your Princess Majestrix awaits news of me, thinking me dead, perchance, suffering. Go back to Vallia, good Vomanus. Give the good news to your princess. Tell her I shall return just as soon as I am allowed. She will understand."

"But what keeps you here? Not Susheeng of a surety."

"Not Susheeng, nor any other girl. I cannot explain. But you will return to Vallia and give my message and my undying love to Delia of the Blue Mountains."

Besides, I wanted him well out of the way when my slave army struck. I didn't want his head stuck on a pike and paraded along the harbor wall.

He shook his handsome head, and thrust his fist down on his rapier hilt so that the scabbard stuck up into the air, arrogantly. "But, Dak, to return without you!"

"Go! For the sake of Zair, go now! Tell Delia I long to clasp her in my arms—and I will, I will, but go, now, before it is too late!"

He stared at me as though, at last, I had taken leave of my senses.

I calmed myself. "All will be explained. And, too, you could return with an airboat to Proconia. I know Vallia does not like using the airboats in the inner sea. I can join you there."

He frowned. Then: "Very well, Kov Drak. I will do as you ask."

We made the final arrangements and then I said "Remberee" to Vomanus and went back to my room that evening to collect all that I might need. I was about to leap onto the windowsill when Susheeng called. It was weak of me, I know. But I felt I could not leave without a kind of warning. After all, she was acting of her nature, like them all. So I went to the door and let her in.

She was magnificent.

She was dressed as barbaric murals showed Gyphimedes, the divine mistress of the beloved of Grodno, to be dressed in the old legends. Kregen is a maze of myth and legend, some of it beautiful, some horrible, all of absorbing interest. Storytellers weave their fantasies in every marketplace and on favorite street corners beneath the sturm trees. The very air of the world breathes a scented miasma of romance and wonder. Now Susheeng stood gracefully before me dressed as a living mistress from one of those old legends.

Her hair was coifed and ablaze with jewels. A thick rope of it had been left free and this hung down, coiling lushly over one rounded shoulder. Her body was clad in strings and ropes of emeralds. A priceless fortune glowed against her white skin. The rosy hue in her cheeks was not entirely artificial. Her eyes gleamed and sparkled from lotions. Barbarically bedecked, more nude than if she had been naked, she glided toward me, the golden ankle bells chiming. The breath clogged in my throat.

"Drak—my Prince—do I not find favor in your sight?"

It was a rote question, as old as man and woman.

"You are exceedingly beautiful, Susheeng."

She swayed toward me. My mind was a jumbled amalgam of Holly, and Natema, and Mayfwy—and then, swamping them all and clearing my head and setting my whole being blazing, came the vivid memory of my Delia of the Blue Mountains stepping so lithely down the rocks clad in those magnificent white ling furs, her figure perfection, her eyes glowing on me, her every aspect so far more beautiful—so—words fail me here. I thrust Susheeng from me so that she staggered.

She dropped to her knees. She amazed me even more. In one hand she had hidden a crumpled gray cloth. Now, moving with a frenzy I found fascinating and appalling, she stripped the emeralds from her so that the strings broke and the gems rolled and scattered wildly about the room. Stark naked she stood, her hair down and the jewels shaken from it. Then—then she wrapped the gray cloth about her thighs, drew it up between her legs, and knelt before me clad in the gray breechclout of the slave!

I didn't want to touch her.

But I didn't want her crouching there at my feet, dressed up as a slave girl, demanding from me what she must know I would not give.

"Get up, Susheeng!" I said. I made my voice harsh and she jumped and flinched, and her naked shoulders shook. "You look ridiculous!"

It was, of course, the end.

Slowly, she stood up. Her breast heaved and she gulped to control herself. She succeeded. Calm, icy, deadly, she stood before me, naked in the gray breechclout.

"I have offered you everything, Kov Drak of Delphond.

You have seen fit in your folly to refuse me. Now—" Her eyes glowed molten on me in the lamplight. She was incredibly beautiful and evil, now that her pretensions had been stripped away. On Kregen there is an expression which means roughly what "my dear" means on Earth, with all the sinister, hating, murderous connotations involved. She used that now, as she turned like a she-leem and glided toward the door.

"You will be sorry, ma faril Drak. Oh, so sorry!"

I knew I had less than a handful of murs to get clear.

The mailed men she was even now whistling up would not know I had a sectrix saddled and waiting; and so I stood a chance. But it was a near thing. As I clattered out of that secret court where a sleepy slave padded his way back to his quarters, I heard the sounds of the hunt rising behind me.

As it was, I got clear away. I belted hard for the warrens and, with the die cast, felt a great lightening of my spirits. Susheeng would no longer enter my calculations to ruin all that I was attempting. So I thought as I reentered the ghetto.

The first person I met as I ducked into the familiar hovel was Holly.

She stood up as I went in and her slight figure in the rustling light from the candle sent a quick pulse of futile anger through me. She smiled. We had scarcely seen each other alone since that first greeting. Now she came toward me shyly, but with the firmness of character and resolve I knew she possessed.

"You've been avoiding me, Stylor!"

The incongruity of it all hit me. I gaped at her.

"Stylor! What—?"

"Holly, dear Holly. I have work to do here. The plans must go on—"

"Oh, fiddle the plans! Can't you see—" She stopped herself. The direct approach was not, in general, Holly's way.

Then, thankfully, Genal, Pugnarses, and Bolan stalked in. They were annoyed because a good smith had been whipped since his production of iron nails was down—because he had been forging pike heads for us.

"We will have to spread the load," I said. "There are, after all, enough slaves to make production light enough—"

"But he was *good!*"

"All the more reason to use him carefully, Pugnarses!" I spoke sharply. Pugnarses gave me an ugly look, but I stared him down. "We are a band of brothers, Pugnarses. We must fight together, or go to the galleys together!"

"We will never do that!" flared Genal.

"Very well, then. Now, listen. We come now to the single most important weapon in our armory." I held their attention; even Holly stood, her hands pressed into her breast, listening.

I told them, then, what the sleeting hail of the arrow storm could do.

"We have a few archers," Pugnarses said. "But few men know the bow. We can make them easily enough, and arrows."

"That is the small straight bow," I said. And I laughed. You who listen to these tapes will know I do not laugh lightly.

It is not exactly true to say that the long English yew bow is the peasants' weapon. Of the famous longbows, only about one in five were made from yew, the others being mostly ash or elm or witch hazel, and only the best and most experienced archers were issued with yew bows. I wished I had the men to use those bows. Their deadly accuracy, their armor-piercing piles, would have laid low the overlords in great droves. As it was, I must make do with what a slave economy could provide.

"It takes years and years of training to make a longbowman. You must start almost before you can walk to pull a bow, to draw it to the ear, to attain that instinctive accuracy and that uncanny speed. Do not think of the longbow, my friends, unless there are men of Loh among you."

"We have a few—some are redheaded, most are not."

"Good, Bolan. We will make longbows for them. But for the main archery strength I shall use crossbows."

My wild Clansmen with their own curved compound reflex bows had some respect for the powerful crossbows of the citizens of Zenicce. I would not be making bows quite like that, not yet, here in the slave warrens of Magdag. I had handled and used the crossbows of Zenicce many times. I knew their virtues and their weaknesses.

"Crossbows?" said Bolan, wonderingly.

"Crossbows," I said. I spoke firmly, decisively. "We will make crossbows and with them we will smash the overlords of Magdag into the dust!"

CHAPTER SIXTEEN

Of pikes and crossbows

The mere manufacture of crossbows and the quarrels they would shoot would not, of course, as with any other weapon, settle the overlords of Magdag.

The men who would use them must be trained.

I insisted that the training be carried out with a great deal of the efficiency and spirit of emulation and success, if without the rewards for failure, that I had applied training my guns' crews aboard the seventy-fours and frigates that sailed other seas four hundred light-years away from Kregen. Volley shooting would be a necessity. Sufficient accuracy should be obtained from individual marksmen so that a wide swathe of the bolts would fall upon the charging overlords' cavalry.

Production was begun as soon as the first crossbow I had designed and seen through its development stages, helped by the slave and worker craftsmen without whom the venture would have been impossible, had been tested and had passed. We began with a simple hand-spanned bow. Once those whom we selected for training had grasped its essential principles, and could put a group of bolts into the targets set up in the alleys of the warrens, we progressed at a jump to bows spanned by windlasses. As a sailor I could handle the simple calculations necessary to arrive at a satisfactory ratio series. The biggest innovation, and one I felt some pride in developing, was what I called the sextet.

One of the main problems with the crossbow is its slow rate of discharge. I have previously mentioned that bows do not fire their arrows or bolts. In every respect the crossbow is inferior to the expertly handled longbow. So men believe. I had so to arrange my crossbowmen as to nullify as many of the disadvantages as possible. We would be fighting from behind barricades. That was essential, as I saw it. So I took a group of six people. The sharp end was the shooter, he who actually loosed the bolt at the foe. To his rear stood or knelt the hander. He took the discharged bow from the shooter and handed him a loaded bow. To his rear were stationed two loaders. They took the spanned bows and loaded them with the bolts, ready for the hander, alternately. Finally, in the rear, were placed the spanners whose task it was to hook on the windlasses and wind like fury until the bows were spanned, when they would hand them to the loaders.

Six men would use six crossbows—and the end result of their labors would be the discharge of a single quarrel. The big difference between that and having the whole six discharge at once was that the rate of discharge could be kept up. And I would naturally place the best shots as shooters. When necessary, say at the final moment of a charge, the entire six could rise and shoot what would be a devastating broadside.

I say men—there were women and girls and young boys in the ranks of handers, loaders, and spanners. Holly, with her tenacious obduracy, insisted on being taught how to handle a bow through all its phases, and she turned into a fine shot.

With the arme blanche I felt we could not expect even a solid phalanx of pikemen to meet and beat down an overlord charge. But once the slaves and workers understood the problems they insisted that they be trained as though they would have to face the overlords in the open. Accordingly, in the inner squares and plazas of the warrens, where overlords and beast guards ventured only in overwhelming mailed strength, and that only when they chased runaway slaves, we drilled and marched and pointed and lifted pikes. The front ranks contained halberdiers on the Swiss model. When I first saw that forest of eighteen-foot long pikes moving steadily across the square I own to a pang of pride and despair and choked affection.

Those men out there, marching with a swing and a tramp through the dust, their throats parched, their lips dry, were slaves and workers, beaten men, whipped cramphs, despised and derided by the scented overlords of Magdag. And here they were marching in ranks and columns together, brothers in arms, shoulder to shoulder, disciplined and dedicated to a freedom that depended on their discipline. And once they had obtained their freedom—what of their so hardly-won and proudly-vaunted discipline then?

That was a problem for revolution, not rebellion. It must come later.

THE SUNS OF SCORPIO

It would come—I had vowed myself that—quite apart from the duty I conceived the Star Lords demanded from me.

We forged a weapon, there in the miasmic odors and the odoriferous mud of the ghetto. We drilled and trained. We built barricades from which we practiced hurling a sleeting storm of crossbow bolts. We devised tricks and traps, things like loops of rope hung between houses, balks of timber to be thrust hock-high across from door to door—for I believed we would have to call down the wrath of the overlords upon us and meet them in the confines of our warrens.

In this, I found to my surprise, I stood alone.

"Soon," said Genal with the lust for battle kindling unpleasantly in his eyes, "Genodras will disappear. The accursed Zim will, for a short space, prevent us seeing the true light of the sky."

I had to stand and take all this without a murmur.

"The overlords retire into their great halls during this time of the Great Death as they await the Great Birth. We workers must grovel in our shacks and hovels, condemned to the warrens. We are not permitted in the halls during their times of use, when all they stand for becomes revealed."

"Aye!" growled the listeners, rough, bearded men, their hands horny with labor.

"Then is the time to strike!" declared Genal. "We are debarred from the great rituals of Grodno, when sacrifices are made so that Genodras, the all-mighty green sun, will reappear. We may never witness the sacred ceremonies. Then, my brothers, then is the time to rise up in our justified wrath and strike down the oppressors!"

Genal, it was clear, had been spending a lot of time with the Prophet. He had caught the intonation as well as the words.

It was a good plan, in the sense that we could sweep up into the city in a great wave of iron, steel, and bronze, and find no overlords to bar our path. I felt sure we could deal with the mercenary guards in the confident strength of our newly-won military skill. Then it would be a matter of driving from one great hall of mystery to another, routing out the occupants at their rituals and slaying them piecemeal. I had no objection in principle to this wholesale killing of the overlords of Magdag; you must remember that at that time I was, besides being very young, thoroughly steeped in the precepts of Zair who hated and detested all things of Grodno. I felt it my binding duty to the Krozairs of Zy to destroy every-thing green on the inner sea, no less than my more nebulous demands from the Star Lords.

If I have given the impression that I am an easy person to live with, then the impression is false. I know I am an ex-ceedingly difficult person to get along with. I know this. I have been told. Poor Holly and Genal found that out, and Mayfwy had been marvelously understanding and undemand-ing. My Clansmen, chief among them Hap Loder, had of course other reasons for submitting to my ill humors. Some-times I felt a sensation I knew must be a cold terror as I con-templated what I would do to my Delia, my gentle, fierce De-lia of the Blue Mountains when at last we settled down to a form of married life in distant Vallia.

As far as killing the overlords of Magdag was concerned I was again brushed by that feeling of doom spreading shadowy wings over me. I had to shrug it off. Didn't I hate everything green about the inner sea, about Magdag and its slavers? I rallied to the plan. It was good. We would catch the overlords with, as the saying goes, their pants down.

"This means we must wait even longer," Holly pointed out.

"Yes." Genal eyed her and, as I had noticed whenever he looked more than casually at Holly—which was almost al-ways—he became hot and most un-Genal like in his reac-tions. Now he said: "We must wait just that little longer beneath the lash; old snake will cut our backs open for just that little longer. But the waiting will be more than worth the pain! For we will squeeze these Grodno forsaken overlords, we will crush them, hall by hall we will tear them apart, sweeping over them like the rashoon of Grodno himself!"

Holly looked at me. Pugnarses looked at Holly, and then swung to glare at me. Genal stared. "Well, Stylor?"

"It is a good plan," I said. "We will wait."

There would be more time to train my little cadre and be-gin to show them what tactical fighting was all about. I thought of my projected barricades with a twinge of regret, but I have always been, like the men of Segesthes, an attack-ing fighter except when I may gain an advantage by fighting in defense.

Genal had mentioned the rashoon, the sudden treacherous storm wind that blows up on the Eye of the World, and for some reason this reminded me of Nath and Zolta, my old oar comrades. Were they even now, perhaps, battling a rashoon on the heaving decks of a swifter? I felt a stifling choking in the warrens of Magdag. How I longed to stand once more on the quarterdeck of a swifter—that huge swifter to whose command I had never reached!

Then I saw the solid phalanx of my friends, the slaves and workers of the warrens of Magdag, marching steadily across the plaza. The pikes all slanted at a single angle. They marched solidly, close-packed, yet there was about those men a swing, a lilt, almost, that lifted me back to reality again. Bolan roared a command and the pikes swung down into their hedgehog of points, neatly, swiftly, as the men had been trained. Once the philosophy of the pike has been shown a man who must fight on foot, and once he grasps the thick haft with its iron bands in his fists and stands shoulder to shoulder with his comrades, he rapidly understands why he is there packed into the pike phalanx.

Bolan's bald head gleamed in the twin suns' light. Some of the men had fashioned caps of leather. Most were bareheaded and their shaggy manes troubled me. Leather— There is no leather so highly prized as the leather of Sanurkazz, the Magdag efforts being quite inferior; but the Magdaggians have the knack of beautifying leather, of adorning it with stampings and colors that make it beautiful and valuable. A lucrative two-way commerce was viable, there, if the red and the green were not opposed.

Sheemiff, the girl Fristle, strolled onto the plaza and stood idly watching the parade. She had, I knew, become a fast hand at loading and handing and was now training hard to become a first-class shooter. In military matters hierarchies of command and order are perhaps at their loosest in a rebellious army whose men all subscribe to the fight with everything they possess. But I had instituted ranks, for I wanted orders given in the heat of combat to be passed rapidly and to be obeyed instantly. Mind you, even then I believe I would far rather have been sitting on a sun-drenched terrace, with Delia by my side, munching a handful of palines and laughing in the fresh air.

But a stricture had been laid on me.

Bare heads and Sheemiff mingled in my mind. I saw myself once more down by the muddy, bloody banks of the river, where the piles of vosk skulls lay hard and obstinate in the sun. "Old vosk skull!" Zolta would call Nath. Yes.

"Sheemiff!" I called. She ran to me eagerly, her slit eyes lighting up, her golden fur sleek and brushed.

"What does my Jikai desire?"

When I told her she looked surprised and disappointed, but she ran off willingly enough. There were some men who swore that a Fristle virgin knew more about the arts of love than a temple maiden from Loh. I wouldn't know about that—then—and dismissed the idea. When she returned, Holly, Genal, Pugnarses, and Bolan, who had dismissed the phalanx, with some of the other leaders, were talking about all the plans we were maturing. Sheemiff walked up to me in the center of the group and held out the vosk skull on her hands.

The uproar around me, as you may imagine, was comical in the still center of the tragic situation brewing. Vosk skulls! What had they to do with the glorious revolution?

I showed those slaves and workers of Magdag just what the skull of the vosk did have to do for us.

I lifted it high in the air. Then, having seen that Sheemiff had washed it thoroughly in the river, and cleaned it, and dried it, I brought it down over my head. I felt the weight come on my own skull. I stared out through those two blank orbits. The nose bone joined them and projected down like a nosepiece of a helmet.

"The overlords call us vosks!" I shouted. "They call us fools and mangy cramphs, and calsanys—and vosks—stupid, obstinate vosks. Very well. The vosk has a skull of a thickness, my friends. Of a redoubtable thickness, as everyone knows, for the piles of skulls by the river attest this and the broken grindstones in the bone mills. So! We take on with pride all the stubborn thickheadedness of the vosk!" I banged the flat of my long sword against the skull. "We are the vosk-helmets, my friends! Vosk-helmets who will smash into the green halls of Magdag and destroy every last overlord!"

They took it very well. Even as some debated and others ran to the river for their own skull-helmets, I felt the ringing in my head. These vosk-helmets would have to be well-padded, with grass and rags and moss.

We set up a vosk skull on a rock and took turns in smashing at it with a variety of weapons. Even I, who had surmised that nature would take care of so stubborn and stupid a creature as the vosk, was surprised at the resistance offered by the skulls. I remembered when we had let loose the vosks in the Marble Quarries of Zenicce—they had been Segesthan vosks, larger than these of the inner sea. These vosk skulls fitted a man's head like a tailored helmet, and they thrust two upcurving horns forward, arrogant now that all the flesh and skin had been stripped away.

Holly grabbed my arm.

"Oh, Stylor—you are clever! They will save many a poor man's life—"

Genal and Pugnarses looked on.

I said: "We are downtrodden, Holly, like the vosk, considered stupid. So we take as our badge of pride the old vosk skull; we are the Vosk-Helmets! From the lowly comes forth the victory."

The Prophet was standing nearby and I had not been able to resist the magniloquence. Afterward, I felt ridiculous. But the people responded, as they do, and the work went on.

Most of the crossbows were fashioned with a bow of horn and wood; some we made of steel. But quantity, for the moment, had to take priority over quality. I put the steel bows into a corps and made sure the best shots were assigned there. We colored our vosk-helmets yellow, purloining the paint from the paint masters on the great friezes. I gave colored scraps of cloth as badges of rank. We drilled. Gradually we were turning into an army.

And all the time the slaves and workers continued their labors on the great halls. Now work was concentrated on just finishing the nearest-completed hall. It was necessary, as I understood, that at least one new hall be finished for this time of the Great Death. It took season after season to complete a hall, of course, within the complex of the massive buildings that could have swallowed all the pyramids at a gulp.

Having discussed the question of overlord spies among us, I had been reassured by my group leaders. We could carry on our work within the complexes of the warrens and lookouts would warn us of any onslaught from the overlords. Of spies, the slaves had experience. A man, acting the slave, acts differently from one who had felt old snake on his naked back, or so the men said. I was not so sure, but in this had to trust those on the spot.

I was aware that despite their willingness to drill and march the slaves were irked by the enforced discipline. Their ideas of rebellion consisted of snatching up a sword and a torch and running like crazy through the streets. Clearly, they became more difficult to hold in check as the time for the Great Death approached. It was also apparent that Pugnarses and Genal were irked. They had drawn closer together of late, and this pleased me. They were often in long, involved, passionate discussions, which would break up as soon as I appeared. I was glad they were more friendly now than they had seemed to be.

Bolan was a tower of strength, his bald head covered by a massive yellow-painted vosk skull. He was manipulating the pikemen into a force I considered might just have a chance against the overlord cavalry. Just a chance, before they were cut to pieces, but that single chance would be all we would have.

Although I had felt it desirous not to use either red or green as colors for the slave army—yellow and blue and black were the symbols and badges we used—the aspect of a religious war was fading. I did not see this clearly then. Zair forgive me—I actually thought I was extraordinarily clever in thus turning the Grodno-worshiping workers against their Grodno-worshiping masters. As the majority of the slaves were for Zair I had even further vague and nebulous plans I could not even acknowledge to myself, and as a consequence I completely overlooked the character of class war that had taken over. I was for Sanurkazz and Zair and the Krozairs of Zy. In that, I failed. I should have taken the longer view. . . .

One night, returning after a crossbow session with the sextets handling the steel bows, I halted on the threshold of the hovel. Genal was grasping Holly in his arms, pushing the shush-chiff she wore down over her shoulders, his lips seeking her soft flesh. Why she should wear a shush-chiff at this time I did not know, but apparently it had inflamed Genal. Holly was gasping.

"No, no, Genal! Leave off! Please—"

"But I love you, Holly! You know that—you've always known it. I'll do anything, anything at all, for you, Holly—"

"You're tearing my shush-chiff!"

Genal's voice broke into an impassioned sob. "And was it for Pugnarses—"

"No—no! How can you say it! I don't love either of you!"

I made a noise outside, and shuffled and dropped my long sword—a thing a warrior only does if he is troubled or scheming or dead—and then went in. We all acted as though nothing had happened. I am sure they did not know I had eavesdropped on their pitiful little scene.

If I had taken more notice. . . . But I considered this affair none of my business. They were both adult; they should be able to handle their amorous problems like adults. Perhaps I was too concerned over trivia like steel crossbows instead of looking at the springs of motivation of those around me, on whom the success of the revolution would depend.

We were all waiting now with a heightened expectation, for daily the green sun Genodras dropped lower and lower toward the red sun Zim, and the time of the Great Death was at hand.

Each day brought the two closer together with an almost visible rate of closing.

The moment Genodras dropped out of sight behind Zim would be the time we would rise. The workers had no care, now, in their passion, that they, too, were thought to own allegiance to Grodno. For them the seasons of oppression at last were to be broken. The whip and the chain were to be banished. No superstition would prevent that.

On what we all knew was the last night Holly came to me. She had donned her shush-chiff, and oiled her body and hair, and she looked very delectable. She laughed at me in her own seemingly modest way, and all the blood surged into her innocent face.

"Why, Holly," I said rashly. "You look charming."

"Is that all, Stylor? Just—charming?"

The hovel did not seem to stink quite so badly in the sputtering, fluttering light of the candle. Genal and Pugnarses were out somewhere. I knew we were making last-minute attempts to create a line of underground communication with the slaves in the dock areas, where the bagnios would provide stalwart fighting-men once the initial attack had begun.

I felt uneasy and put that down to Holly's presence.

A foot scraped at the door, but Holly did not hear, for she came to me, pouting, forcing herself to declare something that her nature made of tremendous difficulty and tremendous significance for her. I moved away, as though casually. I had no desire for Genal or Pugnarses—or Bolan, for that matter—to stand in the role of eavesdropper on me as I had on Genal and Holly.

"Oh, Stylor—why are you so blind?"

Her gentle birdlike movements made me step back again, away from the bed where my mail coat and my long sword were hidden beneath the straw, but with the hilt of the long sword ready to instant hand.

"It will soon be time, Holly," I said.

"Time for war, yes, Stylor. But is war all that obsesses you?"

"I should hope not!" I said.

I looked at her, at her bright eyes, the soft and supple figure beneath the shush-chiff, and the men who entered almost had me. They wore the slave gray, but they had fierce faces of overlords with the down-drooping Mongol moustaches, and they carried swords in their hands. There were four who had wrapped gray cloths about their faces so that only their eyes showed.

My lunge for the long sword was made—I was on my way when the first arrow thunked into the wood—and I did not stop then. I whirled with the long sword—and froze.

"That is better, cramph." The overlord sneered the words.

The bent bow, the nocked arrow, the barbed head—they did not stop me, for the Krozairs make religious sport of striking flying arrows from the air with their swords. No— the arrow aimed directly at the heart of Holly, who shrank back, her hands to her mouth, her eyes enormous, choked with horror.

I dropped the long sword, kicked it under the straw. They took me then, without a struggle, and all the time that merciless arrow remained pointing at Holly's heart.

CHAPTER SEVENTEEN

"A Krozair!
You—the Lord of Strombor!"

I have sojourned for a spell in many prisons in my long life and the one beneath the colossal Magdag Hall na Priags was no worse than most and a lot better than some.

Stripped naked, spread-eagled out against a damp wall, my wrists and ankles clamped in rusty iron rings, chains dangling infuriatingly from the iron hoop about my waist, I waited in the half-darkness partly lit by a ruddy radiance streaming in through the iron-barred grille.

All thought of the rebellion had fled from my mind. This was not because I despaired, but because I had seen a jumbled pile of my group commanders outside my hovel, dead, hideously dead. Bolan, I had seen, running shrieking into the warrens, his bald head glistening in the streaming radiance of the fourth moon, She of the Veils, and with the arrow striking through his left shoulder. All revolt, surely, would be crushed when the green sun reappeared.

The jailers took me up to judgment. They were men, for no half-human, half-beast mercenaries were allowed in the sacred halls of Magdag during the time of the Great Death and the Great Birth. Overlords of the second class, they were of a kind with that Wengard who had so viciously ordered me a touch of old snake.

The room into which I was conducted—pushed and shoved and pummeled—was walled and roofed in uncut stone. A sturm-wood table crossed an angle. Behind this the guard commander sat, all in mail, his long sword at his side. He stroked that ugly drooping Magdag moustache as he spoke.

"You will tell us of the final plans for the rebellion, rast. Otherwise you will die unpleasantly."

I suppose he saw that this did not convince me; he knew as

well as I that they would kill me out of hand. In this, as you shall hear, I was wrong.

"We know of your schemes, you whom the slaves call Stylor. We have samples of your pitiful slave-made weapons. But we would be more exact."

They had been incautious enough to leave me with a bight of chain between my ankles. The chains around my bound wrists would, of course, serve as a weapon. I did not bother to kick the guards next to me. I went straight over the table, wrapped my wrist-chains around the guard commander's neck, and hauled back.

"I will leave you enough air to tell these cramphs what to do," I said, in his ear, low and venomous. He gobbled out a shrieked order to his men to stay back. Impasse.

The door opened and Glycas walked in.

He was speaking in his abrupt, authoritarian way before he was fairly through the opening.

"Send for the prisoner, Stylor. There is a mystery about this slave I would—" Then he saw me. His breath hissed in his throat. His long sword flashed clear of his scabbard.

"I shall cut you down, slave, whether you strangle that miserable guard commander or not." He laughed, his silky, snakelike laugh. "Perhaps I will have him strangled, anyway, for allowing you this much effrontery." He glared around at the paralyzed jailers. "Seize him!"

The death of this Magdag overlord of the second class would benefit no one. I let him go, regretfully, to be sure.

My brown hair had grown long, my trim moustache and beard a trifle shaggy, I was filthy, grimed and mucky with sweat. I stood clear before the table. Glycas kept his sword pointed.

"I am Stylor," I said.

"Your friends have told me a great deal. But they know little of you, slave. You will tell me all I want to know."

"Like, perhaps, where I came from? Where I vanished to? Like, perchance, that you are a foul green-scummed risslaca, Glycas?"

He gaped. For an instant, his composure deserted him. With a jerky strut he bore down on me, the long sword pointed at my breast. He took my filthily-bearded chin in his hand and twisted my head up into the lantern light. Again he drew that hissing breath between his teeth. His fist gripping my chin shook.

"Drak, Kov of Delphond!"

"And now, perhaps, you will free me from these undignified chains, let me have a bath and scented oils, and then provide me with an explanation and an apology—"

"Silence!" he roared. He stood back and still he did not lower the long sword. He would not risk his neck in the same position as the guard commander's. "Enough. That you are Stylor, the wanted slave traitor, is enough for me. What else you have done to my sister, is between us, not of Magdag."

"I have done nothing to the Princess Susheeng," I said, before he hit me. "That is her trouble." Then he hit me.

I was to be used in the rituals to insure the return of the green sun, Genodras, and the rebirth of Grodno.

A medley of emotions tortured me. If I say that in some odd and hurtful way I was glad that this was to happen, I do not believe you will understand. Since this, my third period on Kregen, I had not been myself. Always, I had felt the unseen compulsion of the Star Lords—possibly, I thought then, of the Savanti also—forcing me into actions and deeds that were not truly of my nature. The suffocating sense of that shadowy doom I knew was reserved for me had inhibited me. Strange and mysterious powers had torn me from my own Earth, and I had responded eagerly, gladly. But the doom-laden feelings I could not shake off had soured all my thoughts and actions. Clearly, here in the great Hall na Priags of Magdag, I had been abandoned by the Star Lords, their plans for me betrayed, my usefulness at an end.

I felt, suddenly, free, lightened, ready to be once again plain Dray Prescot, of Earth, and to face that menacing doom with all the callous courage I could summon up.

Captives of the highest rank were used in the ritual games of Magdag to propitiate, entreat, and insure the return of Genodras. We were bundled into iron-barred cages overlooking the great Hall na Priags so that we might see what awaited us and shudder at our fate. I stood gripping the bars, staring out on that fantastic scene as the lamplight and torchlight flickered and flared on the massive walls with their festoons of paintings and carvings, their murals exalting the power of Magdag, their sculptures of the beast-gods, the overwhelming decorative detail.

What I saw astonished me.

Around the cleared area where we would be tortured to death in manners weird and horrible to the mind of a sane man the rows of Magdaggian overlords waited. They waited for the entrance of the high overlord of this Hall na Priags,

who was Glycas, in ceremonial procession. A sigh went up as
the smoke swirled and lifted and the priests and the sacred
guards walked sedately into that vast chamber. Glycas, as
square, as hard, as corrupt as ever marched with the sacred
golden covering held above his head by four nobles. I looked
about. I was astonished.

Every single person present wore red.

Clad all in red, they waited or walked in a rhythmic swing
toward the dais, all in red, and at their sides swung long
swords, broken in half, their jagged edges protruding past the
ripped-away ends of split scabbards.

All in red.

Here, in the heart of Magdag, stronghold of Grodno the
Green!

Here, then, was part of the secret, part of the reason why
only overlords and nobles were allowed to witness these rituals to insure the return of the green sun. We sacrifices, of
course, were not expected to live. And I guessed at a part of
that secret.

The green sun Genodras had been swallowed by the red
sun Zim. What more natural, therefore, since there was now
only a red sun in the sky of Kregen, that the worshipers of
Grodno should seek to placate Zair, the deity of the red sun
Zim! What, indeed! But, how shameful a fact to own in the
world. How they must hate what they now did, clad in the
hated red, parading to the glory not of Grodno, but of Zair.
Begging, pleading, entreating, not Grodno, for the return of
Genodras—but Zair!

"The blasphemers!" A naked man with the marks of the
whip on his back clawed at the bars, cursing. The others with
me in the sacrificial cages shouted and yelled, but the men of
Magdag were accustomed to that. They ignored us.

In that moment had I any pity in my heart for the men of
Magdag surely, then, I would have felt a pang, condemned as
they were by the laws of astronomy to lose their godhead at
each eclipse.

But very quickly they were taking the sacrifices out, poking
them with sharp swords, forcing them into the center of the
cleared area where the torturers waited. What was done was
fiendish, diabolical; and it was all done in the name of religious superstition.

The stink of incense, which has always sickened me, the
noise of shouting, the resonant chanting rising ever and anon,
the shrieks of the victims, the harsh feel of the iron bars in

"I gripped it about the neck and started to run."

my fists, all melded into a hideous series of concussions in my brain. Around the hall were sited huge banners, of red cloth, embroidered with the devices and blazons of Sanurkazz, and of other southern cities, Zamu, Tremzo, Zond, and of citadels like Felteraz, and of individuals like Zazz, and Zenkiren—and Dray, Lord of Strombor!—and of organizations and orders like The Red Brethren of Lizz, and the Krozairs of Zy.

Then I noticed the diabolical cunning in the thinking. As each victim fell to his death one of the red banners was removed, torn into pieces and cast upon the sacrificial fire. Here was an example of the twisted logic available to the fanatical mind in pursuit of a single desired object. And yet each ritual test was designed so that there was a chance, a slim one, perhaps one in a thousand, for the victim to escape and come through safely. If he did so the banner he had saved from the fire was relegated, but he was returned immediately to the cages to await a further trial. This was leem and woflo with a vengeance!

I had a hope I might come through safely.

My test was devilish and simple.

Over a gangway beneath which a series of razor-sharp knives moved jerkily, I had to run carrying a squirming half-grown leem. The leem is furry, feline, vicious, with eight legs, and sinuous like a ferret, with a wedge-shaped head equipped with fangs that can strike through lenk. When full-grown it is of a size with an Earthly leopard. This one was about the size of a spaniel; at once it sought to sink its fangs into me. I gripped it about the neck and started ruthlessly to choke it to death even as long swords prodded me over the gangway. I ran. Men and women of Magdag, laughing, swayed the gangway about so that I staggered and almost lost my footing to plunge bodily onto those circling scythe-like knives. But I gripped the leem which struggled and flailed its eight legs. It could not shriek, for I gripped it. Oh, how I gripped it! And I ran. When I reached the far side men with swords met me and I flung the leem full at them. They cut it down instantly, and sword points prodded my breast, forced me back to the cage.

But I saw the deviced banner of Pur Zenkiren moved away from the sacrificial fire, and I exulted.

I would await my next ordeal.

Feasting, singing, and ritual dancing went on all the time the sacrifices underwent their ordeals, and died. Slowly but remorselessly the victims and the brave red banners lessened in number.

The hideous burs passed.

Then, as though in a daze, I saw, sitting at her brother's side, laughing and drinking wine from a crystal goblet from Loh, the Princess Susheeng. Barbaric and gorgeous, she looked, clad all in red, the blood coloring her face, her eyes brilliant with kohl and her mouth a scarlet pout of sensual desire.

She had seen me run. She had seen me, naked, the sweat pouring down my chest, my muscles bunching with frenzied energy, as I gripped the leem and ran above that pit of death.

When I looked again, after the agonized scream of a poor devil who had failed to draw his head back in time so that the buzz-saw-like wheel of knives had decapitated him, Susheeng was gone.

The sacrificial cages opened by small and well-guarded barred gates onto the great hall. To the rear lay the entrances through which we had been escorted. Beyond them lay the complex of this megalithic structure, one with possibly a score of halls like this, where even now other rituals were being played out in death.

Within the structures, used only during these times, lay kitchens, bedrooms, dressing rooms, and all the facilities the overlords would need. The rear door opened and more sacrifices were thrust in at the points of swords. An overlord in mail gripped my arm. He jerked me back from the bars.

"This way, rast. And quietly."

I followed him. We left the cage and, with six other guards, walked along the stone corridor. I understood then that someone who knew me had sent these men. Seven guards, overlords all, had been considered essential. Along the corridors guards and sacrifices moved, with personal slaves, pampered pets of the palace household, scurrying about their business. They would never be allowed into the great halls at this time.

The leem I had carried had managed to rake one of his clawed pads down my chest. The blood oozed.

The seven guards were overlords of the second class. Their drooping moustaches were extravagantly long. They carried their swords naked in their hands. They had been told about me.

We entered a high, narrow room, hung with brilliant tapestries depicting the hunt of Galliphron when he discovered the succulence of a vosk rasher grilled over an open fire. The guards went out; they backed away from me and the last I saw of them was the tips of their swords.

The other door opened and the Princess Susheeng entered.

She looked pale, the spots of color burning in her cheeks. Her manner was frightened, wild, inflamed, jerky.

"Drak—Drak! I saw you—" She bit her lip, staring at me. I regarded her calmly. She held out a gray slave breechclout and a tunic embroidered with the black and green device of the overseer of the balass. Beneath her arm she carried the balass stick. She was still clad all in red, and her bosom heaved uncontrollably. Her eyes were large and hypnotic upon me.

"Why, Susheeng?" I asked.

"I could not see you die thus! I do not know—do not ask me. I cannot explain. Hurry, you calsany!"

I put on the gray slave clothes. I took the balass. I did not strike her with it.

"You must hide until Genodras returns—"

"It would be better, Susheeng, if I left now, would it not?"

"Ah, Drak! Cannot you stay, even now! Even after I have risked—"

"I thank you, Princess, for what you have done." I looked at her. She was exceedingly beautiful, in her lush overblown way. "I think you have forgiven me for what happened in the Palace of the Emerald Eye."

"No!" She flamed at me. "I have offered you everything! Yet you ridiculed me. Oh, how I rejoiced when those two cramphs betrayed you to my brother! How I thought I would glee in your death, in agony! But—but—"

"Who?"

She shrugged those full shoulders, pouting. "It does not matter. Two cramphs of workers. They have been condemned now—"

"*Who!*"

My face must have worked its usual havoc. She shrank back. "Two overseers of the balass—Pugnarses, I believe, and Genal—"

"No!" I said. I felt the hurt, the agony, there, that I had never felt when a sword bit, when a leem's claws struck.

She saw that. Triumph spurred her on. "They betrayed you! Pugnarses, because the fool thought to wear the mail and sword of an overlord! And the other, because Pugnarses talked him into it, made him out of jealousy of a girl—"

"Holly!" I said.

"Yes," she said, the venom biting. "A disgusting girl—cramph, Holly, who even now awaits my brother's pleasure."

"And the two—Pugnarses and Genal?"

Again she moved those rounded shoulders, indifferent to their fates. She had always taken what she wanted; she still believed she could take me if she tried hard enough. "They are to be sacrifices. It is just. They presumed."

"Just! Is that Magdaggian justice?"

"What do you, a Kov of Vallia, know of Magdaggian justice?"

I gripped her shoulder.

"I would like to find those two—"

"To kill them? To take your revenge?" She let me grasp her and swayed into me, clasping me in her arms. "Ah, no, Drak. No! Let them go. Escape. I have it all arranged. When Genodras returns and the world is green once again—then we can ride!"

"Where to? Sanurkazz?"

She shook her head against my chest. "No. I have wide estates. No one will question the Princess Susheeng. I will create a new identity for you, my Drak. We can return to Magdag. I have wealth enough for us both, and to spare—"

I had had, for the moment, enough of new identities.

She had been clever in not attempting to find a hauberk of width enough to encompass those shoulders of mine, and an overseer of the balass was nicely balanced to move about the megalithic complex without question within the hierarchical structure. I moved to the door. My face was set.

"Where are you—Drak! No! Please—*NO!*"

"I thank you for your help, Susheeng. I do not blame you for what you are. That is not of your manufacture." I opened the door. "If you wish to call the guards, that is your privilege."

She ran to me, caught the gray slave tunic. Outside, a guard detail passed with a sacrifice screaming between them.

"Drak! I will come with you!"

We went out together. She preceded me, as was proper, and she led me through the maze of corridors, avoiding the halls from which floated the horrid sounds of the rituals. There was nothing I could do for those men of Zair now, here in a hive of mailed Magdaggian might. But my blood boiled and my heart thumped the quicker, and I had to hold myself very stiff and straight as we passed those men of Magdag.

Genal and Pugnarses were chained together in a cell, awaiting their call to the sacrificial games.

They looked miserable and woebegone and defeated. I was glad to notice they did not look frightened. They had had time to think, chained naked in a Magdag dungeon.

They saw me over the shoulder of the guard. Their eyes popped and they would have spoken out and so betrayed me once again had I not struck the guard on his chin, above the opened ventail. I took his keys and his sword.

I stood looking at them, as Susheeng hovered uncertainly at the door, peering with frightened eyes into the corridor. I shook the keys before them.

"Stylor—" Genal swallowed. He looked sick. "If you are going to kill us, do it now. I deserve it, for I betrayed you."

Pugnarses, in turn, swallowed. He stared at the sword as a man stares at a snake. "Strike hard, Stylor."

"You pair of fools!" I said. I spoke fiercely, hotly, angrily, feeling all the hurt in me. "You betrayed me because of Holly. Did you not see the pile of corpses—of our own men? The group leaders dead, the glorious revolution finished?"

"We—" croaked Genal.

"I persuaded Genal," said Pugnarses. "I wanted to be an overlord! I thought they would believe two of us more than one alone. I must take the blame, Stylor—"

"And see what the men of Magdag do in return, how they repay your treachery!" My face, I could see, made them believe all was over for them. "I can understand either of you doing anything for love of a girl, and I suppose you thought she must choose one of you! Betraying a rival is a small thing to a man so obsessed with a girl. But you betrayed everyone and everything we worked and struggled for. You betrayed more than me, Stylor!"

I lifted the sword. Both of them stared at me, unflinching.

I reached across with the keys, threw down the sword, and snapped open the locks.

"Now," I said. "Old vosk heads. We fight!"

But first—there was Holly.

I handed the sword to Susheeng. She hesitated. A party of guards moved past a cross corridor. I motioned to them. "A shout, Princess, and how do you explain this?"

She flung herself around, taking the sword, and almost, I believe, the impulse to cut us down mastered her. Then she led us on. The swing of her hips as she walked ahead of us made a fascinating sight.

"Wait here," she said outside her brother's palatial apartments within the megalith. "I will bring the girl."

When she had gone, Pugnarses said: "Can we trust her?"

Genal said: "We have to. She, and Stylor, are our only hope."

"And when we get back to the warrens," I said, "what is to become of her then?"

Genal looked at me, and away. He felt his disgrace keenly. Pugnarses, uncharacteristically, said: "At another time, Stylor, I would have counseled: 'Kill her!' But I do not think you will do that." He eyed me. "Do you love her?"

"No."

"But she loves you."

"She believes so. She will get over it."

"And—Holly?"

"Holly," I said, "is a sweet child. But my love lies far away from here, in another land, and I remain here only because it is a stricture laid on me. As soon as I have finished my work, then—then, believe me, I shall leave Magdag and all its evil ways far behind me!"

I spoke with a passion that forced them to believe. Holly, following Susheeng meekly, came out then, and she saw me and the color flooded her cheeks.

I merely said: "Hurry, Princess."

There was no time, as I saw it, for a traumatic and emotional outbreak. I wanted to get back to the warrens. We all knew what would happen as soon as Genodras reappeared in the sky above Kregen and the overlords of Magdag were freed from their superstitious imprisonment in the megalithic complexes.

Susheeng, it was clear, still believed she could persuade me to accede to her plan. To her it would appear the only sensible plan, indeed, the only and inevitable one.

Why would a man, a Kov of Delphond, choose to return to a stinking rasts' nest of workers and slaves?

We hurried through the corridors. Truth to tell, I was beginning to think we would break clear away without trouble.

"This way," panted Susheeng. "Up this narrow staircase lies a bridge and then a descent to the outside. I dare not venture out while Genodras is gone from the sky. We can wait."

I did not say anything to that. I would not wait.

At the top of that steep flight of stairs, walled with enameled tiles depicting fantastic birds, animals, and beasts, two mailed guards were descending. Torchlight struck back from their mail. Between them they marched a captive, a fresh sacrifice for the ritual games. He was haggard, bearded, filthy. But I recognized him. I moved aside to let them pass.

But Rophren, that certain Rophren who had been first lieutenant aboard Pur Zenkiren's *Lilac Bird* and had failed in the rashoon, recognized me too.

A shout lifted from the foot of the stairs. More torches spattered lurid orange light upon the brilliant tiles.

"Hai! Princess! Princess Susheeng—that man is Stylor! They are escaped slaves! They are dangerous!"

I took the first guard's sword away and chopped him over the back of the neck. He pitched forward and tumbled all the way to the bottom. Pugnarses and Genal dealt with the second guard, who joined the first in a tumbled heap at the feet of his comrades. They started up.

"Run!" screamed Susheeng.

We now had three long swords.

Rophren reached out a hand.

His haggard face looked uplifted, lightened. He squared his shoulders with a gesture at once instinctive and defiant.

"Lahal, Pur Dray," he said. His voice sounded thick, drugged. "Give me a sword. I would be pleased to exchange hand blows with these Zair-benighted rasts of Magdag. You go on and take the women with you."

He knew I could not do that. But he meant it. I looked at him.

"Lahal, Rophren," I said.

"I am of the Red Brethren of Lizz," he said proudly, with a lift of his head. "I wished to be a Krozair of Zy, but the rashoon stopped all my hopes there. Give me the sword. I will die here, and none will pass until I am dead."

"I believe you, Rophren. I will stay with you."

I reached for the long sword Susheeng held. She was looking at me with a wild light in her eyes and she shrank back. "What—?"

Rophren took the sword. He hefted it. The mailed overlords of Magdag were hurrying up the stairs toward us. "It is good to feel a sword in my fist again," he said. "I have been captive too long." He laughed then, and swung the blade. "Stay, as you will, Pur Dray, my Lord of Strombor, you who are a Krozair of Zy. It will be a great fight. Stay and you, a Krozair, may see how a Red Brother of Lizz can die!"

Susheeng was staring at me with all of horror and hell in her eyes. "A Krozair," she whispered. "You—the Lord of Strombor!"

CHAPTER EIGHTEEN

My Vosk-Helmets greet the overlords of Magdag

Truth to tell, all during this imprisonment in the colossal structures of Magdag where I was a sacrificial victim in the ritual games to insure the return of Genodras, I had been half hoping against all reason that the workers and slaves of the warrens would continue our plans, would mount the attack despite the catastrophic loss of their leaders. If ever there was a need for them to put in an appearance, it was now.

Even while the Princess Susheeng shrank back from me, her face a white mask of fury and despair, a seething agony of acrimony I could well understand impelling her to turn from me at last and finally, the mailed men ran up the flight of stairs.

"A Krozair!" she said. Her fists struck again and again at my chest. "A pest-ridden rast of a Sanurkazz pirate! The vilest Sanurkazzian Krozair of them all, Pur Dray Prezcot, the Lord of Strombor!" She was laughing and shrieking now, mad and wild with the frenzy that tore her. Holly came up and took her shoulders and wrenched her away. Holly's face was as blanched and set as those of Pugnarses and Genal. To them it was inconceivable that an escaped galley slave hiding in the warrens might be a Krozair. Krozairs, they knew, fought to the death.

"They come," grunted Rophren. He had wanted to be a Krozair of Zy, and his crisis of nerves during the rashoon had blasted his hopes. But the Red Brethren of Lizz were a renowned order. He had redeemed himself; he would die well. I do not subscribe to the view that a single act of courage can wash out all a man's crimes, as is so often said; but Rophren, for me, had committed no crime save that of being unfit to be a sailor.

181

We stood, Rophren, Pugnarses, and I, with our long swords eager to smite down on the coifs of the advancing overlords. We fought. There were only ten of them and in accounting for five of them I felt I had betrayed my comrades, for Pugnarses was wrestling his sword out of the cranium of one while Genal struggled hand-to-hand with another who sought to cut down Pugnarses from the side—and Rophren was down, on his knees, bending over with his life's blood bubbling through his fingers.

But there were ten dead overlords littering the stair.

We stepped back from the carnage. Pugnarses, with a curse, kicked the bodies down the steps. I knelt by Rophren. He tried to smile. "Say Lahal and Remberee for me to Pur Zenkiren," he whispered, and so died.

Pugnarses and Genal were collecting the swords.

"Why burden yourself with them?" I asked. Susheeng was vomiting all over those brillliant tiles. I knew it was not because she had seen men die.

"We can give them to the slaves!" snapped Pugnarses. "They will fight—"

"As you have just done, Pugnarses? With your blade wedged in your opponent's head? The skill, Pugnarses, the skill."

He swore vilely, bitterly, but he kept the swords.

I approached the Princess Susheeng. She looked up. Her cheeks were stained with tears, vomit slicked on her ripe lips.

"Will you stay here, Princess? You will be safe, for none know now how we escaped."

I felt sorry for her. She had suffered exceedingly; and now she had discovered that the man for whom she conceived she bore a lifelong love had turned, at a single disastrous stroke, into a hereditary enemy. Truly, I think she had suffered enough.

"And are you truly Pur Dray, Krozair, the Lord of Strombor?"

"I am." Did I speak boastfully? I do not think so. Did I speak pridefully? Ah, there, I think I did.

"How can I love a man of Zair?" she wailed.

"You do not love me, Susheeng—"

"Have I not proved it?" she flashed back at me.

I could not answer that. There was no answer.

Holly made a small movement, and I turned, and she stood there, clad in the gray slave breechclout, with a sword in her little fist. "We had best be going, Stylor."

"Yes," I said. I turned back. "Susheeng—try not to think ill of me. You do not understand the compulsions that drive me. I am not as other men. I do not love you—but I think you have touched a chord in me."

She stood up. In that moment, with the tears and the vomit smearing her face, her hair unbound and disarrayed, she looked as close to a human being as I had ever seen her. I thought, then, that if she had the luck to fall in love with the right man she would turn out well. But that is something not of that pressing moment when we stood on the stairs with their florid tiles, in the megalith of Magdag.

"I cannot go with you into the warrens, Drak," she said.

"No. I did not expect you to. Try to think well of me, Susheeng, for red and green will not always be in conflict." I bent and kissed her. She did not move or respond. I suspect that she was trying to hate me, then, and failing. Her emotions had been drained from her, her will power exhausted. "Go down to your friends, Susheeng. As long as we live, we will not forget this moment."

She started to walk down the steps. She moved like a mechanical doll of Loh struts, jerkily, almost tottering at each step. She halted. She looked up. "You will all be killed when Genodras returns to the sky." The words seemed hardly to mean anything to her. "Remberee, Kov Drak."

"Remberee, Princess Susheeng."

She walked away from us, her hated red dress draggling on the flight of stairs, under torches, between those brilliant tiles of winged birds and horned beasts.

We descended the opposite flight and passed out into the brilliance of a day on Kregen when only Zim, the red sun, shone in the sky.

With our news, and with what they suspected, and the wailing over the pile of corpses of their group leaders, the warrens were in uproar.

"The overlords will ride in and destroy us all!" shouted Bolan. His bald head gleamed orange in the light.

We had avoided the half-human guards on our way in. But I knew they would happily fulfill their contracts with the men of Magdag and charge into warrens to discipline us. We faced the kind of decision I think must face any man, any group of men, if he or they wish eventually to taste their rightful portion of life.

Because the orbit of Kregen is slanted steeply to the plane of the ecliptic the green sun during this eclipse appeared to descend at a sharp angle on the red; it would appear at the opposite side at the same angle. I looked about. Were there green tints returning to the orange colors of Kregen?

Soon men and women were running and screaming through the alleys and maze of courts.

"Genodras is returning! Woe! Woe!"

By reason of the place where the green sun was appearing from the red I knew what the men of Zair would say was happening. How that information, that I was a Krozair, had shattered Susheeng! Genal and Pugnarses had little conception; I was still Stylor to them. And I was still their military commander. I ordered the Prophet to be found.

He came up, his beard as defiant as ever. Holly, Pugnarses, Genal, and Bolan gathered at the head of slaves and workers from all over the warrens. I climbed onto the roof of our hovel to harangue them. What I said was a long series of clichés about liberty, freedom, what we had planned, vengeance for our dead. I roused them. I pointed out that from our barricaded warrens we stood a chance of defeating the mailed men.

In the uproar and the driven dust, a furry form glided to the front, leaped up beside me. Sheemiff, the girl Fristle, screamed for attention. When some quiet returned, she shouted:

"We must fight, or we must die. If we die without fighting, what better off are we if we die having tried and struggled to win? This man Stylor, he is a great Jikai—follow him! Fight!"

"My comrades!" I shouted. "We will fight. And we can win by using the weapons we have made and trained ourselves to use. We will fight—and we will win!"

After that there followed all the bustle and hectic activity attending the preparations for a siege as we dragged our clumsy barricades across the mouths of alleys, set our rope and spike traps, brought out the pikes and the shields, the crossbows and the sheaves of bolts. Finally, like a field of daffodils opening all together in the yellow sun of my old Earth, we donned our yellow-painted vosk-helmets. Then, accoutered, ready to fight and die, we took our posts.

Other leaders were appointed to take command of the groups. We four—Bolan, Pugnarses, Genal, and I—would each take a point of the compass, north, south, east, and west, and hold it. We swore to hold until death. We gripped hands, and went to our posts.

I looked up into the sky and saw a white dove circling up there. I swallowed down a knot in my throat. The Savanti, then, had not forgotten me. It had been a long time.

The mailed men, the overlords of Magdag, rode out to crush the slave revolt. With them marched their half-human, half-beast mercenaries: Fristles, Ochs, Rapas, Chuliks, all bent on our destruction.

I placed Holly in command of the sextets of steel-bowed crossbowmen. The shields were raised, carried by lads whose task it was to shield our men from the shafts of the foe. The pike phalanxes waited, ready to thrust out on my command. I intended to leave the Prophet to handle a great deal of my post, that facing away from the city, for I wished to be everywhere the attack was most hotly pressed. Pugnarses had insisted on taking the post facing the city of Magdag. He licked his lips. Though he wore a long sword scabbarded to his hip, he carried a halberd.

We had all snatched time for a little sleep, but a sailor's life had inured me to working through long periods of sleeplessness. The last of the youngsters, boys and girls both, returned from scattering the caltrops in the spaces before the alley openings into the warrens. Various ugly chevaux-de-frise had likewise been fixed across openings. Horses would not face them and I did not think the sectrixes would, either. I would not have dreamed of lifting a zorca against them, and I would have thought twice of the ability of a vove to surmount them. Behind our crude but, I hoped, effective barricades, our weapons in our hands, our eyes bright, and our breaths hard and short, we awaited the onslaught from the mailed men, the overlords of Magdag.

A little wind lifted the dust. Birds were singing with incongruously cheerful notes into the early air, and a gyp—a brown and white spotted gyp, I recall, very like a Dalmatian—lolloped yelping and alone between the caltrops.

The overlords, confident in their muscle, might, and habitual authority in riding down at will the workers and slaves, attacked firmly and in strength and directly. They knew we had made weapons for ourselves, for Genal, not without the agony of remorse burning him, told me he had shown them an example of a halberd and a glaive. Getting a pike and a crossbow out of the warrens and into the palace had not been possible, for obvious reasons. I sensed that Genal, if not Pugnarses, had regretted his weak decision to betray us for love of a girl at a very early stage. Pugnarses—and I believe he could not rid himself of the sight of Rophren dying on the stairs—remained sullen and hating and determined to prove himself what he truly was: a worker, never an overlord.

That first furious onslaught when the overlords tried to charge into the warrens in their usual fashion foundered on the cruel iron spikes of the caltrops and the chevaux-de-frise.

The mailed cavalry drew off, surprised but undaunted, and the half-human mercenaries ran forward to remove the obstructions covered by a brisk barrage of arrows. Looking down from our barricade I could see the quick movements of the Ochs and the Rapas. Chuliks, of course, would be reserved for more positive and noble kinds of fighting. Pugnarses stood next to me. He looked haggard, lean, and wolfish. He said: "Shall we shoot them down?"

An arrow sailed past our heads, to carom from the upraised shield of a young armor-bearer. I looked at him and, instinctively, he straightened up from his flinch and his jaw set stubbornly.

"No. I want to reserve the bows for the overlords."

"Hah!" said Pugnarses. He looked extraordinarily mean.

When a lane had been cleared through the caltrops the mailed might charged again. They came straight for us in a great thundering roll of mail and upraised swords. I lifted my own long sword, the one I had retrieved from the straw of my bed, the long sword that was the gift of Mayfwy. I slashed it down.

At once the shooters of the crossbows discharged their bolts. With a smooth and practiced flow of action the shooters handed the discharged bow to the hander, took a freshly-loaded bow, and let fly with that. Behind the shooter his loaders and spanners worked like maniacs to maintain the rate of discharge I demanded. Bolts whickered through the hot air. Mailed men reared back in their saddles. Quarrels struck through their mail, pierced their mounts, lanced into their faces. A shrill screaming arose. The mailed charge lashed in confusion, like a sea running all crisscross on a rocky coast.

And all the time the crossbows twanged and clanged and scattered their death upon the overlords of Magdag.

The overlords had never experienced this before. They reeled back. Their sectrixes galloped away. Dismounted men ran after their comrades and my marksmen shot them down without mercy, for we expected none.

Six times they charged.

Six times we cut them to pieces.

Because there was nowhere near enough mail to equip all my men I disdained it. Also, I felt a savage affection for people and places and things long past. So I wore a scarlet breechclout strapped around with the leather belt from which swung the long sword. I fancied old Great Aunt Shusha would have smiled could she see me in that moment on the barricades of the warrens. And Maspero, too—for this was a pale replica of the Savanti hunting leathers I had grown to know so well. On my head I wore a yellow-painted vosk skull, like my men, for there were vosk skulls to spare.

On the seventh charge, just as it was falling back in confusion, an uproar began over on the flank of the warrens fronting the river. Here Genal commanded. And here the overlords while keeping us in play with their own mailed cavalry had sent in the Chuliks. Those savage and prideful warriors with their yellow skins and their uprearing tusks had fought through the arrow storm and were now at hand-strokes all along the barricades linking the alley mouths. I had known, given the extent of the warrens, that complete defense at every point would be well-nigh impossible, but the Chuliks had stormed through more rapidly than I liked.

With a shout of good cheer to Pugnarses I hurried off toward the river flank.

The Chuliks met me in a plaza, scattering before them a spray of running slaves who dropped their weapons the better to run.

Everything happened very fast, as is the way during moments of crisis. I shouted to Holly as her crossbows fanned out.

"Fast and accurately, Holly!"

She nodded. Her breast heaved beneath the gray tunic with its mailed coat beneath—a hauberk I had insisted she wear—and the yellow and black badges flashed bravely. She rattled out her orders; the sextets formed, like a series of wedges, and then they went into action. I watched, filled with suspense, for this was a severe trial for my bowmen.

"May Zair shine on you now!" said I. "Shoot straight!"

Over the open plaza the Chuliks, strong and agile, should have reached the slave and worker bowmen with ease. But, for a reason those in command could not at first understand, the Chuliks were falling, lying in heaps and droves across the dust and the bloodied mud. Those that did pass through the arrow storm were met by the halberdiers and the swordsmen of the support groups, protecting the bows. We shot and shot. The Chuliks hesitated; they turned— Holly shouted: "Up, all! *Loose!*"

And every sextet let fly with six bolts.

The Chuliks were never a force in the battle after that.

It raged, that battle; slowly we were forced in, past one barricade after another as the mailed overlords dismounted from their sectrixes and went at it as infantry, with flashing swords. We held them off. The issue hung for some time in the balance.

But the morale of our men, our slaves and workers, grew and increased even as they were being pressed back. For they saw the death toll they were taking. They saw how our armor-bearers, our lads carrying shields, could protect us from the arrow storm until the moment when the arme blanche men stepped out to throw back yet another attack. It went on for a long time, for the overlords could not understand, they could not conceive, that their habitual authority could no longer be imposed. They were used to riding bravely into the warrens and harrying anything they saw. Now, what they saw wore a yellow vosk-helmet and shot a crossbow, or speared with a deadly pike point. They could not understand; but as their losses mounted and they saw their friends writhing in the dust with their mail pierced or shattered, the blood spouting, as they heard the frenzied shrieks of their brothers or cousins in the throes of death, they had to believe they could not subjugate the slaves and the workers.

And still the sleeting hail of the crossbow-shot bolts and quarrels burst about them. There were very many slaves in the warrens of Magdag, and many workers. We had manufactured a great many bolts for the crossbows—a very great many.

The body of longbowmen from Loh performed stoutly, and I used them as snipers and sharpshooters. I did not know how many surprised Magdaggian overlords pitched from their saddles with a cloth yard shaft in them—surprised in the few moments left before they died.

All over the city-end of the warrens slaves and workers were pushing back the overlords and their hired mercenary beast-men.

I sensed the victory within our grasp.

We had fought our way back toward the original line where the conflict had begun. I ordered my pikes to form phalanx ready for what I hoped would be the final charge.

Holly prepared to march in the intervals to give cover. I was covered in a thick paste of sweat and mud and blood. It was not my blood; I looked past the torn-down barricade, out onto the open area from which the overlords had begun their attack and where now a mass of overlords on foot and mercenary beast-men milled. They were saddling up, out there, taking their sectrixes from their slave grooms. Was this their final charge, as we marched out?

I smiled, then, at the thought of mailed men charging my pike phalanx covered by my steel crossbows.

That, as a sight and a terrible retribution, would repay me much.

A single figure rode out toward us. Clad all in white, a long white trailing robe, the Princess Susheeng rode her sectrix out to parley with me, Dray Prescot.

"What can I say, Kov Drak?"

She could not bring herself, I could see, to use any other name for me. She was pale, her moist red lips now thinned, almost bloodless, shrunken. Her eyes glared out on me from deep bruised wells. Her hands fidgeted with her reins.

"There is nothing to say, Princess Susheeng. You and your brother, all the overlords of Magdag, you merely reap what you have sown."

"Do you hate me so much?"

"I—" I began. Then I hesitated. I had hated this woman. I still believed I hated all the men of green. I was young, then, and hatred was easy, Zair forgive me.

"You are a Krozair," she said, with some difficulty. "A Lord, a man of Zair. You could arrange a truce with Sanurkazz—you yourself said the red and the green would one day cease to fight." She leaned over toward me from the high saddle. "Why should not today be that day, Dray Prezcot, Kov Drak?"

"You still do not see. It is not between red and green. It is between the overlords and their slaves."

A harsh discordant shriek shattered the waiting silence as the two armies faced each other. I looked up, shading my eyes. Up there, wheeling in lazy hunting circles, a great scarlet and golden raptor swung on wide cruel pinions.

"Slaves!" Susheeng made a dismissive gesture. "Slaves are slaves. They are necessary. There will always be slaves." She looked down on me, and a spark of her old fire returned. "And, ma faril, you look ridiculous, standing there with an old vosk skull on your head!" She had not forgotten and she was paying me back.

"The old vosk skulls will win this fight, Susheeng."

"I appeal to you, Drak! Think what it is you do! Please—you owe me something, after all—Zair does not hold your true allegiance, you are not of the inner sea, the Eye of the World. Make peace between the red and the green, and we will settle the problem of the slaves—"

Now, in that shining sky as the twin suns of Kregen slanted, close together but separate now, toward the horizon, the scarlet and golden hunting bird was circling with a more deadly intent. A white dove was matching its moves, dive for dive, volplane for volplane. They circled and maneuvered like two fighter planes of a later age. Once again I sensed my own helplessness as the phantom forces of the Savanti and the Star Lords clashed in this world so far from the planet of my birth.

Susheeng saw my face. She moved irritably and I saw that she wore mail beneath that white robe. She twiddled her riding crop and the reins. She said: "I have appealed to you, Drak. Now hear the message I have brought from my brother, Glycas. If you do not all return to your warrens and lay down your arms you will all be destroyed—"

I moved back a pace.

"There is nothing left between us to be said, Princess. Tell Glycas my message is the same as I called him in the dungeon of the great Hall na Priags. He will understand."

A handful of overlords, impatient, were riding out toward us. They carried bows. The bows were bent and strung in their hands. Pugnarses began to walk out to me, tall and ugly with his mop of hair and his sprouting eyebrows. Susheeng lifted her crop.

An arrow arched from the overlords. It struck Pugnarses in the throat. He fell sideways, retching, clawing the arrow that had killed him.

"There!" I shouted, impassioned, savage with anger. "There is your answer to your foul brother!"

She brought the crop down hard on my face, but I turned my head down and the blow glanced harmlessly off the vosk-helmet.

When I looked up she was spurring back to her own kind.

I had to run, zigzagging and dodging, through a pelting rain of arrows, but I stopped to carry Pugnarses back to his friends. Holly bent over him, weeping.

"Prepare to move!" I yelled at my men—my men who were workers of the warrens, and slaves from the gangs, and girls like Holly, and youngsters with their shields. The phalanx stiffened. Holly looked up from Pugnarses' dead body. Genal was at her side. He lifted her up. "Yes!" I shouted at them. "Yes! We fight now in the last battle. We will utterly destroy the evil of the overlords of Magdag." I lifted the long sword. *"Forward!"*

Beneath the measured tramp of the phalanx of slaves the ground shook.

The phalanx advanced. The pikes were all held in their correct alignment, angled forward and upward. The yellow of the vosk skulls glowed in the streaming opaline light. The steel bows of the crossbowmen winked back brilliant reflections. All—everyone in my little army—all moved forward.

With us now were the thousands of other workers and slaves, men and women with snatched up weapons or implements to use as weapons in their hands. The dust rose chokingly. Trumpets shrilled and called. I strode on, wishing I had Mayfwy's mail coat about me now, but moving on, moving on. . . .

I knew, as nearly as a man may know anything, that now we had these arrogant overlords. Against the new weapons of the phalanx and the pike, supported by the crossbows, they would be swept away. Exultantly I strode on. Shouts and rallying cries echoed. Arrows and bolts began to crisscross in the air.

"Krozair! Krozair!" I yelled, swinging the long sword and pressing on, the pikes all about me. Holly's sextets were lavishing loving care in their shooting. "Jikai! Jikai!"

We would win. Nothing could stop that.

In all that uproar, all that bedlam, with the pikes seeming to lean forward in their eagerness to get at these hated mailed overlords of Magdag, I looked up. I looked up. The scarlet and golden hunting bird circled up there—alone. The dove had gone.

"Against Magdag!" I yelled and my sword caught that falling streaming light and blazed like a flaming brand.

The light was changing. Blue tints crept in around the edges of my vision—and I knew what was happening. Arrows fell about me; the pikes were surging forward, stabbing; the halberdiers were hacking and cutting; Holly's bolts were swathing through the mailed ranks and the Prophet and Bolan and Genal were urging the men on. Even as we smashed solidly into that surging sea of armored men and moved on over them, so the blueness limned everything about me. I felt light. I felt myself being drawn upward.

"No!" I shouted. I lifted the long sword. "*No!* Not now! Not now—I will not return to Earth! Star Lords! If you can hear me—Savanti—let me stay on this world! I will not return to Earth!"

I thought of my Delia of Delphond, my Delia of the Blue Mountains. I would not be thrust through the interstellar void away from her again! I could not.

I struggled. I do not know how or why or what happened, but as the blueness grew and strengthened I fought back at it. In some way I had failed the Star Lords. Something I was doing was contrary to what they wanted to accomplish. I had vaunted that I would serve them in my own way—and this was my reward.

"Let me stay on Kregen!" I roared it up at that indifferent sky where the suns of Scorpio cast down their mingled light. Now I was scarcely conscious of the fight raging around me. Men were dying, heads and limbs were being lopped, bolts were piercing through mail, blood was being spilled on a prodigious scale.

I staggered. I was encompassed and floating in blueness. I gripped my long sword with the clutch of death. I felt myself falling, all lifting and exultation gone, falling and falling. . . .

"I will not go back to Earth!"

Everything was blue now, roaring and twisting in my head, in my eyes and ears, tumbling me head over heels into a blue nothingness.

"I will stay on Kregen beneath the suns of Scorpio! *I will!*"

I, Dray Prescot of Earth, screamed it out. "I will stay on Kregen! *I will stay on Kregen!*"